# The Wax Artist

## An Ailsa Rose Mystery

Sarah L King

# ACKNOWLEDGMENTS

My heartfelt thanks goes to my family for their love and support, especially my husband David whose help, once again, was so invaluable during the editing and publishing process.

I would also like to thank my draft readers K.J Farnham, Alexandra King, David King and Diane Robertson for their time, effort and feedback.

# One

## Spring 1803

I'd watched him die on the North Bridge scores of times. It never got any easier to witness it.

Today I prayed I wouldn't have to. I had an appointment to keep; a duty, however unwanted, to perform, and I could not afford to be delayed. I could not keep those who had summoned me waiting. Of course, the spirits had other ideas. They always did. Halfway across the bridge, I felt time slip back a little, sensed the lost stones grow up beneath my feet. Shuddered along with their tremors, and braced myself for their fall. I saw him then, the lithe young man with a book in his hand, standing where he always was against the low stone wall. He turned to look at me, smiling and tipping his hat as though it was me that he'd been waiting for. Then he stumbled, the ground beneath him shaking with an uncommon violence as the ghost of an abutment gave way. My heart swelled with the urge to cry out, then broke with the knowledge that it was futile.

This happened long ago, I reminded myself. There is nothing you can do about it now.

I turned away, not wishing to look as the crumbling stones finally betrayed him, gifting him to the earth below. Under my feet, the ground stilled as time slid again; forwards now, the past surrendering to the present, the old acquiescing to the new. When I looked back, the bridge had healed, and the man was gone.

Gone, at least, until the next time I saw him. I recalled his small nod, his smile, and wondered who he'd been waiting for. Wondered if they were the reason why he returned to that same spot, time after time. Wondered where he was now. Roaming the valley perhaps, with all those other restless souls? I gazed over the wall, regarding the spirits of Edinburgh's drowned and dispossessed as they wandered the barren land which lay beyond the markets sheltering in the shadow of the bridge's great arches. I pitied them the loss of their watery grave. There had been a loch down there once, known as the Nor Loch, but it had been shrunk long ago by draining. All that remained of it was now obscured from view by the earthen mound which grew bigger each year, fed by the builders' waste of the New Town.

The old gave way to the new; it was how it was meant to be. But that wasn't to say that the past didn't mourn its losses.

A sharp gust of wind brought me back to the present, and I found myself reaching up to shield my bonnet from its grasp. My thoughts returned to my appointment, and my earlier urgency gripped me once more. The dead might have all eternity to rue their lot, but I had only a few minutes to get to Hill Street.

I hurried across the bridge, glad to leave its haunting sights behind me, and made my way towards George Street, the great wide boulevard which ran through the centre of the New Town. I didn't come here often, but I never found it difficult to negotiate my way around. I was used to navigating the old part of the city, its webs of wynds and closes piled high by the centuries. This place was the work of mere decades, built under a regimen of order and symmetry to tempt the city's wealthiest inhabitants away from their chaotic, antiquated dwellings. I found its vistas unappealing, but not confusing.

I rounded the corner on to Frederick Street and stopped for a moment, feeling out of breath. Immediately I noticed the quiet; this side of town might always be busy with Edinburgh's well-to-dos, but it was peaceful to me. It was still new enough that it was mostly only the living who walked its immaculate streets. I breathed deeply, noting rather begrudgingly that its air smelt better, too. I took the final steps of my journey at a steadier pace, conscious of the company I was about to keep. It was bad enough that I was here, dressed in my best but still not quite passing muster, my dress well-worn, the soles of my shoes thick with Canongate filth; I didn't need to appear flustered as well. I needed to seem composed, refined. I needed to be all those things I used to be. I caught sight of my reflection in a window, sighing my disapproval at my flushed cheeks and the frizz of red-brown hair escaping my bonnet. I thought once more about those poor souls roaming that desolate valley between the towns, utterly out of place and time. For a moment I understood how they must feel.

I found my destination with ease, about halfway down Hill Street. The house was just as Jane had described it: identical to all the adjoining houses, fashioned in a grey stone and punctuated by neat lines of sash windows. Elegant, Jane had called it, when she'd brought the invitation to me. I hadn't commented; I'd been too absorbed in reading the little card's details.

*Mrs Charlotte Andrews requests the pleasure of your company... Thursday next... two o' clock...*

They want you to perform a reading, Jane had explained, but that detail had only perturbed me more. Why were they seeking such a service? And why had Jane been foolhardy enough to mention my name?

I made my way along the lane which ran behind Hill Street, where I assumed I would find the servants' entrance to the house. Although I had an invitation to visit, I didn't believe that invitation extended to the likes of me wandering through the family's front door. I knocked briskly on what I hoped was the correct door, and after a few moments Jane answered. She looked different in her maid's attire; younger than her twenty-five years, with a red glow in her cheeks and sweat on her brow which hinted at the relentless nature of the work. She liked it here, she'd once told me. It reminded her of growing up in the border country. Sometimes, at night, she could even hear corncrakes calling out from the surrounding fields, upon which streets had not yet been built.

'I'm glad to see you, Miss Rose,' Jane said, beckoning me to come inside. 'The family are expecting you. They will receive you in the parlour.'

I nodded and smiled, partly in agreement and partly out of amusement at her formality. It was not really so long ago that we worked together in the tavern.

'How are you, Jane? We didn't get much chance to speak when you called the other day.'

'No – sorry, Ailsa. I had to go to market, and I was in an awful rush to get back to help the Misses Andrews dress for dinner. There aren't many of us here, so I must help with everything,' she said, lowering her voice.

'But you are well? Still happy?'

Jane nodded. 'I don't miss tavern work, if that's what you mean. Come on, I'd better take you up and introduce you. It is after two now and you shouldn't keep them waiting, and the mistress will scold me if I'm caught blethering downstairs. Although, perhaps you'd best take those shoes off first. I think they're beyond even the boot-scraper's help,' she added, with a wary glance at my feet.

I did as I was bid, then followed Jane up the stairs and into the parlour, a well-appointed room at the rear of the house, fashioned in a pleasing pale green. The colour reminded me of my home in Paris, and before I could prevent it, its many hues flashed before my eyes. Greens, yellows, reds. A touch of blue along the staircase which led to our apartment. I pushed the thought from my mind, fixing a smile on my face and gave a polite bow as Jane announced my arrival to the family, who were enjoying tea around a fine mahogany table in the centre of the room. Four intrigued faces turned to examine me; a woman in her middle years, who I presumed to be Mrs Andrews, two younger women who were likely the Misses Andrews, and a fair-haired man of whom I knew nothing at all. Their interrogative stares made me conscious again of my faded dress and stockinged feet. I'd had finer clothes back in Paris, but those were gone now too.

The older woman spoke first. 'Ah, Miss Rose. Very pleased to make your acquaintance. Please, do sit down. Jane, bring up a fresh tea set, with another cup for Miss Rose.' Her voice was soft but commanding, its notes surprising to my ear. Not Scottish, I thought. English. She smiled slightly at me; if she was irritated by my lateness, she didn't show it.

Jane left promptly with her orders, cutting me adrift as I fumbled with a heavy wooden chair. In the end the man rose from his seat to assist me, prompting a stifled giggle from one of the young ladies. Her mother shot her a stern look.

'Miss Rose, allow me to introduce Mr Henry Turner, and my daughters, Miss Clara and Miss Grace. Thank you for coming to attend upon us this afternoon. It is a fine day, I see. I hope your journey across town was not too arduous.'

I thought briefly about that young man, about how this time I couldn't bear to watch him fall. Arduous, indeed.

'Not at all, Mrs Andrews. There was a little wind on the bridge, but then there is always a wind blowing between the towns.'

My remark prompted more laughter, this time from both sisters. They were strikingly different to look at; one shared her mother's slender, dark features, with near-black hair and deep brown eyes, whilst the other was fair, blue-eyed and a little plump. Neither of them could be much more than one-and-twenty, and both were beautiful in their distinct ways. I imagined the suitors were lining up for their hands.

'It was Grace, my youngest daughter, who prompted our invitation to you,' Mrs Andrews continued, giving a nod of acknowledgement to the fair-haired girl. 'I understand you're acquainted with our maid, Jane. Grace tells me that Jane has shared some stories of your…talents. My daughter has an enthusiasm for these matters, and was inclined to make your acquaintance so that you might be able to read her leaves.'

Of course. Typical Jane. The matter had unfolded much as I expected, but that didn't mean it rankled any less. I could hear my mother's warning echo in my ear.

*Be careful who you trust, ma chérie.*

'I'd be happy to oblige you,' I replied.

Jane returned briefly with the tea set. She managed to avoid catching my eye, which was just as well as I couldn't be sure I wouldn't scowl at her. After she'd laid out the required wares and left, Mrs Andrews retrieved a key and unlocked the tea chest which sat atop a mahogany table across the room. I watched as she filled an attractive porcelain bowl with leaves before placing it in the centre of the table.

'I'll let you do the honours, Miss Rose,' Mrs Andrews said.

'In fact, Mrs Andrews, I'm afraid the practice requires that each person makes their own cup of tea. Leaves first, then hot water. The leaves must remain in the bottom of the cup.'

Mrs Andrews curled her lip, partly at me and partly at Grace, who shrank a little across the table. I was being tolerated. But then, my sort always were.

'I see. Well, girls, you heard Miss Rose. You too, Henry. Make your tea.'

I watched with some amusement at the show of refinement and delicacy as one by one, each concocted their brew. I realised how unused I was to company such as this; too accustomed now to the rough manners of the tavern, to the clink of ale mugs and the stink of whisky and sweat. It had been many years since I had sat and enjoyed tea in a room such as this. The thought unsettled me, and I brushed it aside.

'Miss Rose, that is an unusual accent. Pray, do tell us where you are from,' the elder sister, Clara, said as she stirred a spoon in her cup.

I felt the heat grow in my cheeks as four pairs of eyes bored into me. I worked hard to conceal my accent, but it could always be detected by a well-attuned ear.

'I spent my childhood in France,' I replied. 'But I have lived in

Edinburgh for many years now.'

Grace gave a little snort. 'France, indeed! Jane never mentioned that. I do hope you're no admirer of Monsieur Napoleon, Miss Rose.'

'Upon my word, Grace!' Henry interjected before I could answer. 'What an assertion to put to Miss Rose. I am sure that, given her long residence in Edinburgh, she is no friend to the revolution. Am I right, Miss Rose?'

I nodded. 'You are indeed, sir. On the question of Monsieur Bonaparte, I would say that I welcome the current peace. Long may it last.'

'Yes, yes, very good,' said Mrs Andrews, before sipping her tea. 'I presume I may now drink this, and that we may dispense with all talk of politics.'

I nodded my agreement, and poured a cup of my own. I hadn't answered badly, but when in polite society it was very often impossible to say the right thing.

'Have you any family in Edinburgh, Miss Rose? Parents, or siblings, perhaps?' Clara's dark gaze remained intently upon me as she pursued her line of questioning.

I shook my head. 'I'm afraid not. I have no siblings, and my parents are dead.'

A half-truth, but I wasn't prepared to part with the full story of my upbringing. Indeed, I didn't know the half of it myself.

'That is sad, being alone in a strange city,' Grace lamented. 'We are strangers here too, but at least we have each other for company.'

'Hush, hush,' her sister urged, 'or you shall be revealing all our secrets and there will be no point in Miss Rose's divining for us at all. Although, I must agree with my sister that it is sad – and unusual.'

Unusual. Perhaps it was in her world, but it was all too common in mine. Clara continued to regard me, and I wondered if she felt as I did, if she could sense the chasm between us. The valley between the towns. The empty space which separated our lives. After a moment she looked away, and I decided it was best to move on.

'Has anyone finished their tea?'

Henry sat back in his chair, his casual pose seeming to mock me. 'I confess I have finished, but I am going to decline a reading from you, Miss Rose. I mean no offence, but such amusements are the preserve of young ladies with heads full of novels and nonsense.'

I nodded, inwardly cursing Jane once again. This was exactly why it wasn't worth my trouble to do readings. Too much risk. Too much unbelief.

'Oh, do ignore him, Miss Rose. He is an utter blockhead,' Grace said. She pushed her cup towards me. 'I asked Mama to invite you here. I would like to go first.'

I took her cup, examining the messy, wet swirls of leaves clambering up its sides. 'You are a young woman of great sensibility, Miss Grace. I see that you love to dance and that you play the piano very well.'

Grace beamed at me. 'Yes, indeed. Yes, it's true. My playing is far superior to Clara's.'

Henry clicked his tongue in disapproval. 'Dear Grace, how easily led you are. Most young ladies in Edinburgh will like to dance and to play the piano. Mere guesswork, and that is all.'

'You are happy more often than not,' I continued, undeterred by Henry. In truth this was turning out to be an interesting cup. 'But I can see your circumstances have been difficult of late. There has been a division in the family, I believe. Yes, a separation, leading you here to Edinburgh.'

I didn't need to have the sight to understand that I'd touched a nerve. Mrs Andrews sat bolt upright, sending the remainder of her tea swishing around her cup.

'An easy supposition, Miss Rose, if you've read the newspapers in these last twelve months.'

'I have not, madam,' I replied, 'but I shall leave that line of enquiry as it is, since it is clearly vexing.' I looked back at Grace. 'Is there anything in particular you wish to know?'

'Marriage,' her mother snapped, before Grace could answer. 'Can you see anything on the matter of her marriage?'

I looked back at Grace's cup. In truth, I could see little. Her leaves were scattered all over the place, much like her feelings. 'You will have many suitors to choose from, and you will have a difficult decision to make. But I see that you will be happy.'

Grace giggled. Mrs Andrews, however, was far from impressed.

'That is all very well, but do you have a name? Who will she marry?'

'I'm afraid I don't have a name, Mrs Andrews. Sometimes during a reading, names will make themselves known, but it is rare.'

'Well yes, I imagine that would be far too specific,' Henry scoffed.

'Indeed. Let us see whether you have better luck with Clara,' Mrs Andrews said, tight-lipped. 'My dear, pass Miss Rose your cup.'

Clara did as instructed, her cool fingers brushing mine as we leaned across the table. I felt her feelings as they seeped from her skin; restlessness, anxiety, panic. Love. I caught her gaze for the briefest moment, watched as she extinguished the spark. I wondered how often she had to bury those feelings beneath that well-rehearsed serenity. In my hand her cup grew warm, the neat arrangement of soggy leaves readying themselves to reveal her secrets.

Then I looked down, and realised it wasn't the leaves that were speaking to me at all.

A dark corridor. A flash of yellow paint. A man, his lips upon a woman's neck.

A flickering candle, running with molten wax, its wick almost spent. A stone staircase. A woman's body tumbling down, a soft blur of muslin and limbs.

A face, running with blood.

Her face.

Her blood.

The vision broke, torn apart like pages from a book. In my

hand her cup shook, and the delicate porcelain cracked. The red trickled away, succumbing to the black, and I knew what was coming next. I knew before I saw him. I knew before I heard him cry.

'Pierre,' I whispered, just as the ground greeted me, and the darkness swallowed me whole.

# Two

I hadn't seen Pierre since the night I left Paris. He'd not liked the fact that we were leaving, and had made his feelings on the matter very clear, banging on every wall and stomping on every floor as we hurriedly packed our things. My mother had pleaded with me to make him cease his noise, reminding me that we must not draw attention to ourselves. As if I could ever make Pierre do anything. No amount of yelling at him ever did any good, but I tried anyway.

Arrête, Pierre! Arrête!

You're running away, he'd said. Tu as peur. You're frightened.

Of course we were frightened. I'd tried to distract him with a game, and to reassure him that everything would be alright. Yes, the next inhabitants of this house would be just as nice as me. No, they wouldn't be Jacobins. Yes, I was sure they would always want to play.

You shouldn't be scared, he'd insisted. Je n'ai jamais peur.

Of course he was never scared. He would be a brave boy forever.

As we left, he'd stood at the window, his pale hands pressed hard against the glass. I waved, but he didn't wave back. My mother shook her head, reminding me of all the warnings she'd given me. I should have stopped talking to him years ago. I'd given him too much encouragement, let him become too attached. I'd never been able to make her understand that the dead don't let you simply ignore them.

Besides, I'd explained, he was helpful. He would show me things, important things that I needed to know. That we needed to know. We'd been able to leave, thanks to him. For that I was grateful. He was my friend - I would miss him.

And I had missed him. But getting that message from him in the middle of Clara's reading had been a bit of a shock.

My fainting episode had brought the Andrews' reading to an abrupt end. I had woken to the blurry sight of Jane, frantically waving smelling salts under my nose. I was still on the floor, and my shoulder ached badly from the fall. Mrs Andrews had retreated to the sofa, keeping her distance, while Henry and Clara assumed statuesque poses in front of the fireplace. Only Grace had remained by Jane's side, chattering all the while about what I must have seen and who Pierre might be. I felt weak, as I often did in the aftermath of a vision, but I forced myself to my feet. I wanted to leave, and fortunately the family were only too happy to oblige. After Henry fulfilled his duty by offering to order a carriage for me, and I fulfilled mine by declining, I set off on foot for my home in the Canongate.

'Take good care, Ailsa,' Jane called after me from the doorway.

I'd smiled, trying to reassure her. Above her, a quick movement at the window caught my eye. I couldn't be certain, but I sensed that Clara had been watching me too.

*

That evening in the tavern I struggled to keep my mind on my work. I was still feeling the draining effects of the vision; my thoughts were foggy and my concentration spent, and I wasn't helped by the atmosphere at Franny's, which was as raucous as ever. It was a warm spring night; the air was hot and my head was full of drunken voices. I craved silence. I wanted the world to stop for a moment, just so that I could make sense of it all.

'I hope it isnae a man,' Franny said after I spilled a second mug of ale. She wiped her rough hands on her apron, half-smiling at me as she waited for my response.

'Of course not,' I answered, rather more abruptly than I'd intended.

'Glad tae hear it. I ken yer a guid lass,' she replied, 'but I also ken when somethin's up. Ye look awfy pale. I hope yer not sickening.'

I shook my head. 'Just tired, is all.'

'Aye, well, as long as that's all.' Her keen blue eyes studied me for a moment longer, before shifting towards a group of gentlemen gathered in the corner of the room. 'See if they want any more port. If it gets quiet later on, ye can get away early.'

I thanked her, feeling guilty for not being entirely honest. I could have at least told her I'd fainted, lest it happen again tonight, but I worried that such an admission would have only prompted more questions I didn't wish to answer. When I'd come to work here, I'd made the rare mistake of talking a little about my experiences with the dead. Jane had been enthralled, hanging on my every word and demanding every delicious detail. Franny, however, hadn't approved. In the end she had taken me to one side and asked me to stop filling Jane's head with stories. It was the only time she'd ever spoken to me so sternly. I hadn't given her occasion to again.

After I'd served those men their port and brandy, I settled myself on a wooden stool beside the bar. I was suffering some discomfort in my feet after being on them all day, and my shoulder still hurt after my earlier fall. I just needed a moment, to gather my thoughts and to recover my strength. If only a moment was all it ever took. In truth, the images Pierre used to share with me could sometimes weaken me for days, depending on how vivid they were, how potent. It had been so long that I had almost forgotten how they made me feel. He wasn't the first spirit to communicate with me in this way, nor had he been the last. But his messages had always had the most powerful impact.

My feet throbbed as I ruminated on the same handful of questions. I hadn't heard from Pierre in years. Why was he contacting me now?

What exactly was he trying to tell me about Clara Andrews?

And why?

In the past, his messages had been for my mother and I. Tell your mother to be careful, that man has a bad temper. Take care around him, he likes you. Don't wear pink, he likes it. Don't go out today, he will have a carriage waiting for you. Something bad is going to happen, but I don't want you to leave.

I hadn't wanted to leave either. And in the end, running away hadn't done us any good. My mother was dead anyway, and I was all alone. Just another sorry story for genteel girls like Clara Andrews to pity.

But what was Clara's story? And why did Pierre think it ended with her lying dead at the bottom of some stairs?

Why had he seen fit to warn me about Clara's fate, but not my mother's?

I sighed heavily, forcing myself off the stool and back to work. In the corner the chorus of gentlemen's voices reached a crescendo as they drank and debated the day's events. For a moment I envied their port and their politics, their parlours and their comfortable beds. I'd lived in their world once, or a version of it, at least. My life had revolved around drawing rooms, card games and the best claret. A governess and a library of books. Sumptuous dinners and the finest dresses. But whilst their world embodied power, mine only ever orbited it. And when that power had gone, there had been nothing left to cling to.

'You're looking very serious this evening, Miss Rose.'

One of Franny's regulars, Angus Campbell, stood grinning at me, and I realised I must have been wearing a very odd look on my face. I forced a smile in return.

'Dinnae bother with her, Angus, she's oot o' sorts,' Franny

interjected, shaking her head at me. 'And I've told ye before, ye can call her Ailsa! None o' this Miss Rose nonsense in here,' she added with a chuckle. Her plump cheeks glowed pink as she grinned at Angus.

'Your usual?' I asked him, trying to ignore their teasing.

'Aye, thank you,' he replied, recoiling as Franny swept past him. 'She terrifies me. Reminds me of my mother.'

'She has a good heart. She just likes to look after people. It's in her nature, I suppose,' I replied, pouring his drink and handing him a mug of his favourite ale.

'Aye, well, I'd say a bit of mothering is no bad thing for you, this evening,' he observed, staring squarely at me. He had nice eyes; I noticed that the first time I served him a pint. Green, flecked with a chestnut colour which made them look almost brown in the dim tavern light.

'Perhaps. Unfortunately, my mother is long dead,' I replied.

'And mine is back home in Glendrian. So, here's to being motherless,' he said, raising his drink in a mock-toast, 'and being taken under the wing of Franny Fergus.'

I laughed, far louder than intended. Across the room, Franny shot me a stern look as she gathered up the empties from the gentlemen who had now departed.

'I am sorry about your mother, though,' Angus said, his voice quieter now. I liked his accent the most; it was quite unlike the Edinburgh tongue I was accustomed to. There was something soft, even musical about it. Franny had told me once that he came from the north. They spoke a different language up there. Lived in different ways. It had been a clumsy remark, but it had left me feeling curious.

'Do you want to talk about it?'

He'd fixed those eyes on me again; I felt them search my face for a response. I shook my head, unable to bring myself to say anything more. I seemed to have spent far too much time thinking about the past today.

'Off duty tonight?' I asked, determined to change the subject.

'Aye, thankfully. First night off in what feels like an age. It's the price you pay for being a young man in the Town Guard, Miss Rose. You get to work every hour God sends so that the old ones can rest easy.'

'Do you like it, though? Being a guardsman can't be dull, I'm sure.' I chose my words carefully. I knew fine well what being a guardsman involved at times.

Angus shrugged. 'Oh, at times it can be. It can also be dangerous when there's a brawl or a riot, or even just a big crowd for a hanging. But it keeps me fed and out of trouble and besides, I'm in good company - a lot of the guardsmen come from the highlands too,' he added, with a grin.

'They must be a constant reminder of home,' I pondered, half to myself. 'I can't decide if that would be a good or a bad thing.'

Angus took a large mouthful of his drink, wiping his mouth with the back of his hand. 'That depends on how you feel about your home, I should think. Do you miss yours?'

I looked at him quizzically. I'd never told him where I was from. Clearly, like Clara Andrews, he had well-attuned ears. I thought again for a moment about my mother, about our home with the bright walls and fine furniture. About Pierre.

'Sometimes,' I replied.

'Is that why you're looking so glum tonight?'

'No. I've just had a difficult day.' I paused, trying to decide how much I should say. I needed to say something, to someone, to let at least some of what troubled me pour forth and relieve the pressure which was building in my head. 'Have you ever seen something and just not been able to make any sense of it at all?'

Angus laughed into his mug as he took another mouthful. 'Every day, Miss Rose. Every day.'

'What do you do about it?'

His face grew serious as he weighed up my question. 'Depends what it is. Usually, I try to decide if it's worth looking into, or best left alone, and that decision depends on how serious I think it might be. Is this thing you saw a serious matter?'

I thought about Clara's bloodied face, those empty eyes staring at me as she lay on the floor. It could hardly be more serious, if it had happened. But it hadn't happened, not yet. I could hardly tell a guardsman about a death I'd foreseen, about which I had no real information other than the broken shards I'd witnessed in a dream.

'Not really,' I lied. 'Franny is right – I'm just out of sorts today.'

Angus finished his beer and gave me a small nod. 'Well, if you ever need my assistance, you need only ask, Miss Rose.' He rose swiftly from his seat. 'But now I must bid you a good evening.'

I couldn't tell from his expression whether he believed me or not.

*

Franny kept her word and let me leave early that evening. The walk back to my home in the Canongate was a moonless one, and I felt grateful for the light offered by the lamps which illuminated my way, no matter how dim and sporadic they were. I was still feeling unsettled after the day's events; the images I saw whirred around my mind so relentlessly that they had caused a headache. I longed for my bed, to find the sanctuary which I knew only sleep could provide. Whilst ever I was awake, I would keep going round in the same circles, scrutinising everything I saw, trying to extract from it the tiniest details in the hope of finding clues to solve the riddle. Who was the man I saw with Clara? Did he push her? Did she fall?

If I knew who he was, would I be able to stop her from dying?

Around me Edinburgh's closes and wynds spread their tentacles into the darkness, with only occasional sounds left to betray that their inhabitants were still abroad. The soft tinkling of someone relieving themselves against a wall. The moans of men and prostitutes as trading began for the night. The squeals of the town's animals as they found dinner in putrid gutters. In the distance I heard raised voices; guardsmen, no doubt, keeping order. I walked faster. The last thing I needed after today was to fall foul of an old man wielding a Lochaber axe.

Then, behind me, a different sound. A scrape, a thud, the clatter of a tin on the cobbles. I spun around, peering into the darkness.

'Who's there?' I asked.

Only silence answered me. Nearby the lamplight flickered, but revealed no shadows. No one stepped forward. My heart beat a little faster. I hadn't sensed I was being followed, but now, standing there, I felt sure I was being watched. The only thing I couldn't be certain about was whether my observer was living or dead.

'Who's there?' I tried again. 'Can I help you?'

'Joanna?' a voice called back from the darkness. 'I can't find my box.'

The shuffling sound resumed. I breathed a sigh of relief, almost smiling as a bent figure emerged from the shadows. I knew who it was.

'Alice,' I said softly, helping the old woman to her feet.

Alice looked wildly about her, her yellowing eyes darting in every direction. She cut a sorry figure, even in the darkness, her shawl threadbare and her white hair barely contained by a filthy cap. I felt a familiar pang of pity rise up in my gut as I retrieved her little tin which had fallen nearby and handed it to her.

'It's me, Alice. It's Ailsa. I live near to you, remember? What are you doing out here at this time of night?'

Alice shook the empty tin. 'I lost my coins. Have you seen Joanna? I've been looking everywhere but I cannae find her.'

'Oh, Alice.' I wrapped my arm gently around her shoulder. She was so tiny and thin, I always feared that she would break into pieces under even the lightest of touches. 'Let's get you home to bed.'

The old woman gave me a toothless smile, which I took as acquiescence, and together we walked the final yards to our homes in one of the Canongate's towering old buildings. Once a fine home for Edinburgh's wealthiest inhabitants, Anstruther House, as it was known, had long since been divided into a set of grim, cramped dwellings. It was dark, damp and reeked frequently of disease, but life in a single room with a tiny window was all I could afford on tavern wages. It was also far better than the alternatives. I'd experienced the city's lodging-houses briefly after my mother's death, cramming into damp cellars and sleeping on bare floors with countless others. I could still recall the odour of decay, and the relentless itching caused by the lice.

I guided Alice up the stairwell, which was thankfully quiet. Only a couple of people passed us, squeezing by on the narrow steps. At one point, Alice cried out, quite without provocation, earning her a few choice words from an unkempt-looking man lingering nearby. People always seemed to be wary of Alice, with her frailty, her ramblings and her begging. I couldn't understand it. I could only feel pity for her.

'Come on,' I beckoned her. 'Here's your door, Alice.'

'But where's Joanna? Is she inside? I've got to make Rab his dinner afore he goes back to the bakehouse.'

'Yes, of course, you'd better go in and get on,' I replied.

I'd learned long ago that it was best not to contradict her. Her mind dwelled in the past, in a time when there was a Rab and a Joanna. In a time when she wasn't all alone.

Perhaps I was wrong to pity her. Perhaps she was the lucky one because, in her mind at least, she'd managed to escape.

Helping Alice had spent the last of my energy, and I fell into my bed, exhausted. Around me Anstruther House creaked and groaned as its many inhabitants settled down for the night. I closed my eyes, determined to embrace the dark, but soon found myself tossing and turning as the day once again replayed in my mind. Grace's delight. Henry's disapproval. Clara's poise. Clara's fall. My fall. Angus's words this evening: is it worth looking into, or best left alone?

I had to investigate; I knew that. But where to begin?

That was the question I failed to answer, time and time again, until outside the street lamps faded and finally my fevered mind succumbed to sleep.

# Three

I slept deeply that night, waking late the following morning with a heavy head and no recollection of my dreams. The day which greeted me through my little window was bright, the sunshine peering through the gaps in my faded curtains, illuminating the dust which lingered in the air. I lay in my bed a few moments longer, in no hurry to get on with my day which was, given my delicate state, mercifully empty. Outside my door, the building was quiet; most, I guessed, would be at work or at the markets by now. Only tavern workers and prostitutes slept all morning and the latter, who lived and worked on the ground floor, would be in bed for some time yet.

I smiled, thinking of those women, fast asleep, still wearing their garish dresses and smudged rouge. It amused me to think of this once fine home now operating as one of the city's many brothels. I wondered what the house's original noble owners would have thought of that, if they would have been shocked to see how far this towering stone building had fallen. Maybe they wouldn't care. I cared, although I wasn't sure why. Perhaps I welcomed the reminder of how low something could sink, and yet still survive.

*So quick to judge, ma chérie!*

My mother's voice intruded. Not her real voice, of course; for all my gifts, I'd never been fortunate enough to hear her from beyond the grave, no matter how often I had willed it so. No matter how often I had craved her advice, or even welcomed one of her lectures.

'This is hardly a genteel house, Maman,' I whispered. I couldn't help it; even imaginary voices sometimes needed answering.

Reluctantly I dragged myself out of bed and began dressing for the day. A cursory glance at the table beside the hearth revealed a small amount of bread, wrapped up in cloth. In the midst of yesterday's events, I'd forgotten to buy any provisions. I supposed a trip to the market would do me good; the High Street air, though usually thick with the stink of the tanneries and flesh-markets, was air nonetheless. A bit of sunshine and a change of scenery might help me think things through, to gain the perspective I needed. I still had no idea how to proceed with the information I'd seen in my vision, and although I suspected I was expecting too much of a simple walk, it was worth a try.

I grabbed my bonnet, then swallowed down a morsel of stale bread and the mouthful of water which remained in my jug. I would need to visit the wellhead later, too. Just as I was about to leave, there was a knock at my door. Alice, probably. She would often turn up in the morning, looking for Joanna, or for food. I wrapped the rest of the bread back up for her. It wasn't much, but it was something.

Today, however, it wasn't Alice. Instead, upon opening the door, I was surprised to find Jane standing there, her cheeks flushed from climbing up Anstruther House's many stairs.

'I hope you don't mind me calling,' she said. 'The Misses Andrews asked me to check on you.'

'Not at all, although I can assure you, I'm absolutely fine. Please, come in.'

'That's a relief,' Jane replied, breezing past me. 'The Misses have been very vexed about what happened yesterday. Your fainting gave them a real fright.'

'Vexed? Have they, indeed?' I suppressed a smirk. Even in the circumstances, I couldn't help amusing myself with the thought of those two delicate young ladies having an attack of the nerves on my account.

'They have talked of little else. They cannot help but wonder what you must have seen, Ailsa, and how terrible it must have been.'

Ah, I thought. How quickly we arrived at the real reason for Jane's visit.

'Jane, I would thank you not to mention my abilities to anyone else. Yesterday was a difficult and exhausting day for me. In truth, I rarely do readings now, and certainly not for those I don't know. I made an exception when you asked me – indeed, I felt unable to refuse given the sort of people your employers are – but it isn't something I wish to do again. I think yesterday's events show why these things are best avoided.'

Jane bit her lip and I was pleased to see looked genuinely regretful. 'I am sorry, Ailsa. I suppose my mouth ran away with me a wee bit one night. Miss Grace is very easy to talk to and so interested in these matters, that I could hardly help myself. But Ailsa, I must ask you, what did you see?'

Jane's wide blue eyes implored me; it would have been so easy to have just given in, to have told her everything and to have invited her help. But what good would that do? Anything I told her would likely find its way back to Clara, and I couldn't be sure of the result of that – hysterics, at best, or at worst, my arrest, if the family decided that it was me who was the threat. No, I decided. I needed information from Jane, that was certain, but the less she knew, the better.

'I had a vision yesterday – a powerful one, which caused me to faint. But it was nothing to do with the Andrews family. I was contacted by an old friend, the spirit of a boy who lived in my home in Paris. The message was about my mother.'

'Your mother?' Jane's eyes widened further. 'What about your mother?'

'Well, you know that she is dead. It was about her death.' I spun my web of lies rapidly, hardly able to believe what I was saying.

*Wishful thinking, ma chèrie.*

And indeed, it was. I wished more than anything to understand what had happened to her. To really understand it, beyond what I had seen, beyond what was known.

'But your mother, didn't she...?'

'Yes,' I snapped. 'I know what was said.'

I really had said too much to Jane in those early days of our acquaintance.

*But you know that cannot be true, Ailsa. You know I wouldn't have left you like that.*

'That must have been a shock, to get a message such as that after all this time.' Jane gave me a considered look, and I wondered for a moment if she doubted the truth in my story. 'I'm sorry to have troubled you, Ailsa. I'll tell the Misses Andrews that your fainting fit had nothing to do with them. I'm sure that'll put their minds at ease.'

I mustered a smile. 'I hope so. Jane, I hope you don't mind me asking, but there was one thing which did intrigue me yesterday. I saw something about a rift in the family. Mrs Andrews became quite agitated when I mentioned it, and started alluding to a story in the newspapers. Do you know anything about that?'

'Yes, of course, as does most of Edinburgh! Honestly Ailsa, I know you're not one for gossip, but sometimes I think you must live under a rock. You know, of course, that the family are fairly new in town-'

'Indeed,' I interjected, ignoring her condescension. She had spoken in much the same tone on the night she told Franny and me that she was leaving to go into service. The finer sort, lately arrived in town, was how she'd haughtily described her new employers.

'Well,' Jane continued, 'you perhaps didn't know that they came here all the way from London.'

'I didn't know that, although I did note their English accents.'

'Aye, and you might also have noted that there was not a Mr Andrews present yesterday. That's because, whilst Mr Andrews is currently in town, he lives at a different address. Mr and Mrs Andrews are estranged, you see, on account of his affair with Lady Henrietta Arbuthnot. I heard it was the talk of London last year – a real scandal, with some sort of trial in the courts involved. Anyway, all I really know is that now Mrs Andrews wants a divorce, and that's why she's here.'

'Mrs Andrews wants a divorce?' I repeated with a raised brow. The revolution had brought divorce to France, opening its door to wives as well as husbands, but I didn't know that it was possible here.

Jane nodded. 'Very brave, I'd say. Or foolish – I suppose time will tell. Many a woman of her standing would put up with her husband's behaviour rather than risk ruin like that. But apparently, she is settled upon it; the moment the trial was over, she travelled with the young ladies to Edinburgh. I don't think Mr Andrews had much choice but to follow her and agree to the divorce.'

I gave a wry smile. 'She must really dislike her husband, although from what you've said, it sounds like he's given her more than sufficient cause to feel that way. But why would Mrs Andrews need to come here for a divorce? I can understand wanting to leave London in those circumstances, but why come here, specifically? Do they have other family here?'

Jane shrugged. 'Not as far as I know. As I said, I don't know all the details. They do go out into society but I think folk talk about them, as you'd expect. Mrs Andrews and Miss Clara are quite bothered by it, but Miss Grace doesn't seem to notice. She's too busy being on the lookout for a husband, I think.'

'I thought as much from reading her cup,' I mused, half to myself. 'And what about Miss Clara? She's very beautiful. I imagine the young men about town are falling all over themselves to be acquainted with her,' I added, as casually as I could manage.

'Well, they might be, if she wasn't so serious. I think Mrs Andrews would like to find husbands for them both, but Clara is very cold about the matter. She's an odd one – more interested in her accomplishments than anything else.'

I thought about the feelings I detected when I touched Clara's hand. All that agitation, all that love. Clearly there was a great deal going on beneath that icy exterior.

'I see. Thank you, Jane. Sometimes it is good to be able to fill in the gaps of things I see during readings.'

'You're welcome Ailsa.' She walked back towards the door. 'As long as there's nothing else for me to tell Miss Clara and Miss Grace?'

I shook my head. 'There isn't. Oh, but before you go, what's the story with the gentleman, Henry Turner? It was a great pity that he wouldn't allow me to do a reading for him.'

Jane laughed. 'Aye, no one who works in the house has worked him out, either. A clever young man, that's for certain, trying to make his fortune in the banks or some such sort of work, just like Mr Andrews. He's a distant cousin, I think, on Mrs Andrews' side of the family. The mistress is very proud of him, dotes on him like the son she never had. Miss Grace said her mother was delighted when he wrote to say he'd be joining them. Personally, I think it's strange, following them up to Edinburgh, given the circumstances. Most folk will run away from scandal, not towards it. He must be very loyal.'

'Yes,' I agreed. 'He must be.'

Or, I thought, he is another member of that family with whom there is more going on than meets the eye.

\*

After Jane had left, I lost no time in heading out to the market. The morning sunshine had kept its promise, and the day was warm and bright. We'd had little rain during the past week, leaving the roads dusty, their filth not washed away but instead baked to the surface. The air was hot and putrid, and my earlier hunger quickly abated as I made my way along the High Street, the great spine which meandered up the hill towards the ancient castle. The streets were busy, even by Edinburgh's standards, and I found myself weaving my way through a crowd at the dairy stalls which wrapped themselves around the Tron Kirk. The noise was raucous, the gin-drinking women who ran that market holding court as they sold their wares. I moved on at a pace, deciding against buying any cheese today.

On days like today the town seemed to fold in on itself, and any relief I felt at being outside increasingly gave way to a growing tightness in my chest as I approached the Luckenbooths. I liked this part of town the least; the streets were narrow and gloomy, the great piles of ancient buildings casting shadows no matter the time of day. Beyond this cramped arrangement of tenements and shops was the Old Tolbooth, the town's gaol and the home of its Guard, looming like a spectre in front of the old church of St Giles. The street here too was busy, but I did my best to hurry past, walking so fast that my sides began to hurt. I could never bear to look at that building, or at anyone surrounding it: dead or alive, they were wretched souls to regard. I held my nose, guarding against the foul stench which seeped from the Tolbooth's walls, like a cesspit filled with misery and death. I thought then of Angus, and wondered how he could bring himself to work in a place like that.

'There! There's Joanna! Help me, Joanna, please help me!'

I turned around, alarmed to see Alice being hauled along by two guardsmen. Their large tricorne hats momentarily obscured their faces, but as they drew nearer, I saw that one of the men was Angus.

'Alice,' I called, running towards her, 'what's happened? Are you alright?'

'She's far from alright, miss,' replied the other, much older guardsman. 'Caught thievin' doon the market under the brig.'

I looked squarely at Angus, who seemed to shrink back from my gaze. 'I'm afraid it's true, Miss Rose.'

I shook my head at them both. 'Poor Alice. She will be hungry. I was just heading to the Grassmarket to get some provisions for us both.'

Angus frowned at me. 'Is this woman a relation of yours?'

'No. She's my neighbour. Have pity on her; she has very little means and becomes confused easily. I assure you, she's harmless.'

'Harmless?' the other guard scoffed. 'Try telling that tae the man she stole fae at the greenmarket!'

'So, you're going to lock her up for what, exactly? Stealing a few bruised vegetables off some miserly traders? What would you rather, sir – would you rather she starved?'

The man shrugged. 'The law's the law, miss. Isnae up tae me tae ignore it in favour o' charity. It's ma job tae keep vagrants like her aff the streets.'

Between them Alice struggled against their firm grip, muttering and pleading for her freedom.

I looked at Angus. 'And would you agree with this?' I challenged him.

'He is right, Miss Rose. We can't pick and choose the laws we like.'

'I see,' I replied, indignant. 'And what happens to her now? A night in those dreadful cells? The poor woman won't survive it.'

'Och it's no' so bad,' the guard replied cheekily. 'A straw bed for the nicht and a bit o' gruel for her dinner.'

'And after that?'

The man shrugged again. 'It's no' up tae us what happens tae her after that.'

I shuddered, looking at Alice's frightened, desperate eyes. 'All that for the sake of some vegetables! Can you not see the injustice, sir? What became of those vegetables, anyway? Were they spoiled?'

'No,' Angus interjected, 'she was caught with them. They've been returned to the stalls.'

'So, no harm was done then, was it?'

Angus sighed, looking at me with heavy eyes. 'Perhaps – perhaps if you would vouch for her, if you were to take her home...'

'Angus!' the guard interrupted. 'Ye ken we cannae dae that.'

'Come on now, Dougie, the old woman hasn't confessed to anything. And who's to say she didn't intend to pay for those vegetables? That man down at the market didn't even give her a chance.'

'That's because he kens she's a thief,' Dougie retorted.

'Alice carries a tin about with her,' I added. 'It usually contains some coin, which would prove she had the means to pay, would it not?'

'Perhaps,' Angus replied. 'Have you got your tin with you today, Alice?'

Alice shook her head. 'Dropped it doon the market,' she replied, her eyes cast down. 'Too much in ma hands. Wis tryin' tae find it when that man started tae shout at me.' She looked up again then, fixing me with a hopeful stare. 'Am no' a thief, Joanna. You believe me, don't you? I just wanted some tatties. Rab likes tatties for his dinner.'

'Of course, Alice,' I answered her, before addressing the two guardsmen. 'It sounds to me as though an ill-tempered trader has jumped to the wrong conclusion about an old woman who had simply dropped her money and was trying to retrieve it. Wouldn't you both agree?'

Angus nodded, relinquishing his grip upon Alice's arm. 'I would, Miss Rose.'

'I cannae believe this.' Dougie threw his arms up in the air, releasing Alice who ran straight towards me.

I felt a smile spread across my face. 'Thank you, Angus.'

He gave me a brisk nod. 'Aye, well, I just hope I don't live to regret it.'

I led Alice away from the Tolbooth, taking her with me as I began to walk down the winding West Bow towards the Grassmarket. Once again, my day had taken an unexpected turn, and any hope I'd harboured of mulling over the information Jane had provided was now gone. Alice was unpredictable at the best of times, and I was responsible for feeding her and seeing her home safely. Thoughts of anything else would have to wait.

Just as we got a little way along the Bow, Alice stopped. She stood still for a moment, gazing around her, as though realising where she was for the first time. Fearing she was about to run from me, I tried to grab hold of her arm but she snatched it back, resisting with an indignant squeal. Then she moved away, not running but limping along as fast as her aged frame could manage. Confused, I followed her as she headed down a narrow close opposite the Assembly Room, where the old part of town's dances took place.

'Alice,' I called. 'Where are you going?'

I rushed through the grim, damp space, feeling thankful when it expanded quite quickly into a courtyard. There, in the middle, Alice stopped, her yellowing eyes staring straight ahead, writ with a sort of captivated horror.

'Alice?' I said gently. 'What is it, what's the matter?'

She raised her hand, pointing a crooked finger towards a crumbling old house in the centre. It was only then that I realised where I was. I felt my heart begin to beat a little faster as I looked up, knowing already what had drawn her here. A house with a fearsome reputation, renowned for the presence of evil spirits. A house so haunted that no one had dared to live in it for over a century. A house I had never ventured near because I couldn't bring myself to look at it.

But now I was looking at it. We were both looking and, I realised, we were both seeing the same thing. At the window on the first floor, a man's face – pale, sombre, and staring down at us.

'The Wizard of the Bow,' Alice whispered, her voice shaking.

Horrified, I pulled on her arm with all the force I could muster, all but dragging her away. It seemed that I wasn't the only person I knew who could see the dead, after all.

# Four

A family beset by scandal. A woman seeking a divorce. Two sisters with very different ideas about their futures. I mulled these scant details over in my head as I served drinks on a busy Saturday evening in the tavern. More than a day had passed since I'd spoken with Jane, but it remained the case that those were the only facts I had in my possession; anything else was mere conjecture. The picture Jane had painted of Clara was quite different from the one I'd perceived from my vision, or from that brief touch of her hand. I felt sure that underneath all that careful composure was a young woman in love, harbouring a well-kept secret. The question remained, was it the secret itself that was deadly, or its revelation?

I ran my hands down my apron, wiping sticky ale deposits from my fingers. I'd been working since lunchtime; my feet ached and my head felt muffled by the constant noise and exertion. I struggled to work long hours now; I had turned one-and-thirty in March, and my bones felt the weight of every year which had passed. I wasn't old, but I wasn't young anymore either. It was a thought which sat quite uncomfortably with me, forcing me as it did to reflect upon what had gone before, but also to acknowledge what was in front of me. I was likely too old for many things now; for marriage or for children, not that I particularly desired either. The future only promised more of the same – more evenings in the tavern, more nights alone. It was enough to make me melancholic, to hanker after a friend, dead or alive, to keep me company. I had people in my life – Jane, Franny, Alice – but those were acquaintances rather than friends. In truth, I'd not had a friend since I came here.

I'd not had a friend since Pierre.

My thoughts drifted wistfully back to my childhood friend, who had remained so even as I had grown up. He'd been stuck in eternal youth, but I'd promised never to leave him behind. Except, in the end, that's exactly what I'd done.

'How's Alice?'

Angus's voice pulled me into the present. I turned around and put on my friendliest face. He'd done me a good turn yesterday; I could set aside my self-pity for him, if not for myself.

'She's well, thank you. I took her something to eat this morning before I left to come here and she seemed in good spirits. She's likely forgotten all about yesterday already. She doesn't tend to remember much,' I added, pouring him a mug of his usual ale. 'It's on the house. Well, it's on me, to say thank you.'

He gave me an appreciative smile. 'As long as she's alright, and as long as my superiors don't find out about it.'

I frowned. 'I'm sorry. I was so concerned about Alice that I never even considered the trouble I might cause for you. That was thoughtless of me.'

He shook his head. 'There was reason enough to let her go, once we'd got her side of the story, although that wasn't a decision for a mere guardsman to make,' he added, more than a little sarcastically. 'But don't worry, Dougie's a good man; he'll not say anything.'

'Alright, as long as you're sure.'

'I am. Alice is lucky to have you, you know. If you hadn't intervened yesterday, she'd probably be facing a spell in the Bridewell by now.'

I shuddered at the mere thought of poor, frail Alice ending up in the House of Correction. 'Indeed. I must try to do better as far as keeping her fed is concerned, then she won't have cause to go down to the market and get herself into any more trouble.'

'I do wonder at the responsibility you take for Alice. It's very good of you. It's not like she's family.'

I shrugged. 'It's no hardship. Alice has no one, but neither do I.'

'Aye,' he replied. 'I know that feeling.' He took a large gulp of his beer. 'How are you getting on with that thing you couldn't make any sense of?'

I groaned. 'Oh. I got a bit more information about it from someone, but a lot of the details still don't make any sense to me.'

'Such as?'

I hesitated for a moment, unsure how much I should say. Quite clearly Angus read my expression because he let out an amused laugh.

'Come on, Miss Rose. You don't have to be specific. Keep names out of it and so forth. But try me - I like a good riddle.'

'Alright. Why would a woman need to come all the way to Edinburgh from London to divorce her husband?'

He gave me a quizzical look. 'That wasn't a question I was expecting.' He paused for a moment, and I found myself enjoying the thoughtful expression on his face as he contemplated the answer. 'Well, our laws are different. Anyone – man or woman – can get a divorce here. I think things are different down there.'

'Aye, they are,' interjected Franny. I had been so preoccupied with the problem in front of me that I hadn't realised she was listening.

'Go on,' I urged her.

'Doon there they can only divorce if they take their grievance tae the parliament. A man can dae it if his wife's been tae bed with another man, but I dinnae think she can if it's the other way aboot. Aye, an' there's those trials - ye must a heard o' those trials, Ailsa. What're they called? Criminal somethin' or other.'

'Criminal conversation,' Angus added. 'Aye, the newspapers love reporting on those.'

Franny screwed up her face. 'Well, I dinnae ken aboot that. I just ken what I hear talked aboot in this place.'

'So what happens at these trials? Who is on trial?'

Franny leaned in towards me, as though ready to impart some salacious gossip. 'Let's say a man finds out his wife is takin' another man tae her bed. A rich man, a man o' means. He might decide tae sue him first, get a bit o' money from the whole sorry affair, then divorce his wife afterwards. It's a scandalous business, though, as Angus says.'

'I see,' I replied, the pieces of the puzzle falling into place. Jane wasn't exaggerating when she talked of the extent of Andrews' ladies' recent hardships. What bearing any of it had upon what I saw in my vision, I still couldn't fathom.

Angus grinned at me. 'But now I'm really curious. What have you got yourself caught up in, Miss Rose?'

'Nothing,' I said quickly. 'Just trying to make sense of something I'd heard about.'

Angus nodded. 'You see and hear some interesting things, from the sounds of it.'

'Aye, an' she talks a lot o' nonsense, for all her clever ways,' Franny scoffed.

I shook my head. 'Never mind her,' I said, answering the look of confusion on Angus's face. 'You know what? I might have lived here for all these years, but sometimes I feel as much a stranger as I did on the day I arrived.'

Angus finished his ale. 'You're from France, aren't you?'

I eyed him sharply. 'Did Franny tell you that, or are you good at detecting accents?'

'Franny told me. I'd never have guessed. If anything, you sound English to me.'

I smiled slightly, thinking back to my days in the schoolroom, the endless recitations I was forced to undertake to remove all hints of French inflections from the unfamiliar words. My governess was English, and thorough.

'Do you know about the exhibition that's just arrived from France?'

'No?' I asked, only half-listening now as I served drinks. The tavern had grown even busier, and I was wary of Franny chastising me for being idle.

'Aye. Over in the New Town, on Thistle Street. It's been there for a few weeks now. Madame Tussaud, I think her name is. Specialises in making wax models of people – it's supposed to be quite the spectacle. Very lifelike figures, apparently. Anyway, I thought it might be of interest to you, since it's something from your homeland.'

I forced a smile. I remembered hearing of the waxworks, of the renowned exhibit at the Palais Royal. Of the death masks she'd made of guillotined royals and revolutionaries. I hadn't known that she'd come to Edinburgh, though. My stomach churned as I felt my worlds overlap a little.

'It is – very interesting, I mean. Thank you.'

He cleared his throat, shifting on his stool. 'If you'd like to go, I could always accompany you. It would be my pleasure.'

'Well, I'm not sure, I…'

Franny nudged me in the ribs. 'Dinnae be daft. Go an' see it.'

I drew a deep breath, sensing I had little choice in the matter. Maybe Franny was right; maybe I was being daft. After all, it was just an exhibition.

'Alright. Thank you.'

He supped his beer, his expression unreadable behind the rim of his mug. 'As I said, it would be my pleasure,' he replied.

*

I fell wearily into bed that night, every limb screaming in indignation at the hard labour they'd just endured. At some point I'd have to tell Franny that I couldn't work such long hours, but I knew now wasn't the time. In recent months she'd lost Jane and a couple of others to service; the arrival of more and more New Town families had offered them an alternative to tavern work, and I knew Franny hadn't yet found suitable replacements. My body would just have to bear it, and besides, I needed the money, especially as I was increasingly feeding Alice as well as myself.

*You were not made for that sort of work, ma chérie.*

'You didn't leave me with much alternative, Maman. Unless you wished for me to spend my life on my back.'

My imagination didn't bother to retort.

I turned over, trying to ease the pain in my shoulder. It was still giving me trouble after my fall at the Andrews' reading. The Andrews' reading: I shook my head at the reminder of it. There was little point in ruminating on any of that tonight; I was far too tired and besides, the information I'd discovered about the family's recent history hadn't got me any further forward in understanding the meaning of my vision. If I was honest with myself, I was beginning to doubt that I would ever get to the bottom of it.

Outside the streets were noisy; trouble was brewing, as it often did when drink was involved. Nights like that set me on edge, took me back to another time in my life. I knew Edinburgh wasn't Paris; rioting, when it occurred here, had always been quelled, in the end. But I'd seen how disorder could escalate, how quickly it sowed the seeds of revolt. How ready it was to tear everything down. I might not be in Paris anymore, but Paris still haunted me. It was always there, a part of me, forever melded with my soul. Angus's talk of Madame Tussaud's models had been an unwelcome reminder of that.

*Women like us are always vulnerable, Ailsa. We hang on the gold threads of others but are easily torn away.*

Except, I had no gold threads anymore. No fine clothes, no opulent rooms, no life of leisure. All I had now were memories, packed tightly between the stones of this tiny, damp room in which I lived my life. I had a few plain dresses, a couple of bonnets, a handful of books. I served ale for a living and had visions I kept to myself. My life was utterly unremarkable, but it was mine, and though lowly, was solidly built.

When I eventually slept it was fitful, disturbed intermittently by the commotion outside and the confused images those sounds produced in my mind. I dreamt I was back in our apartment in Paris, playing cards with Pierre and drinking wine. He was there too, slouched on the sofa, his waistcoat undone by his burgeoning belly, his lazy gaze watching my every move. He asked why I played by myself, whether I wanted a partner, and I couldn't explain about my dead friend so I just smiled and wished my mother would join us so I could escape to my room. He drew closer and I could smell him, all stale sweat and liquor-laced breath. I felt his hands reach towards me, but as soon as they touched my skin they began to melt like wax and I knew, without seeing, that Pierre had lit a match.

'Pierre! Maman will be displeased,' I cried as bit by bit, his fat form lost its shape and pooled on the floor.

But Pierre just grinned at me, and the next thing I knew I was standing at the bottom of a staircase. Above me raised voices echoed, punctuated by the thuds of footsteps on the wooden floor. I strained, trying to hear what was being said, but only managing to pick out words – something about love, about escape. Something about scandal. A woman screamed and I ran up the first couple of steps, brushing my fingers over the bright yellow paint which illuminated the wall.

I paused, realising the noise had stopped. My feet grew warm as beneath me, the floor softened and steps disappeared. I tried to walk up but couldn't; I was no longer climbing but wading as the world around me disintegrated into swirls of colourful wax.

'Help! Help!' I cried out, sinking deeper into the thick, hot pool. 'Maman? Pierre? Anyone?'

But no one answered. Outside the night finally grew silent as, trapped in my slumber, I felt the wax fill my lungs, encasing me completely, and swallowing me whole.

# Five

I watched the pale face staring back at me, flecked by the little black spots which tarnished my mother's old mirror. Her hazel eyes were heavy from nights of disturbed sleep, but her curls of auburn hair had been cajoled into pleasing order, pinned back with a few loose strands hanging fashionably at the front. Her pale blue dress was a favourite one, bought second-hand but so seldom worn that it almost passed for something new. It hung from her thin frame in places, despite the smoothing effects of her stays, but she decided she looked acceptable enough. In fact, she looked nice. Genteel, almost. But would she pass for a New Town lady? Perhaps. She smiled at me, just long enough for me to remind her not to be vain, not to forget her place now. Her smile faded, and I turned away to fetch my bonnet and shawl. Angus would be here any moment, and I didn't wish to keep him waiting.

*You used to wear that colour all the time in Paris. It was my favourite on you, do you remember? You had so many beautiful dresses!*

I ignored the reminder as I adjusted myself a final time. If I thought too much about it, I might be tempted to change, and then I really would be late.

I hurried out into the street, where we'd agreed to meet around eleven o' clock. It was a dull Wednesday morning; rain threatened to fall from the dark clouds gathering above, and the air had grown cooler than it had been in recent days. I was glad of my shawl, and pulled it tighter around my shoulders as I looked for Angus. I still felt uncomfortable about this outing; I wasn't sure viewing the exhibition was wise, given the memories it would likely provoke. I'd been in a morose sort of mood for days already, brought low by vivid dreams and a plaguing notion that I wasn't ever going to understand the meaning of my vision. I wasn't sure why it mattered – Clara Andrews was nothing to me, and yet…

And yet, she appeared to be in some sort of trouble. I couldn't stand by and let it happen. I couldn't wait until I read about it in the newspaper, or heard about it in the tavern. I couldn't live with that knowledge. I couldn't live with myself.

'Good day to you, Miss Rose,' Angus called as he approached, mercifully disrupting my thoughts. 'I beg your pardon for being a little late.'

I smiled. Like me, he'd made an effort, embellishing his usual shirt with a brown waistcoat and matching coat, a handkerchief tied around his neck and a grey tricorne hat upon his head.

'Don't worry - it's barely a moment past the hour. We could have met near the bridge, if that would have been more convenient,' I added, realising then that I didn't actually know where in the city he lived.

'Not at all, Miss Rose. I offered to accompany you. Shall we walk?'

I nodded. 'Yes. But please, Franny is right; you can call me Ailsa and let us dispense with Miss Rose altogether.'

He let out a little laugh, and though we were walking side by side I found myself turning towards him, trying to interpret his countenance. He looked cheerful, his lips hinting at a smile, but the manner of his body seemed less controlled, perhaps even nervous. I wondered then if I'd been too forthright.

'If you'd prefer to keep to Miss Rose, that is also acceptable to me,' I added, after a few moments' uneasy silence.

'No, not at all, I…' he paused, as though gathering his words and putting them in careful order. 'It feels strange to call you Ailsa, is all. I would not presume to address someone like you in such familiar terms.'

'Someone like me? I work in a tavern.'

'Aye, you do, but you're not from those places, are you?'

He sighed, clearly conscious of his struggle to explain. I understood him, though. Perfectly.

'Forgive me for asking, but where are you from? I mean, I know you're from France. Actually, don't answer me – it was impertinent of me to ask.'

'No, it's fine,' I said. 'My early life in Paris was a fortunate one. My mother provided well for me – I had a nice home and a good education. Very good, in fact, for a girl. I think my mother dreamt of me becoming one of those salonnières.'

'I had thought right then; you are from a wealthy set,' Angus replied, pondering the details I'd given him. I wondered if he'd noticed how scant they were. I wondered if he'd guessed the parts I'd left out.

'I'm not from the nobility,' I added quickly, 'although we had certain connections, and…it became apparent that we needed to leave. Maman arranged everything, and so we came here, but unfortunately not many months after we had settled in the town, she passed away.'

'That must've been hard, being on your own in a strange country.'

'Hmm,' I mused. We were approaching the bridge; I could sense the change in the wind as it picked up around us. Although, if I was honest with myself, I knew that wasn't the only reason I felt suddenly cold and exposed. 'Anyway, enough about me. What was it like for you, growing up in Glen-?'

'Glendrian. Nothing like Edinburgh, or Paris, I'd imagine. Think of a tiny village, low stone dwellings sitting under the biggest sky you've ever seen. Around you there's just the green and the brown of the land as it rises into hills and then disappears into the sea. No tenements. No streets. No markets. Just your few wee homes and the land you live off.'

He smiled, catching his hat as the wind lifted it from his head. He took it off, and I noticed for the first time the deep black of his hair. I realised then that I'd never properly studied him in daylight before; his straight nose, his slim lips, the redness in his cheeks disrupting an otherwise pale complexion.

*Très beau. And I think he is around your age. Quelle chance!*

It was true. He couldn't be more than thirty years old.

'It sounds wonderful,' I replied, refocusing my mind on his story. 'I can't think why you'd want to leave.'

The smile faded. 'A hard life in a beautiful place, where the land doesn't always provide. I'd started forming a habit of going away – seeking work in other places, kelping and the like. I'd heard of others leaving for the towns and thought, well, why not? I thought I could find a better life here.'

'And did you?'

He laughed, shaking his head. 'No. I found a hard life in a not-so-beautiful place. But though the pay in the Guard is poor, it's regular and it's enough. And I've got used to this town, for all its dirt and smoke.'

His story had so absorbed me that I'd barely noticed any detail of where we had walked since leaving the bridge. Now I found myself standing on an orderly-looking street of new, grey stone buildings, identical in character to those I'd seen on my visit to the Andrews' house. I followed Angus as we walked past a multitude of doors, stopping only as we reached a final dwelling on the corner. I swallowed hard, staring at its black door, flanked by windows which, I immediately noted, were all screened by thick curtains. Outside, a simple notice announced the exhibition: The Grand European Cabinet of Figures.

'I believe this house is usually used for dancing classes,' Angus said quietly, nodding towards the sign. 'This is quite a change; don't you think?'

'Yes, indeed,' I replied. I gave him a smile, hoping he wouldn't detect how grim I was feeling.

I followed Angus inside and into a hallway, where he purchased two tickets – he wouldn't let me pay for my own, no matter how much I protested. There was no queue, and there seemed to be few visitors around. Perhaps word hadn't spread quite yet. Or perhaps this exhibition wasn't to New Town tastes. After taking Angus's money, the ticket seller, a thin young man with mesmerizingly dark eyes, handed me a small paper pamphlet.

'A guide to the wonders and spectacles of Madame Tussaud. She is here today, talking to visitors about the collection,' he enthused with a thick French accent. 'Mais faites attention, monsieur,' he added, addressing Angus, 'some things can be difficult for the ladies to see.'

'I'm sure I shall be fine, thank you,' I interjected, a little irritated by his insinuation. But he had already turned his attention away from us and towards the paper laid out in front of him on his little table. Wondering what could be more important than his guests I peered over at it, and saw that he was sketching. I supposed I should not be surprised that a young man working for an artist, was also an artist himself.

We made our way into the first room, where it took a few moments for my eyes to adjust to the dim light. Whether out of style or necessity to protect the displays, all daylight had been extinguished by the drawn curtains, and the candelabras only sparsely lit. Two gentlemen stood in the middle of the room, talking to a small woman with a French accent who I presumed to be Madame Tussaud. I studied her for a moment, noting her simple but elegant dress and animated smile as she answered their questions about her work in her somewhat hesitant English.

'I think that must be her,' Angus whispered rather too loudly.

Our attention earned us a nod of acknowledgement; it was polite, but I felt the heat of embarrassment rise in my face. I didn't like to be caught staring, but also, something about the keen look in her eye told me we'd been examined just as closely.

The lack of light also unsettled me, and I found myself walking closer by Angus's side. We were greeted first by royalty; countless wax mannequins stood tall, perfectly sculpted down to the minutest detail, and all dressed in their finery. Angus was drawn immediately to the figure of la reine, Marie Antoinette, a spellbinding vision in her wide dress and powdered wig, her bright blue gaze staring off into the distance. I watched, a little amused by his reaction as he circled around her, his mouth agape, as though he wasn't looking at a model but was meeting the queen herself.

'I never knew what she looked like,' he said, as though explaining himself to my unspoken thoughts.

We moved around the room, perusing the other figures of France's rich and powerful, as they once had been; images of a bygone time, suspended now in permanent animation by Madame Tussaud's magical touch. Le roi, the sixteenth Louis, stood near to his wife, and flanking the royal couple were countless comtes, comtesses and other members of la noblesse. Near to the far wall one figure of a woman caught my eye. Unlike all the others she wasn't standing but lying down on a fine, gilded sofa, her raised arm partially obscuring her face as she slept. She was unmistakeably beautiful; her hair golden, her face serene, lips hinting at a smile. I drew closer, opening the pamphlet to find the figure's description.

'Madame de Sainte-Amaranthe, modelled by Monsieur Curtius,' I said aloud. 'Interesting that she's not one of Madame Tussaud's figures. I wonder how she came to be here.'

'Perhaps she's someone important,' Angus suggested. 'Do you know who she is?'

'I don't, I'm afraid,' I replied, and I didn't. Something was familiar about that name, but I couldn't place what it was. 'But it's certainly a captivating image – whoever she is.'

Angus grinned. 'I'm glad you agreed to come today. I felt certain you'd enjoy it.'

Above us a sudden thud startled me, followed by the tinkling of piano keys and animated chatter. I frowned, confused momentarily by the sound. Then I remembered: dancing classes.

Together we moved into the next room, a smaller space which seemed even darker than the first. In here too it was quiet and empty, and again the models stood tall and orderly, but unlike in the previous room there were no bodies – only wax heads, mounted on wooden poles. I felt the air disappear from my lungs as I absorbed their details; their eyes half-closed, their expressions grotesque, their blood appearing to trickle from open mouths and run down their severed necks. Whereas the previous room had exhibited the dazzling riches of the ancien régime, this room reeked of the revolution, and Madame la Guillotine was centre-stage.

At once I felt myself begin to spin; it confused me at first, as I was sure I was rooted in horror to the spot. Then I realised it was not me but the room which was moving, groaning and straining, perhaps protesting against the horrors it contained. The heads began to move too: one by one their eyes opened to look at me, their mouths pronouncing all manner of noises. Some screamed, some cried, others begged for help. I felt Angus's soft touch on my arm, heard his words of concern running like a current under the almighty din, but though he was next to me I knew he couldn't reach me. I knew I had already slipped too far away.

'Stop, please stop!' I heard myself say.

I pushed my fingers into my ears, pressing hard, but it did no good. The voices only grew louder, more insistent. Aidez-nous, they cried. Vous pouvez voir. Vous pouvez entendre. Aidez-nous! Then, in amongst the chorus, a voice I recognised. A face I recognised.

'Help me, ma petite,' he said, his wax tongue lolling from his broken jaw. 'For your mother. Help me for your mother.'

Hot tears filled my eyes as I ran from the room. I could hear Angus calling after me as I found myself back in the hallway. The voices seemed to follow me too, their pleas as constant as they were loud, their faces forever fixed in my mind. I collapsed on to the cold stone floor, crying out, desperate to be free from his horror, to be stirred from this waking nightmare. Somewhere in my periphery I became aware of footsteps on the stairs, of figures dressed in white muslin. Of pretty young faces, peering at me. Someone touched my shoulder, tried to stir me from the ground. Spoke in a voice I knew.

'Miss Rose? Are you quite well?'

The voices began to fade, my eyesight becoming clearer as the heads ceased to dominate and the tears my eyes had harboured began to fall. In front of me stood Clara Andrews, a look of deep concern etched upon her face. To her side was Angus – he was bent down, trying to talk to me, but I couldn't focus on what he was saying. All I could see was Clara, and behind her, the staircase, rising along a backdrop of bold yellow paint. As one vision subsided, the memory of another took over, and my head throbbed with the pain of it.

'It's here,' I gasped. 'Here is where it happens.'

Then I got to my feet and I ran from them both.

# Six

I'd never run like this in my life. Not even as a child. Not even in Paris, with the heat of the revolution bearing down on us as we fled in search of sanctuary. I'd sat in a carriage then, dressed as a servant girl, fixed to the spot while others steered my fate. I'd never reacted, never shown fear, even though I'd felt it canker in the pit of my stomach, rendering me unable to sleep or eat. I'd felt it all keenly: the loss, the terror, the disorientation of leaving my world behind and adopting another. But I'd worn a mask and credited myself with betraying nothing. The world was like the stage, my mother had always told me. We assumed our roles, and our fortunes rose or fell depending upon how well we executed them. I cherished my parts: faithful daughter, diligent scholar, innocent mannequin. I'd performed them well. I was bereft without them.

My shoes clattered hard on the ground, the growing heat scorching my lungs as I panted for want of breath. The sun had come out, at once illuminating and oppressing me as I dashed back over the bridge. The New Town passed into the old; the streets narrowed, the crowds and the dirt accumulated. Still I ran, winding my way past bodies and spectres, not caring to distinguish between the living and the dead. It didn't matter who saw me, who understood that I was aware of their presence on these ancient streets. Today I would not heed their careworn faces, or hear their half-remembered tales. I was weary of their awful mysteries. I just wanted to be home.

Finally, I reached the Canongate. I slowed my pace; my legs felt weak and every part of me burned with exertion as I limped the final yards of my journey. I drew nearer to Anstruther House, unable to remember ever being so happy to see its tall, faded glory. A few familiar faces hovered outside, greeting me with surprised expressions and reminding me what a sight I must be: a red-faced, breathless wreck in an ill-fitting blue dress and bedraggled bonnet. What was I thinking, going to that place today, and surrounding myself with all those ghosts? It had been asking for trouble.

I hobbled inside, dragging myself up the stairs. The air in the stairwell was cool, laced with dampness and dust, and I found myself possessed by a fit of coughing which I tried hard to suppress. Desperation weighed on me like a stone in my gut. I didn't want to draw any more attention to myself; I just wanted to be inside my room, with the door bolted behind me. I just wanted to shut everything out. With a sigh of blessed relief, I made it to my door, and turned my key in the latch.

'Have you any bread? I've had naught to eat today.'

Alice's voice echoed behind me. I sighed, trying to calm the waves of turmoil which swelled within me, and struggling to muster some compassion instead. I rushed inside, grabbing at whatever lay on my table. A morsel of bread, thoroughly dried out, was all I had to offer. Better than nothing, I supposed, and besides, I hadn't the appetite for it. I darted back out into the stairwell and handed it to Alice without a word to her.

'Thank you. Have you seen...?'

'No!' I called.

I fled back inside and closed my door to any further questions. I knew it was unkind, but I'd had my fill of other people's burdens for the day. Besides, Alice would forget. She always forgot everything.

I lay down on my bed, surrendering myself to the comforting familiarity offered by my soft pile of blankets. The sun outside had warmed my room, although not uncomfortably so, and I found the heat conspired with my physical exhaustion to lull me towards sleep. I didn't try to resist – in fact, I welcomed the refuge it offered. I desired a deep, dreamless slumber, capable of erasing all that I'd seen today – if only for a little while. I didn't want to think about France, about the bloodshed, about him. I didn't even want to think about seeing Clara, about the piece of her puzzle which had fallen into place the moment I saw her standing near to those stairs. I closed my eyes. All of that could wait until I had rested.

A knock at the door disturbed the peace. I forced my eyes to remain shut, determined to ignore it. It was probably Alice, looking for more food. That bread hadn't been sufficient, but it was all I had.

'I've nothing else to give you, Alice,' I called out. 'Please, leave me alone.'

'Ailsa? Ailsa – it's me. It's Angus.'

My eyes flew open. Angus. In the midst of all that had happened, I'd almost forgotten that I'd been with him. I'd been so determined to run from that place that I'd run from him, too. What must he think of me? I hauled myself off my bed, straightening my dress and smoothing down my frenzied hair. I didn't even dare to glance in the mirror; that might be enough to prevent me from answering the door altogether.

*It's good to see you have such a care for your appearance again, ma chérie.*

'Not now, Maman,' I hissed.

I opened the door, greeting Angus with the best smile I could manage, though doubtless it was grim. Wordlessly, I bid him to come inside.

'Ailsa, are you alright?'

The concern on his face made tears prick in the corners of my eyes. Tears of self-pity or tears of shame – I wasn't sure which. I sat back down on my bed; my head was now aching and for a moment I feared I might faint. Angus pulled up a chair beside me. He leaned forward, frowning but silent, awaiting an explanation. I knew I owed him that, at least. But what to tell him? And where to begin?

*At the beginning, Ailsa. Start at the beginning.*

The beginning – yes. I drew a deep breath.

'Angus, I am deeply sorry for my behaviour today, and for any embarrassment I may have caused you in making such a scene. That place – it brought back a lot of bad memories for me. About Paris; about what happened there. I told you earlier today that we had to leave…'

He nodded. 'Yes. I assumed you left because of the trouble there.'

'That's correct. As I said then, although we were not high born, my mother and I, we moved in aristocratic circles. At first, we thought that the strife wouldn't reach us, but as time went on it seemed to seep into everything. In the autumn of ninety-one my mother decided that we should leave. It was not long after the king had tried, and failed, to flee. That really alarmed her; she didn't know what was coming next, of course, but she seemed to sense it wouldn't favour us. And, of course, she was right.'

'So, how did you come to be a part of such society? Did your mother marry well?'

I gave him a sad smile. 'If only it was such a happy circumstance.' I drew another breath, preparing myself to tell a seldom spoken tale. 'My mother's name was Delphine Rose. She was an actress and a celebrated beauty in Paris. She was also a courtesan, and during her life was the mistress of a number of powerful men. The last of these was the Comte de Rocrois – probably the wealthiest and most generous of them all. He provided us with luxury, but as is often the case in these matters, it came at a price.'

Angus shook his head. 'You don't have to tell me, Ailsa. Not if you don't want to.'

'No, it's alright. Much time has passed and I've learned to live with it – or I thought I had, until today. The comte was kind and cruel by turn. He would beat my mother one day, then lavish gifts on her the next. As I grew older, as you might expect, he turned his attentions to me.'

'Oh God, Ailsa,' Angus said, and I watched as he curled his fists.

'No. He didn't…I mean, he was never successful. My mother made sure of that, as did a friend of mine, Pierre. But I disliked him - feared him, even. Over these past years I had managed to forget him, but recently I have found him creeping back into my thoughts, sometimes my dreams. Then today, at that exhibition, there was a waxwork…'

'Of him?'

I nodded. 'Yes. The comte didn't leave with us; my mother didn't include him in her plans. He lost his head to the guillotine, several years after we fled. His was one of those gruesome death masks we saw.'

'Now I can see why you were so distressed.'

*You see? He understands. You don't need to say anything more about it.*

No, I thought. I owed him a full explanation, whatever the consequences.

'There's more,' I began, 'although I'm not sure you'll understand. Most people don't, in my experience.'

He raised a curious brow at me. 'Go on.'

'All my life I've had certain abilities – some would call them gifts, although I'm not sure I'd regard them as such. Sometimes images take over in my mind, and I see things which haven't yet occurred. Other times I see the past; people who have departed from this world but whose spirits linger here. They speak to me and I can speak to them. My friend I mentioned, Pierre, was one such spirit. He looked out for me, helping me avoid the comte's advances and later, confirming my mother's worst fears and helping us to escape from Paris. He's been in my thoughts a lot recently, too.' I paused, trying to measure Angus's reaction. His face, however, remained impassive. 'And now, I'm sure, you think me quite mad. Or at the very least, you think what I've told you is a lot of nonsense, just like Franny does. I suppose I should be grateful for that. In times past, I would have been ducked in the

Nor Loch and burnt at the stake.'

To my surprise, Angus placed his hand over mine. His skin was rough, but warm, and I felt unexpectedly reassured by the gesture.

'I believe you. I'm not sure I fully understand what you've told me, but I don't think you're mad. So earlier today, at the exhibition, was it the comte's spirit that you saw?'

'Not exactly. It was more like a vision. Those horrid death masks began to move and talk, crying out at me to help them. I can hardly understand it myself; I've never experienced anything quite like it. It was overwhelming, and all that fear and horror I felt in Paris came flooding back to me. I think that was why I reacted the way I did.'

'It must have been dreadful.' He gave my hand a small squeeze before withdrawing his. 'I'm sorry. It was my idea to visit the exhibition. I would never have suggested it, if I'd had the slightest idea of its effect on you.'

I smiled, genuinely this time. 'Oh, how could you have possibly known? Mine is not exactly a predictable tale.'

He returned my smile. 'That's true. One thing still puzzles me, though.'

'Oh?'

'Your name – Ailsa. Did you change it, when you came here?'

I frowned. 'No, it's the name my mother gave me. I suppose it is an unusual choice for a French girl, but my mother was anything but ordinary.'

Angus stared at me, and I could tell he was mulling over the details. 'It's intriguing though, isn't it? Your mother gave you a Scottish name, and chose to flee to Scotland. I just wondered if you had a connection to this country, beyond finding sanctuary here? Perhaps some family of your mother, or even your father?'

I shook my head. 'My mother never spoke of my father, and I always felt I shouldn't ask – I don't know why. I suppose I wish I had now, given that she's no longer here. She died just a few months after we settled in Edinburgh. It was very sudden.' I bit my lip, willing myself to say nothing further on the matter. I had revealed enough about myself for one day.

'Yes, of course. I'm very sorry.'

'It was a long time ago. Eleven years, in fact.'

I was feeling rather exhausted now; both the afternoon's trauma and the effort of explaining had wearied me greatly, and my head pounded like a fierce drum beat. I knew that only sleep could restore me; there was never anything else for it.

'Forgive me, Angus. I am very tired.'

He got to his feet. 'Of course. I will leave you to rest. Before I go though, can I ask you one last question?'

'Yes?'

'Just before you ran away, you said something about this being the place where it happens. What did you mean by that?'

I stared at him. I had been so caught up in telling him about the past that I'd almost forgotten about Clara, about the staircase and the yellow wall. I thought for a moment about admitting him into my confidence on this also; his eye for detail and natural curiosity would certainly be assets in solving this particular puzzle. But what did I really have to tell him? Some half-formed images I barely understood myself about some unknown threat to a young woman I knew next to nothing about. No, I decided. I had told him enough for today.

'I don't remember,' I replied. 'I was so caught up in the vision. I doubt it was significant.' I lay down on my bed, obscuring my face before he could see the lie upon it.

'I see.' Angus walked towards the door, ready to let himself out. 'Get some rest now, Ailsa. I'll see you soon.'

'Angus? How did you know which door here was mine?'

He turned around, his face set in a sort of half smile, though his eyes were serious.

'I asked folk. You know, not many of your neighbours know your name, but most knew where I could find the auburn-haired woman in the pretty blue dress.'

I let out a sleepy chuckle, enjoying his favourable description of me. 'I can see why you're suited to being a guardsman.'

'I'm good at getting to the bottom of things, Ailsa. If you ever need help with anything, you need only ask.'

From somewhere between sleeping and waking I mustered a muted reply, and heard the distant creak of the door as he left. Then all was darkness and silence for a little while.

\*

By the time I woke it was late in the afternoon. I lay in bed for a few moments, contemplating the last remnants of spring sunshine as it fell behind growing cloud outside my little window. I wasn't expected in the tavern that evening, which was fortunate since, although my headache had abated and my mind had cleared, I still felt weary. I was also hungry, having not eaten since the morning and having given the last of my bread to Alice. I needed food and perhaps some air; my little room had grown stuffy, the air both hot and wet as warmth and dampness mingled. I forced myself out of bed and changed into my grey dress, packing the blue one away. I'm not sure what had possessed me to wear it; fine, flimsy and ill-fitting, it harboured pretensions I could no longer own. Pretensions to something I hadn't been for a long time.

After buying a roll from one of the nearby shops which was, thankfully, still open, I walked down the Canongate and away from the bustling town. To the south-east of my home the city simply fell away, the harsh streets suddenly replaced by soft grass, the towering tenements giving way to a backdrop of imposing hills known as the Salisbury Crags. I had on occasion walked up those steep rocks, sitting for some time at the top and admiring the city as it stretched beneath me in one direction, and as sea and country sprawled in the other. Today, however, I was short on both time and energy, and contented myself with a meander around the bases of those rugged cliffs as I breathed the cooling air and gathered my thoughts. It had been a difficult day, with far too many intrusions from my past. But I had also learnt something more about Clara Andrews, too. Something vital. I still didn't know exactly the nature

of the danger she was in, but I knew now the scene of her demise.
*Always jumping to conclusions, ma chérie. How many staircases with
yellow walls might there be in Edinburgh?*
My imagination tried to cast doubt, but I brushed it aside. No.
It was too much of a coincidence, seeing her there today, standing
against that fatal backdrop. My vision had spoken to me of candles,
of wax – that had to be why. It had to be that building, that
staircase. The question was, what possible danger could a genteel
young woman encounter at the place she attends to perfect her
dancing?

That question still preyed on my mind as I walked back up the
Canongate towards my home. The evening light was dim, the grey
clouds above hastening the dusk and bringing the lamplighters out
a little earlier than usual. Around me the streets and closes emptied
into the tenements and taverns as the need for beer and sustenance
overcame the city's work-weary residents. I thought for a moment
about carrying on up the street to Franny's; not for a drink, I didn't
want that, but for the solace of some company. However, I quickly
decided against it. Franny would only want to know every last detail
of my afternoon with Angus, and I feared I didn't have the
strength to recount it. I didn't have the strength for a great deal, it
seemed, as lifting my feet became such an effort that I tripped and
fell, right into a gentleman who was lingering nearby.

'Good God, woman, watch what you're doing!'

The man spun round, his steely blue gaze meeting my thousand
muttered apologies. He was a tall, fair-haired man in his middle
years, exquisitely dressed in a dark coat and white linen shirt, a
cravat tied around a high collar. A real coxcomb, and someone
who would have been handsome for his years, if it hadn't been for
the mean twist of his mouth. He watched as I got to my feet,
withholding any offer of help.

'You see, Henry. This is the difficulty with the taverns in this
part of town. All the gin-soaked nymphs collapsing in the gutters.'

I peered beyond him as another man emerged from his shadow.
This one, however, I recognised: a younger man, fair-haired and

equally immaculately dressed. At the Andrews' reading I hadn't taken in Henry Turner's features properly, but I did so now. He was rather unattractive, in truth, with a bulbous nose and thick lips which made his blue eyes seem tiny by comparison. He stared at me, and I saw a flicker of recognition pass over his face, but he didn't own it.

'Yes indeed, sir. Most inconvenient,' he replied.

I watched as the two gentlemen walked away, recalling the remarks Jane had made to me just days ago. No one knew what to make of him, she'd said. His motivations were a mystery, particularly concerning why he'd chosen to remain with those who had sunk so low in the eyes of London society. To me he seemed in every way typical of a young man in his position; imbued with privilege, infected with arrogance. But, as my vision about Clara had shown, everyone had their layers, their secrets. I wondered what Henry's were. I wondered why he hadn't wanted me to read his cup.

The evening air and that unpleasant encounter had sharpened my mind. If I was going to discover the meaning of my vision, I had to find out more about the Andrews family. There was no other way to proceed.

# Seven

A broth recipe: that was my cover story. I had decided upon it in the small hours, as I lay in bed and tried in vain to sleep. The world around me had been dark and quiet, and on any other night I would have drifted off without an effort. But I had been too restless, and instead of being a place of repose, that deep silence afforded me the space to think. To scheme, if I'm honest. My thoughts were not merely the idle wanderings of the mind, but the rudiments of a plan which, I knew, would not allow me to rest until I had exorcised it. I had to gain access to the Andrews' home, and to do so I had to contrive a reason to call on Jane. I had to need something from her. Around the stroke of three in the morning, my stomach growled, and – yes! That was it: a recipe. She'd always talked of her mother's cooking, always offered help when she'd cast a disapproving eye over my meagre, plain diet. It was a believable reason to call and besides, some wholesome food would not go amiss, especially as increasingly I fed Alice as well as myself.

Despite the barest amount of sleep, the following morning I rose early and made my way to Hill Street. I knew that no hour was too early for Jane, since her long day began around five. I shook my head, realising that she had been toiling for several hours already. I knew that working in a tavern could sometimes be grim, but nonetheless I would never understand what had possessed her to go into service. Outside it was drizzly and cool; heavy rain had fallen overnight, and the streets ran with murky water as nature washed Edinburgh's filth away. The Old Town air was damp and putrid, and I was almost relieved when the wind on the bridge caught me and swept me along into the cleansed orderliness of the newer streets. Perhaps new Edinburgh was beginning to grow on me, after all.

I arrived at the Andrews' home and made my way to the servants' entrance. As much as I wanted to gain access to the family living above stairs, it was unthinkable that I should call at the front door in any circumstance, never mind at such an early hour and without an appointment. I would just have to see what I could learn below stairs. It took several anxious moments for my brief knock to be answered; when it was, I was disappointed to see that it was not Jane but a man, middle-aged and balding, his face stern and disapproving.

'Yes?'

'Good morning. I'm looking for Jane. I'm a friend – my name's Ailsa. Ailsa Rose.'

'It's not her day off, and she's busy with her duties. I'm afraid whatever it is will have to keep.'

The man moved to shut the door, and I swiftly lodged my foot in the way. This wasn't going well, but I wasn't ready to be defeated just yet.

'Please, sir, it is rather urgent. It concerns a poor acquaintance of both myself and Jane. A matter of Christian duty, you might say,' I added. In desperate situations, there was never any harm in appealing to the Almighty.

The man pursed his lips at me, but I could see he was about to relent. 'Alright,' he said, opening the door wider, 'you may have a few moments.'

The comforting smell of warm toast greeted me as I followed the man inside and down a set of stairs into the servants' quarters. He directed me towards the kitchen where Jane sat at a wooden table in the centre, tucking into her breakfast. She looked up at me as I walked in; her mouth fell open and she dropped her spoon.

'Ailsa? What are you doing here?'

'Good morning, Jane. Sorry to disturb you. The man who answered the door said you could only spare a few minutes. I hope you don't mind but I have a favour to ask.'

'Oh, Mr Collinson did, did he?' Jane snorted, taking another spoonful of her porridge. 'Mr Turner's new valet - only been here five minutes and thinks he runs the house! You'd best sit down, then.'

I took a seat at the table, opposite Jane. The room was cosy, warmed by the range upon which pots simmered, emitting delicious smells and making my stomach growl.

'Are you cooking this morning?' I asked her.

She shook her head. 'No. Just keeping an eye while Mrs Simpson is up with the mistress. She's up with the larks, is Mrs Andrews. No doubt she's nipping Mrs Simpson's ear already about something or other. Anyway, what can I do for you, Ailsa? You said you had a favour to ask.'

'Yes, that's right. Do you remember my neighbour, Alice?'

Jane gave a slow nod. 'Aye, I think so. The old woman – rambles on a lot?'

'Hmm, yes. Well, poor Alice doesn't fare well, and I've been trying to look after her, making sure she eats and so on. I'm not much of a cook, though. I remember when we worked together, you used to talk about your mother's recipes, and I wondered if I might trouble you for instructions on making a simple broth?'

'Of course, although my writing isn't up to much, Ailsa. But I know those old recipes by heart, so I can tell you, if you want to write it down?'

'Yes, thank you.' I looked about me, realising I'd nothing to write upon.

'Here.' Jane rolled her eyes and handed me some paper and a pencil from a nearby drawer. 'Just don't tell Mrs Simpson I gave you that, or I'll be in the suds.'

She began to dictate the ingredients and method while she

finished her porridge. I scribbled down her instructions, keeping half my mind on the task at hand and the other half on observing what was going on around us. Disappointingly, though, that wasn't a great deal: neither the cook nor the valet returned, and seeing any member of the family in the servants' quarters was highly unlikely. I wanted to contrive a way to go upstairs, but I was at a loss to identify a reasonable excuse. When we finished, we were still alone, which at least allowed some time for a few carefully chosen questions.

'So how is life here, Jane? Does the family fare well? I hope they felt no further distress after my reading.'

Jane shook her head. 'No, they soon forgot about it, don't you worry about that. The family are much the same as ever. Mrs Andrews keeps to the house a lot; she pays a few calls but doesn't seem keen on venturing too much into society, which I suppose is to be expected. The young ladies keep a busier schedule, promenading about town and attending dancing classes at a place on Thistle Street. They must enjoy dancing as they spend a lot of time there. I think Mrs Andrews hopes they will impress at one of those balls they have at the Assembly Rooms on George Street, and that they will find husbands that way.'

'Mrs Andrews is very keen to see them both married,' I mused.

'Well, it's little wonder, really, what with the divorce and all. Miss Grace told me that it's important that their futures are secured.'

'And Miss Clara? What does she think?'

Jane shrugged. 'Miss Clara doesn't blether the way Miss Grace does, so it's hard to say. She keeps her own counsel. Although...' Jane paused, and I realised she was trying to decide if she'd said too much.

'Although?' I prompted, my interest piquing.

'I probably shouldn't really say this, but I heard Mrs Simpson and Mr Collinson talk of an argument between Miss Clara and Mr Turner. Apparently, they were overheard raising their voices at one another, and Miss Clara was seen running from the room in tears.

Mrs Simpson remarked that she'd never seen her like that before. She's normally so reserved.'

'Do you know what the argument was about?'

'No, but whatever it was must have really upset Miss Clara. She's barely spoken a word to anyone since. And if Miss Grace knows what happened, she's keeping tight-lipped about it, which isn't like her.'

I wanted to dig a little further, but unfortunately at that moment we were interrupted by a short, thickset woman walking into the kitchen. She wore an irritable expression on her flushed face, her red hair curling wildly from underneath her cap. She peered at me, wringing her hands on her apron.

'Who's this?' she asked Jane.

Jane immediately rose from the table. 'Mrs Simpson, this is Miss Rose, a friend of mine. Mr Collinson let her in - she had to speak to me about an urgent matter, but she is just leaving.'

Mrs Simpson waved a stray arm towards me, half in acknowledgement, half in dismissal. 'Yes, well, I think she'd better. You've work to be getting on with. Miss Grace will be ringing her bell soon.'

Jane frowned. 'It's usually Miss Clara first, Mrs Simpson. She is quite well?'

Mrs Simpson puffed out a heavy breath as she attended to the pots on the range. 'The mistress says she's already risen and gone out. More dancing classes, apparently. Don't get any work-shy ideas, though. There's a nip in the air today after all that rain. The fires will need extra attention.'

'Yes, Mrs Simpson,' Jane replied. 'I will just see Miss Rose out.'

Jane led me back up the stairs and towards the servants' door. I followed meekly; I knew there was nothing to be gained by probing any further. What Jane knew amounted to very little and my continued presence would only cause trouble for her. Some of what she had said had been helpful, though. I knew now that there was some conflict in Clara's life, although whether that was relevant to my vision was far from certain. I also knew that her presence at the exhibition house yesterday had not been an isolated occurrence but a frequent habit. The likelihood of that place being a danger to her had increased, although I was still far from understanding why.

'Sorry about her,' Jane said in a whisper as she opened the door and let me back out on to the lane. 'She's always cross. The mistress doesn't have a housekeeper so the whole lot falls on Mrs Simpson. She means no harm, though.'

I gave her a thin smile. 'I know you're happy here, and I'm glad of it, but I can never see the attractions of service.'

'Aye, well, there are worse lots to have in life. It'd be easier if the family had more of us, though. I run about from dawn till late at night, doing everything for everyone. Although not for Miss Clara today, it seems.'

'Is that usual, for her to go out so early, alone?'

Jane glanced over her shoulder briefly, before lowering her voice further. 'To be frank with you, Ailsa, she's been acting oddly for a while now. She's always been an independent sort, but recently it's like she doesn't want anyone near her. She's been even worse these past few days since she argued with Mr Turner. I don't think she has gone dancing this early before, and never on her own - she usually goes a little later with Miss Grace. But I suppose it doesn't surprise me that she has.'

'And what of Mr Turner? How has he seemed since this argument took place?'

Jane rolled her eyes. 'The same as ever. Can do no wrong in the mistress's eyes. A real gentleman about town, is that one, with his dandy clothes and his new valet all to himself.'

I thought about my encounter with him last night, his face lit by the street lamps as he gave me an indifferent stare. No one seemed to know much about Henry Turner, but the glimpses of his character that had emerged didn't appear to be favourable. Unpleasant young men were not necessarily dangerous, though. If they were, most of the eligible ladies in the country would be in trouble.

\*

After leaving the Andrews' residence I took the short walk on to Thistle Street. I wasn't sure why I headed in that direction or what I expected to achieve, but something propelled me there nonetheless. An insatiable curiosity, I suppose, or the hope that I might be fortunate enough to see something important, however unlikely that was. After all, I could hardly wander into that building; I had no business being in those dancing rooms, and I didn't dare venture anywhere near that exhibition after causing such a scene. Memories of my vision yesterday still taunted me; his dreadful face still loomed, large and heavy in my head. I couldn't risk a repeat performance.

*You always were so nervous about him. I don't know why. I protected you, didn't I?'*

'I know, Maman,' I whispered. 'But I still had to witness what he did to you.'

I shuddered, pushing all thoughts of the past from my mind as I reached that now familiar building on the corner. To my surprise, the door through which I'd entered yesterday was closed, and the sign alerting passers-by to the exhibition was nowhere to be seen. It was early, I supposed; it had been much nearer noon when Angus and I had visited yesterday. Presumably it hadn't opened yet. I wandered down the lane which ran down the side and to the rear of the buildings, looking for a second entrance where it might be presumed the dancers would gain access. Once again, everything appeared to be locked up; the place was deserted, and no sound came from within. Perhaps the classes hadn't started yet, either. But if they hadn't, then why did Clara leave home to come here so early?

'Can I help you?'

A voice from above startled me. I followed the sound, looking up to see a woman leaning out of an open window on the second floor, shaking out rags.

'I was told there are dancing classes here. Am I in the right place?'

'Aye, but Mr Bernard doesn't start his classes until eleven. If you come back in an hour, he should be here by then.'

'So, there's no one in there at the moment? A friend told me about the classes here and I'm sure she said Mr Bernard taught classes all morning.'

'I'm afraid your friend was mistaken,' the woman replied, beating her cloths with her hand. 'There's only me here. I come in first thing to clean before his students arrive.'

'You're the only person in the building?' I pressed her.

She beat the cloth harder. 'For the dancing. Can't speak for that French exhibition downstairs – that's nothing to do with me. Not heard anyone, though.'

I thanked the woman, and watched as she retreated back inside. I didn't know what I expected to find here this morning, but this certainly wasn't it. Clara Andrews wasn't here. She'd gone out this morning, without her sister, and concealed her true whereabouts. Worse than that, she'd given a terrible excuse – if I could establish so easily that she wasn't really at dancing lessons, then her family certainly could. Her behaviour was secretive, but it was also reckless and, as Jane had said, it was odd. There had to be a reason for a young lady of her standing to behave in such a way. I thought again about what I'd seen in my vision, and what I'd sensed from the touch of her hand. She had been worried about something; I'd felt her turmoil, but I'd also felt love. The existence of a secret lover would certainly explain her behaviour; I wasn't quite the woman of the world that my mother had been, but I knew enough about it to know that. But that could only be part of the story, surely? A lover might lead her to scandal, to ruin, but why to the sort of danger I had foreseen?

Deep in thought, it took me a few moments to notice how the air around me had grown cooler. A breeze got up and began to whisper my name, carrying an ethereal voice towards me. A boy's voice, soft and unbroken. Rooted to the spot on that lonely lane, I thought I saw a little face peering at me around the corner, a pair of deep brown eyes boring into my soul. Then I heard a sob; a loud, echoing cry which seemed to bounce off all the walls around me and strike me from every direction. Help, the voice wailed. Help.

'Pierre,' I whispered. 'Is that you?'

I readied myself for a vision, but it didn't come. Instead, the sobbing stopped; the breeze abated. The face disappeared. My question was left hanging in the now still air, but I knew the answer; I had recognised those eyes and that voice straight away. Whatever was going on, Pierre wanted me to uncover it. He wanted me to save her. If only I knew why.

'I will get to the truth, Pierre,' I promised. 'I don't know why she matters to you, but I will help her.'

I owed him that much, at least.

# Eight

Angus didn't come into the tavern that night. That wasn't unusual; he only came in when his guard duties allowed, and his absence meant he was probably on watch through the night. But I was anxious to see him, after all that I'd told him. After all that I'd held back. I knew he'd sensed I wasn't being entirely truthful; I'd been too tired at the time to realise it, but when I thought now about the way he'd turned his back, and the way he'd left, it seemed obvious. He knew I'd been lying when I said I didn't know the meaning of my own words – of course he knew. He was good at getting to the bottom of things. But I'd already told him so much about myself. I shuddered every time I thought about how much I'd said about my past and my abilities. I felt so exposed, and the more I thought about it, the more his absence felt less like bad luck and more like ridicule.

Maybe he had the night off, and had gone somewhere else for a drink.

Maybe he was avoiding me.

Maybe he thought I was mad.

I meandered wearily around the tavern, last night's lack of sleep finally catching up with me. It had been a slow start to the evening but it was getting busier now, and for a while at least I could hide from my doubts and throw myself instead into the repetitive motions of serving drinks, taking coins, smiling nonchalantly. It was a boisterous crowd tonight, thirsty for ale but friendly enough. I knew I wasn't as talkative as normal, that I was distracted, my eyes constantly creeping towards the door and hoping to see Angus's smile. I couldn't help it. I didn't know why it mattered so much to me, but I wanted to make sure that he would still come here. That he would still buy his favourite drink and talk to me, just as he'd always done.

Of course, Franny never missed a thing.

'Lookin' for Angus?' she asked, nudging me in the ribs.

'No!' I bristled. 'I'm just tired tonight. Didn't sleep well.'

'Oh, aye?' she replied, winking at me. 'It wis like that, wis it? I kent it wis warmin' up between you two, but I never thought ye'd go tae bed with him that fast!'

I almost spilled the beer I was pouring. I stared at her, open mouthed. No one had ever spoken to me like that, not even my mother, for all that she could be brazen at times.

'Dinnae look at me like that, lass. He's a guid man. Ye could dae worse than Angus.'

'You're always telling me to keep away from men,' I retorted.

I walked away with a full jug in my hand. I hoped to end the conversation there, but she followed. I shouldn't have been surprised; Franny was infamously persistent.

'Aye, I ken, but no' Angus. No' guid men like him, Ailsa. How was yer day with him yesterday? Did ye enjoy the exhibition?'

'Yes, it was very interesting. We had a very nice day together.'

I put the jug down on one of the tables, giving the men sitting there a brief smile. Then I walked away again, hoping Franny wouldn't follow. I wasn't telling her anything else. How could I? She'd tell me it was all nonsense, that I'd made a fool of myself. That I'd let a perfectly decent man slip through my fingers. If I was looking for a husband, then she'd probably be right. I was more concerned that I might have lost the chance of his friendship.

'Ye think ye'll go oot together again then?'

I sighed, stopping and turning to face her. She wasn't going to let this go.

'I don't know. Why don't you ask Angus himself, if he ever comes in here again.'

Franny frowned. 'What dae ye mean by that? Ye didnae upset him, did ye?'

'No, but…'

She didn't let me finish. 'Ye need tae put yer airs and graces tae one side, lass. I ken ye must have had a different kind o' life at one time, but no' now. Angus would be a guid catch. He's a kind man, an' he thinks the world o' you, I can tell. I've been around long enough tae ken that look in a man's eyes.'

I glared at her. I knew I shouldn't, but I couldn't help it. I knew how much my life had changed; how much my circumstances had reduced in the years since my mother's death. I didn't need Franny to point it out.

'I'm not looking for a husband,' I snapped. 'Like you, I'm happy to be on my own.'

I expected the bite in my answer to end the conversation, but to my surprise, Franny shook her head, her eyes suddenly heavy with a sadness I hadn't seen before.

'A man an' some bairns would've made me far happier than running a tavern tae the end o' ma days. But it wisnae tae be.'

'Oh Franny, I'm sorry…' I began, but this time it was Franny who walked away.

Inwardly I groaned. I was so tired - so out of sorts, as Franny would say. I needed to go home and to bed, before I upset anyone else.

\*

Unfortunately for me, closing time was not quick in arriving, nor did the crowd of drinkers quickly disperse. If anything, the place grew busier still, the lively chatter building towards an unbearable crescendo as the hours wore on. Some of the men, a real ragged-looking group with fraying shirts and filthy slops, started up some singing, earning them disapproving looks from some of our more discerning guests. That was the thing about the tavern; it attracted all sorts, from the richest men down to the poorest. Although they didn't drink together, they did, for a brief time, share the same dimly lit space in this shabby little corner of the city. It fascinated me, and I'd once asked Franny why the finer sort would choose to drink in places like this.

'It's away fae their world, I suppose,' she'd replied, her own voice full of wonder, as though the thought had never occurred to her before. 'Away fae their society rules an' games. Perhaps it makes 'em feel free.'

I'd thought about the comte then. Tucked away in our resplendent home and shielded by my mother, I'd known so little of how men such as him spent their time. Given what I often witnessed now during an evening's work, perhaps that had been for the best.

Certainly, the tavern seemed to liberate them, for it was often the best dressed who were guilty of the worst behaviour. That was undoubtedly true tonight. They might have disapproved of the singing, but the well-to-dos were quite content to make their own scene; staggering around half-blind from drink, laughing raucously and making more than a few lewd remarks. It wasn't anything I hadn't seen before, but my mood meant that it grated more than a little on my nerves. Such was my distracted, irritable state of mind that it took some time before I noticed some familiar faces in amongst that particular crowd. In fact, I might not have noticed at all if one of their number hadn't placed an unwelcome hand upon my backside as I removed the empty bottles of port and old hock from their table.

'Kindly remove it, sir,' I hissed through gritted teeth. I always objected to such behaviour, even on a good night, and I had no ability to tolerate it now.

The man pulled his hand away sharply, apparently alarmed by my manner. Good. I wearied easily of his sort, thinking that money could buy them anything. I liked to remind them that not everyone was for sale.

The man beside him laughed loudly. 'Even the tavern luckies won't have you, James!'

My ears pricked up at the voice jibing his friend; I knew its haughty, well-spoken tones from somewhere. I glanced to one side, keen to satisfy my curiosity. There he was: the man from the previous night, the one who'd sneered at me as I'd pulled myself back up out of the gutter. He caught my gaze for a moment, but there was no flicker of recognition. Of course there wasn't: women like me were nothing to him. And there, sat beside him, was Henry Turner. I felt my heart leap into my throat, and instinctively my eyes darted away and back to the army of empties scattered all over the table. It was unlikely that he'd noticed me, since his eyes were barely open. He slouched in his chair, head lolling backwards, a stupid smile fixed on his face as his body succumbed to inebriation.

'No matter,' the man, James, replied, 'what you can't take, you can just as easily pay for.'

His crude remark earned him some more laughter, which he basked in as he drank thirstily. His head wobbled unsteadily atop his neck, and his eyes rolled. The last thing he needed was more port. I finished collecting their bottles and moved on to clearing an empty table nearby. Here I worked more slowly, listening to their conversation. I wasn't sure why; the ramblings of a group of drunken men were unlikely to reveal anything of import. But for some reason Henry Turner intrigued me, and I needed all the information I could gather if I was ever going to get to the bottom of my vision about Clara.

'Yes, indeed,' the sneering man was saying, 'but the difficulty in paying for such pleasures is that often you will get more than you bargained for. Even the genteel houses are rife with the pox.'

'But Charles, that is the last thing on a man's mind when he gets tempted into one of those dark wynds by a creature of the night. All sense and reason abandon the mind,' James replied, almost falling from his chair.

'That's because the mind is full of port,' Charles scoffed. I watched as he nudged Henry, who judging by his silence must have been almost sleeping. 'And it is no excuse. We should try to be more like young Henry here. He never goes anywhere near a bawdy house. Not in London, and not here.'

Henry had his back to me, but I could tell by the nod of his head that he briefly stirred. Whoever this Charles and James were, they'd helped him get into a sorry state this evening. I wondered if this was normal for him, to get quite so drunk. I wondered if he was trying to drink his cares away. I wondered if his cares had anything to do with Clara.

Henry slurred a response; I strained to hear it, but it was utterly unintelligible. The men seemed to understand it, however. They both laughed wickedly at him, as though he'd just told a joke in very bad taste.

'It pains me to see him like this,' James said as their laughter abated.

A shadow fell over Charles's face. 'He's made a fool of himself, James. But he'll learn. We all do, in the end. And it's nothing that cannot be resolved, if he keeps his word to me.'

He looked up, catching my eye again and this time, seeming to notice me. His stare hardened, and his lip curled into a look of sheer revulsion. I felt the colour rise in my cheeks and quickly, I looked away.

'Come, James, let's drink up and see Henry home. All the filth of the streets seems to have gathered in here tonight.'

I didn't look over again, but I felt them get up and leave as I hurried to finish the work I had been lingering over. I hoped he hadn't realised I was listening, but I sensed that he knew fine well that I had. For some reason, that thought made me uneasy. There was something about that man which told me that I'd be wise not to cross him. Pity, then, that I already had. Twice.

\*

I couldn't get that man's face out of my mind, even as I fell into bed that night. I was exhausted and should have been able to sleep easily, but the conversation I overheard kept running through my mind. What had Charles meant, when he'd said that Henry had made a fool of himself? And what did he mean about fixing it, if Henry kept his word? I tossed and turned, listing the possibilities. Was it all about a woman? They had been talking about women, but that wasn't unusual; many men did once they had a drink inside them. Or had he made a fool of himself in his profession, damaging his reputation in some way? It was possible; after all, Jane had intimated that Henry was ambitious. Or was it something that, try as I might, I couldn't even guess at? I knew virtually nothing about Henry; he'd remained an enigma ever since he hadn't allowed me to read his cup. All I knew were the scant details I'd seen and heard. An argument with Clara, the cause of which was unknown. A propensity for drunkenness in the Old Town taverns. A friendship with an unpleasant gentleman of whom I knew nothing except his name. And now I knew that there'd been some foolish act on his part, presumably in his recent past. None of that really told me anything. It certainly didn't shed any light on the mystery surrounding Clara. If anything, each piece of information I learned seemed to provoke more questions than ever.

I sighed, turning over once again and determining to sleep. I would never be able to work out any of this if I was tired. Indeed, part of me believed that I might never be able to work out any of it at all. My thoughts slowed as sleep began to crawl over me, and they wandered lethargically towards Angus. He would be able to help, I knew that. If only I had dared to ask him, when I'd had the chance. It was probably too late for that now. He'd probably already decided that I was deranged, an embarrassment best avoided. Or, like Franny, he'd decided that I was a woman full of pretensions to a life she no longer possessed. Either conclusion would be enough to frighten him away. No. I would have to work this out on my own. I couldn't depend on anyone else. I hadn't had anyone for the last eleven years; there was no point in thinking that could change now.

But still, as sleep finally wrapped me in its comforting embrace, it was Angus who kept returning to me, placing his hand over mine, his imagined touch washing up like waves against my skin. My waking self would have been appalled, but safe in my slumber, I allowed myself to savour that moment, and to dream of others which would never come to pass.

# Nine

The rain poured down as I hurried along the High Street, the great, heavy droplets battering the ground and forming streams which ran apace along the gutters. Water soaked through the cloth I'd draped over the basket I carried, and every part of me was drenched; my shawl, my bonnet, my stockings. Inwardly I cursed my ineffective shoes; the soles had thinned, and I had hardly needed a wet Edinburgh day to remind me that they needed to be replaced, or that I should have had the good sense to wear pattens. The streets were quiet; even the town's spirits seemed to have made themselves scarce, and I saw barely a soul, either living or dead. Apparently, I was one of only a few who had been foolish enough to venture outside during such a deluge. I needed food, and with the very best of intentions for the day ahead, had decided that I would use Jane's broth recipe to make a warm meal for Alice and me. But as the water climbed up my skirts and began to weigh me down, I wondered if I should have stayed in my room.

I reached the top of the Lawnmarket, my head bowed against the ceaseless torrent, my thoughts fixed on Alice. I hadn't seen much of her since the middle of the week, when I had spoken to her so harshly. I shuddered at the recollection, and for a moment I wondered if she'd been avoiding me. It was certainly out of character for her not to appear at my door, rambling about Joanna and Rab and begging for a morsel of food. It seemed unlikely that she'd remember how I'd spoken to her, but that did nothing to ease my conscience. If anything, I felt worse. I gritted my teeth, determining to regard this dreadful outing and the meal I would produce from it as a sort of penance. It was the least I could do, after being so unkind.

*And what about the young man you have frightened away? What are you going to do about him?*

I pulled my sodden shawl firmly around my shoulders and ignored the imagined question. In truth, I didn't know what to think about Angus. It hadn't been so long since I'd last seen him, yet given the circumstances in which we'd parted I'd hoped to have seen him again by now. The fact that I hadn't left me feeling foolish. I'd talked to him about myself, my past, and my secrets. The likelihood that he had been repelled by what he'd heard stung me more than I cared to admit. Cold water dripped from the edge of my bonnet and on to my face. I wiped it away with the back of my hand, and brushed all thoughts of Angus to one side. I didn't have time to think about him, or to mourn for a blossoming friendship I'd probably already lost. If I was going to ruminate on anyone, it should be Clara Andrews. The unanswered questions which still surrounded my vision were more than enough to preoccupy my mind.

I turned to walk down the West Bow, the change of direction allowing a gust of wind to bite at my soaked form. My teeth chattered and I huddled down against it, walking so fast that I was almost breathless. Like the rest of town, the Bow was deserted, eerily quiet except for the wind which whistled between its collection of antiquated abodes. I traced a path directly down the middle of the winding street, the torrents of rainwater cascading from the roofs of the towering tenements removing any possibility of seeking shelter beside them. Fighting the urge to give up and return home, I clenched my jaw and fixed my thoughts on the bowl of warm food which would later be my reward.

'Ailsa.'

The sound of my name being called alarmed me, for I was certain there was no one else around. I stopped and looked about me in every direction, even glancing up in case it was someone calling out from a window. But no wave, no smiling face greeted me. Shaking my head at what was surely my imagination, I continued on.

'Ailsa!'

The voice was louder this time, so loud in fact that it seemed to surround me, its insistent tone pulsing down the Bow and along its assortment of narrow closes. Above me the sky rumbled, the grey clouds blackening as they greeted the coming storm. The rain beat the ground as though it was a drum, providing accompaniment to the high, melodic voice as it sang my name, over and over. Was it a voice I knew? I couldn't be sure; there were too many competing sounds.

'Pierre?' I called out in hope.

I listened but heard no affirmation. After a moment the day grew lighter once more, and the rain began to abate. The voice, too, faded.

Then, to my side, came a sharp, loud creak. Startled, I watched with my mouth agape as the iron gate guarding the nearby close swung open of its own accord. I stifled a gasp as I recognised the narrow passage; it was the same one which Alice had run down just a week ago. I shuddered, thinking of that face at the window, of all the stories I'd heard. The invitation was clear, but I knew exactly where it led, and it was somewhere I did not wish to go.

'No, thank you,' I whispered. 'I've no time to play your games.'

I turned away, intent upon continuing my journey down to the market. I would not be drawn into the darkness; I would not fall prey to malevolent spirits. I had enough problems to contend with as it was.

'Ailsa!'

A cold breeze wound itself around my fingers and I felt a small hand tug mine. My resolve wavered as images ran uncontrolled through my mind. A deck of cards, scattered across a wooden floor. Fine green curtains, pulled hurriedly shut. The cries of the mob as they grew ever closer in the street below.

A burning candle, its wax running like tears down its sides.

'Pierre? It is you, isn't it?'

He didn't answer me. Instead, the tugging on my hand grew stronger, beckoning me into the close. After a moment I relented, following his lead down the narrow passageway. The dark, dank space quickly enveloped me and I felt my heart begin to quicken in my chest. I took several deep breaths but they provided little comfort, the moist, putrid air I inhaled settling heavily in my lungs. All the while, my mind raced. Why did Pierre want me to come down here? Didn't he know what surely lay in wait for me?

What if I was wrong – what if it wasn't Pierre leading me here at all?

I arrived in the courtyard, greeted by the rain which had intensified once more. I wrung my hands, discomfited by the realisation that Pierre – or whoever it was – had released me from their ethereal grip. Just as it had done the previous week, my gaze fell upon that house, that empty, haunted place which had terrified the city's residents for more than a hundred years. I stared warily for a moment at its dilapidated stone and rotting wooden door, unable to tear my eyes away. I recalled the face Alice had spotted at the window, recalled the name she had given him – the Wizard of the Bow. I'd seen that face then too.

I could see it again today.

I blinked, trying to erase the image, but when I looked again, I realised it had only multiplied. Two figures watched me now; I saw their shadowy visages staring out of the gloom, and sensed their lifeless eyes gazing at me from another time. Everything I'd heard about what occurred in that house raced through my mind; all those tales of a brother and a sister delving into dark magic and even darker desires. Witches, they'd been called back then, and although belief in such things was now consigned to the past, the town still marvelled at their story. They'd hanged, of course, but, according to local folklore, that hadn't stopped them from returning to the earth. For what purpose I didn't know, and I'd no intention of finding out.

'Why did you bring me here, Pierre?' I muttered under my breath.

But no answer was forthcoming. I turned away and made a swift exit back down the close, resolving to stay clear of that house. The dead liked to tell their stories in their own words, and I doubted I had the stomach for the secrets those two spirits would whisper, if ever I gave them the chance.

*

I made my way quickly around the stalls of the Grassmarket, buying what I needed under the weight of an incessantly gloomy sky, before returning up the West Bow, this time resisting giving even the close leading to that awful old house another glance. I had to visit one more market, as Jane's recipe required some ingredients which would be best purchased from the vegetable stalls under North Bridge. Inwardly I groaned; it was the market I least liked to visit, partly because of its position on the site of the old drained loch, riddled with spirits, and partly because of the fleshy stink emanating from the slaughterhouse which sat beside it. At least the heavy rain had lightened to a drizzle, making my journey less miserable as I slipped past the Luckenbooths and down towards the under-bridge. Town had grown busier too, and as I drew closer to the bridge, I could see that a crowd had begun to gather. I peered in front of me, wondering what on earth had caught their attention.

'There's an auld wummin up there. Says she's going tae jump aff the brig,' a man in a scruffy hat said to me, answering my furrowed brow as he walked the other way.

'How terrible,' I remarked. 'Is anyone trying to help her?'

The man shrugged. 'Isnae much tae be done when folk're like that. She disnae ken where she is – keeps ramblin' aboot gettin' intae the loch, like it's still there.' He shook his head. 'Should prob'ly be in the madhouse.'

My stomach lurched with dread at his remarks. 'This woman – what does she look like?'

He shrugged again. 'I dinnae ken. Like an auld wummin. Dressed in claes like rags. Prob'ly a beggar.'

'No,' I muttered to myself, 'it can't be.'

Clutching my basket in one hand, I lifted my dress above my ankles and began to run. It probably wasn't Alice – there were many old women in the city who would match the description given. But I had to be sure, and besides, did it matter who it was? Someone was teetering on the edge of a bridge, desperate. I couldn't ignore that; I'd never been able to ignore that. Not since the day I'd left Maman in tears. The air in our little rooms had been so cold that day; my words had been so hot. I'd struggled to breathe. I'd struggled to say sorry. If only I'd come back sooner, I might have found her before...

*Arrête, ma chérie. You know that is not how it happened.*

I didn't know anything, except what was said. She must have been melancholic, must have taken too much laudanum. It must have been hard, leaving France. It must have been too much for her.

She must have been desperate.

I reached the bridge, pushing my way through the group of people who had huddled around to watch the spectacle. My insistence was met by some objections, but I didn't care. I could have offered up a few choice words of my own to these men and women who'd decided to stand and gawp at such a scene of misery. The same gruesome individuals who relished a hanging, no doubt. They wouldn't have been out of place in Paris a decade ago, getting drunk on blood lust and chaos. I couldn't abide it. I stared hard at each of them, and they must have seen the ice in my eyes, as one by one they moved out of my way until, finally, I saw her.

Alice.

The little old woman sat on the bridge's shallow wall, her shoulders hunched, her feet dangling towards oblivion. Tenderly I approached her, keeping my movements deliberate and slow. The last thing I wanted to do was startle her. The wind was blowing characteristically hard, whistling its warning through the valley. I felt sure one strong gust would carry Alice away, but somehow she remained stoic against it. She was staring down, muttering inaudibly to herself, but she seemed peaceful enough. I began to hope that she was just confused, that she hadn't any intention of jumping and giving this crowd their satisfaction.

'Alice?' I spoke her name softly. 'Alice? What are you doing?'

She turned her head ever so slightly and gave me a smile, her whole face seeming to brighten at my presence. 'You're the lass who lives near me,' she said.

Her acknowledgement took me by surprise. 'Yes, that's right. My name's Ailsa. I've been to the markets today, Alice, and I'm going to make us a nice broth. Why don't you come down from there and come home with me?'

The smile faded, and she shook her head. 'No' today. I'm gonnae see Joanna today.' Her gaze returned to the ground below.

'I don't think Joanna is coming to the bridge, Alice. In fact, I think she's in your rooms with Rab. They'll want their supper soon, won't they?'

I reached out a hand and placed it delicately on her arm, but immediately she snatched herself away from me.

'No!' she insisted. 'They cannae be! They're gone. Joanna, she…she went into the water. I'm gonnae go doon an' see her.'

Desperation began to rise up in my chest, and for a moment I felt light-headed. I glanced over the side of the bridge. Far below the marketplace had been cleared, people positioned on its perimeter like statues, staring upwards, anticipating the inevitable. I looked back at Alice, but she'd turned her head away from me and had returned to her rambling. I was losing her. I wanted to reach out and pull her back, but I knew that one wrong move would send her over the edge.

'Alice,' I tried again, 'the water's gone now, see? It's been drained. I don't think Joanna can be down there anymore.'

To my surprise, Alice began to laugh, her tiny frame emitting a deep, bewildering sound which seemed to bite at me from every direction. She looked squarely at me with those yellowing eyes, no longer glazed with confusion, but sharp with a madness I hadn't seen in them before.

'Of course she is,' Alice replied, extending her arm and pointing into the distance. 'Look, can't you see her? She's doon there.'

I followed her crooked finger and found myself looking towards the earthen mound which rose up in the middle of the valley. In front of it a handful of sheep grazed on the now dry land, and children played on the nearby slopes which had once formed the banks of the loch. I shook my head, my eyes darting across the scene as I tried to understand what she was pointing at. If there were souls wandering down there today, I couldn't see them. I couldn't see anyone who might be Joanna.

'I'm sorry, Alice. I really don't think she's there.'

'Aye, she is,' Alice insisted. 'Don't you see? How pretty she looks in that dress, with her hair all loose, just like when she was a girl. So black, like Rab's. See how it blows in the wind!' She laughed again, and a shiver ran through me.

'Was Joanna your daughter, Alice?'

I must have heard the name a thousand times, but to my shame, I'd never asked.

Her smile faded, but she didn't answer me. 'Look at that water,' she said. 'Shines in the moonlight, ye ken. They say it's no' very deep, but it's deep enough. No! She's going in…no! She's gone…I cannae see her…she's gone under…'

Alice's voice broke as deep, wracking sobs overtook her. Tears rolled down her face, large and heavy like the raindrops which had again begun to fall. She looked at me, and for the first time I could see it in her eyes – all that pain, all that suffering. Everything which the confused fog she lived in had concealed. All her delusions, her sanctuaries, had been stripped away and now she was here. She was here and she couldn't bear it.

'I'm coming, Joanna,' she whispered.

'No!'

I tried to grasp her arm, but it was too late. I could only watch as her frail frame took brief flight, before tumbling to find earth where she'd hoped to meet water.

# Ten

My room was dark and cold, even as the midday sun warmed the city outside my window. I shivered, pulling my blankets tighter around myself as I huddled back down in bed. I had lost all sense of how long I'd been lying here – a day, two perhaps. Time had become a strange concept to me; like a length of rope full of knots, tangling around me, tightening then loosening its grip in turn. It raced by and yet also stood still, because around me nothing changed. The curtains stayed shut. The door stayed locked.

Alice stayed dead.

I turned to face the wall. I wanted to sleep, to force myself into that black state where thought might be evaded, but I couldn't. I stared at the wall, greyed now by the surrounding gloom, trying to overwhelm my senses with its blankness. But even it provided interest, every flake and crack inflaming my mind, encouraging it to roam. I had no control over its movements as it darted repeatedly over horrors which would forever be etched on my memory. The look of agony in her eyes. The pain expressed by her hollow laugh. The willingness to die for someone who was already long dead.

The unsettling notion that she both knew exactly what she was doing, and yet was still deluding herself, right until the very end.

I hadn't gone down into the valley. Many others did, rushing down to take in the spectacle, to confirm death. To capture the full story so it might be repeated at dinner that evening, so that wide-eyed children might be told about the mad old woman who dashed her brains out after throwing herself from the North Bridge. I hadn't needed to see her lying there, broken and bleeding. Such a scene might satiate some appetites, but not mine. I saw enough death; I lived it, every day. I absorbed it, was haunted by it. And so, I'd walked home, my basket in my hand, still half-laden with my good intentions. That basket had sat in the corner of my room since, its contents untouched, uncooked, uneaten. I didn't want it. It wasn't mine. It was meant for Alice, but it was no good to her now.

How could I eat, when I had so badly let Alice down?

Guilt gnawed at me; I felt its poison grow in my empty stomach, rising like bile into my throat. I'd been so unkind to Alice recently, and worse than that, I'd dismissed my unkindness as unimportant because I knew she wouldn't remember. More damning proof of my callousness would be difficult to find, and I would never forgive myself for it. Even when I had been considerate, I'd thought of my duty to her as little more than passing her a bit of food, or making sure she found her way back to her lodgings at night. I humoured her ramblings, but I never inquired about them. Until the day on the bridge, I'd never asked about Rab or Joanna. I'd assumed they were family, but I'd never taken the trouble to learn their stories, to understand what they meant to Alice. Even now, all I knew was that Joanna had been her daughter. I didn't know what had happened to her. I didn't know why she was no longer here.

It was good of me to look after Alice, Angus had once told me. I groaned at how I had accepted his compliment, pressing my face hard into my blanket, as though I might suffocate my shame. I had done so little for her. I should have done so much more.

Angus had knocked at my door some time ago. Or at least, I had some memory of hearing his voice calling to me from the stairwell, asking me to let him in. I could have dreamt it; when I'd slept, I'd had such vivid dreams, and now I wasn't entirely sure what was real or what was imagined. I didn't suppose it mattered, but I believed that he had visited, that he'd stood for some time, tapping and saying my name in turn.

'I'm sorry I haven't been in the tavern recently,' I'd heard him say. 'The captain's had a few concerns and we've all had to take some extra patrols, but that doesn't matter now.' He'd paused for a moment, and I'd held my breath. 'Franny seemed to think we'd parted on bad terms —'

I'd wanted to answer the door then, to demand to know what else Franny had said. I recalled sitting up, staring at the dark old wood which separated him and me. Part of me had wanted so badly to let him in. But another, more forceful part of me knew I couldn't face him.

'I told her we hadn't,' he'd continued, 'at least, I mean, I didn't think we had, but if I've upset you in any way then I am truly sorry. I'm concerned about you, Ailsa. I know Franny is, too.'

The tender way he spoke those words had made me weep all the more. I didn't deserve such care, not when I'd cared so little for Alice. I'd burrowed back under my blankets, biting down on my fist to stem my sobs and calm my uneven breath. Angus had remained at the door a while longer; he didn't make another sound, but I could feel the warmth of him penetrating my little cell. I rejected the comfort it offered, but when finally he left and the cold resumed, I was, in spite of myself, bereft.

Sometime later, there were other visitors. Franny came; she didn't knock, perhaps having received word from Angus that such an attempt would be futile. Instead, she put a note under my door, offering her condolences and assuring me that I could take a little time for myself before returning to the tavern. My tears had run over her unsteady hand as I berated myself for my thoughtlessness. I hadn't even considered the impact that my absence from work would have upon her. I hadn't thought about anyone other than myself.

Finally, a little while ago, Jane had come. Like Angus, she'd knocked and had been persistent about it. So worn down was I at that moment that I had contemplated opening the door to her and allowing myself some consolation. But then, as Jane always did, she began to talk. She was very sorry about my friend, she'd said. She'd heard that I'd been there at the bridge, that I'd witnessed it all. It must have been awful. Did I know that it was the talk of the town? Even Miss Grace had remarked upon it, had wondered whether I'd had any visions, or whether I'd communed with Alice's spirit since. Miss Grace was most taken with the notion of speaking with the dearly departed, and had got it into her head that I could return to Hill Street to perform such a feat – once I was no longer in mourning, of course. And Miss Grace offered her condolences too, of course.

'Ghoulish, self-centred young lady,' I'd muttered to myself as Jane's soft footsteps indicated her departure from my door. I felt terrible about many things at that moment, but not about that.

*But you still want to help her sister, yes? Or have you forgotten your promise to Pierre?*

I rubbed my face hard with my hands, as though trying to erase it all. Clara tumbling down the stairs. Clara arguing with Henry. Clara running off to goodness-knows-where. Clara and her secrets. What was any of that to Pierre? Perhaps it was nothing. Perhaps Pierre's recent appearances had been little more than my imagination, conjuring the past and playing tricks on me. God knows, I would deserve it. In the end I'd done nothing for Pierre, just like I'd done nothing for Alice, or Maman.

*You know yourself better than that, ma chérie. Your instincts are good. If it wasn't for you, we might never have left Paris…*

'If it wasn't for Pierre, we might never have left Paris,' I retorted, correcting the voice in my head. 'Not that leaving did us any good in the end…'

My voice cracked, and my mouth felt like it was full of sand. I might be able to go without food, but I would have to drink something soon. Or, perhaps I wouldn't. Perhaps I would let nature take its course.

*Don't think like that, Ailsa!*

'Why not?' I rasped. 'You did! You did, and you left me!'

Maman's voice fell silent. Of course it did; it held no answers. It couldn't speak for her, couldn't tell me what was going through her mind that afternoon. Couldn't explain where she'd got the laudanum, how long she'd been taking it, whether she had known what she was doing.

Whether she had meant to die.

I sat up, the pain of thirst spreading from my mouth to my head, swelling and pulsating behind my eyes. I caught sight of my reflection in the mirror, stared emptily at its sickly skin and dull features. I'd never been a great beauty, having inherited none of my mother's golden-haired, blue-eyed traits. She had been tall, slender and graceful; I was small and thin, even thinner now after years of a meagre diet, and I was a great deal clumsier. In many ways, it was fortunate that I hadn't remained in Parisian society, as I would have made little success of it. As a girl, I had been quiet, bookish, and awkward; I was happier in the company of spirits than of those who lived and breathed. I had been that way for as long as I could remember - quite the embarrassment for the daughter of a courtesan! Certainly, I could never have followed in my mother's footsteps.

*I never wished for you to follow me. You know that.*

I did know that. I knew she saw a different path in front of me, although I was never quite sure what that was. She encouraged me in my studies, told me of the importance of being cultivé, even though she'd received little education herself. You have a wonderful mind, she would tell me. It is a gift from God, and you must not waste it. When my other gifts began to materialise, she encouraged me to embrace them, and to hone them, too. She never doubted me, never presumed madness as many others would have. Speak to the dead, she would say. Learn from them. But be careful, always. They will have their reasons and their motives, just like the living.

'Can you see spirits too, Maman?' I'd asked her once, when I was just a girl.

She'd laughed, and shaken her head. 'No, I have different talents,' she'd replied. 'But if each of us makes the best of the gifts we are given, then we can be very powerful indeed. This is especially important for women. The world helps us less.'

It was true; she hadn't had my gifts, but she had always had a sight of her own, especially when it came to me. Sometimes I had felt as though she knew me better than I knew myself. It was little wonder I felt so lost without her, even after all these years.

It was little wonder that I couldn't accept that she'd chosen to leave me.

*It is your choice to remain alone now, Ailsa.*

I lay back down, bracing myself for an imagined onslaught about Angus, about how I should have answered the door to him, how kind he is, how handsome. How, at the very least, I should nurture his friendship. In Paris, my mother had steered me away from the company of young men, perhaps deciding that those who surrounded us were quite unsuitable. But in those brief months we spent together in Edinburgh, grappling with our rapidly reducing circumstances, she had begun to speak to me of marriage. It had been in vain, of course; as newcomers in dubious circumstances, we had no good connections. Yet, she persisted - perhaps, seeing the poverty we were slipping into, she sought finally to save me from destitution by more conventional means.

Perhaps she already knew she wasn't going to stay.

'Why did you leave me, Maman?'

My mind, of course, couldn't answer, and her voice remained silent. As the hours passed, I heard nothing more about Pierre, or Clara, or Angus. I suppose I had run out of things to say to myself; I had no more words, no more tears, even, for those had dried up with the advance of the desperate thirst which now gripped me. I must have slept again awhile, because when I woke the sky outside was black, the town around me silenced by the marching of the night through its streets. Indeed, the only sound I could hear was a gentle wind, whistling through the old panes on my window. Delirious, I staggered from my bed and dragged open the thin curtain which had shut out the world for a day or more. The night was unusually clear, and the stars greeted me, glittering and bright against their vast backdrop. I found myself staring at them awhile, mesmerized by their mysterious beauty. An odd calm grew over me, and I began to imagine that each of those stars was a face, someone who'd passed on, looking down and watching me. It was a childish notion of heaven, I knew that, but I let it comfort me nonetheless. I pointed a shaky finger at a different star in turn, naming them. Maman. Pierre. The comte, even. My father? Perhaps – I didn't know if he still lived or not.

Alice.

I picked a little one for her, shining timidly but no less beautiful for it. It sat in the middle of a row, flanked by two other small stars. I drew a line through them with my finger, joining the three of them together in the sky. Alice, Rab and Joanna. It was the least I could do. Alice had searched for them for as long as I'd known her. I could only hope that she'd found them now.

'I'm sorry, Alice,' I whispered.

But her star just watched, distant and indifferent as I crawled back under my blankets and tried not to think about everyone who'd gone, and everything I'd lost.

# Eleven

Early the following morning, I finally left my room. Dawn was breaking, and I found myself bathed in glorious pink-orange light as I made my way along the silent streets to the wellhead nearby. Desperation for water had finally got the better of me, and I found myself scooping it up and drinking with my hands as I filled my stoup. The feeling of the cool liquid running down my throat restored me a little, but I was greatly weakened by hunger and by the malaise which still troubled my spirits. It was a struggle to carry my heavy stoup home, but somehow, I managed. During those black night hours, a change had come over me; a sort of instinct to survive had materialised, overpowering my grief and melancholy, and telling me to carry on. Its voice was small but insistent. Take little steps, it said. Water first, then food. Then look at the day before you, and decide what you must do with it.

You still have things to live for. You still have things you must do.

As I walked back towards Anstruther House, I stopped to rest often, lifting my eyes to that bright sky which illuminated the city with its promise of a fine day. Angus had spoken to me once of enormous skies. I hadn't understood what he meant at the time, believing such things to be impossible under the shadow of tenement buildings and crowded streets. But now I could see the hint of it, the possibility. Such wonders were always there, I supposed, if you were prepared to look for them. I drank in its glow one more time, then returned to my room, where I set about taking those steps towards sustenance.

*

I left my room again at around midday, after preparing and then dining on a rather frugal brose I cobbled together from the ingredients still sitting in my basket. I'd struggled at first to even touch the items, finding the thoughts they provoked too upsetting. However, eventually a grave sort of hunger overcame me, and that little voice once again gave its instruction. You must use what you have, and you must eat. Alice would not wish you to starve yourself out of guilt. Your mother certainly wouldn't. You must go on.

It was right. In the end, there'd been something comforting about cooking on my little stone hearth. And that dour combination of barley and hot water was perhaps the best I'd ever tasted.

I walked along the Canongate's main thoroughfare and then up the High Street towards Franny's tavern. If I was going to move forward, I needed first to ensure that I had some employment to return to. I found Franny easily enough within, sweeping the stone floor, her plump face red and shining after a morning's hard labour. I was relieved to see that the tavern was quiet yet, with just a handful of men enjoying some lunchtime refreshment. I gave a couple of familiar faces a small smile, before turning my attention to Franny. She leaned momentarily on her broom handle, a tender look watering in her blue eyes.

'Oh, Ailsa,' she said, striding towards me and wrapping her arms around me. 'Am so sorry aboot Alice. I ken she meant a lot tae ye.'

'Thank you,' I replied, humbled by her warm gesture and trying hard not to cry.

After some moments she released me, regarding me with that

familiar inquisitive gaze. 'But what are ye doin' here? Did ye no' get ma note?'

I nodded. 'I did, thank you. I appreciate your kindness, but I'm ready to return to work, if you'll have me.'

'O' course, o' course – only, dinnae hurry back, Ailsa. Take more time, if ye need it.'

'I don't, thank you.' I gave her as reassuring a smile as I could manage. 'I think it's best to keep busy.'

Franny nodded. 'If you're sure. Ye look very pale.'

'I'm always pale, Franny. Honestly, I'm fine.'

'Alright.' She sounded unconvinced. 'Tomorrow night?'

'Yes, tomorrow night. The sooner, the better.'

Franny regarded me carefully once more. 'Alright,' she said again. 'But take good care, lass. It wis a horrid thing ye saw, an' tae see it happen tae someone ye cared for…well, it'll take some time before yer fully recovered.'

I drew a deep breath. 'I'll be fine. I've seen plenty of awful things in my life.'

'I ken ye will have, but still…' she clicked her tongue in mock-disapproval. 'Yer no' so guid at listenin' tae advice, eh?'

I shrugged. 'No, perhaps not.'

'I'll see ye tomorrow night, then. Mind an' let me ken if ye have a change of heart, though.'

'Of course. Oh, one more thing while I'm here. You wouldn't happen to know where I can find Angus, if he's not on duty? He came to see me while I was unwell, and I wanted to thank him.'

A broad smile spread across her face. 'Aye. He bides at the top o' the West Bow. Temple's Land, I think the place is called. If ye ask aroond there, ye should find him.'

I gave her shoulder an affectionate squeeze. 'Thank you, Franny. I appreciate your help.'

'Ailsa?' Franny said as I turned to leave.

'Yes?'

'That man has been awfy afeared for ye. Make sure ye find him; he'll be ever so glad tae see ye.'

I nodded a silent promise, then made my way out of the tavern before Franny could spot the colour growing in my cheeks. If I was honest with myself, after everything that had happened, I would be glad to see him, too.

*

I found Temple's Land easily enough. Sitting near the summit of the Bow, it was a tall, unwieldy-looking building, its weary stones clinging to the smaller, timber-dressed building next door. Like so much of old Edinburgh, the buildings on the Bow were ancient, their fine but faded features hinting at a once glorious past. I didn't know how ancient, although I'd often wondered. I'd asked Franny once, about the age of some of the town's most antiquated dwellings.

'They look as though they've stood for centuries,' I'd mused.

Franny had given me a funny look, as though she couldn't fathom why I'd want to know about such things. She hadn't given me an answer.

I was relieved to find Temple's Land occupied such an elevated position, which meant that I wasn't forced to walk past the entrance to the Wizard's house; that particular abomination sat a little further down. With a small shudder and a determination not to think any more about that place, I walked inside and ascended the narrow stone stairwell. A cool dampness lingered in the stale air, and I was struck by how closely this place resembled my own home in Anstruther House. But then, there was no reason it shouldn't. Many of the city's inhabitants lived in the same way, crammed into tiny rooms carved out of once grand homes.

There were few people around, and I found myself having to knock on a handful of doors to find out where Angus lived. His neighbours were, on the whole, about as welcoming as mine, but among the dirty looks and terse words I did manage to ascertain that he lived in one of the small rooms, right at the top of Temple's Land.

'He's a guid lad,' remarked the old woman who told me his whereabouts. 'For a guardsman.'

I smiled my agreement, trying not to notice how much her wiry hair and toothless smile reminded me of Alice.

Breathless by now, I made my way up the final flight of stairs. Look for the damaged door, the old woman had said. The one with all the scratches marking the wood. And sure enough, it was there, just as she'd described. What she hadn't mentioned, however, was the man lingering immediately outside it. He leaned against the wall, his head down, his face shaded by the gloom. He was filthy, barely dressed in what remained of his ragged clothes, and the smell coming from him was fetid. I took a step back, covering my nose with the back of my hand.

'Can I come past you, sir? I'm here to see a friend.'

He turned to look at me, and I gasped as I caught sight of his narrowed, opaque eyes. His movement caused a fresh stink of rot to waft towards me, and I had to force myself not to retch. It was disgusting, but also strange; it wasn't often that I could smell as well as see the dead.

'Oh! I'm sorry, sir,' I began. 'I thought...'

'You can see me?'

'Yes, but I'm not...'

He grinned at me through gritted teeth. 'If you're gonnae see John, you can gie him a message from me. Tell him Tam kens what he did.'

'I'm not,' I replied hurriedly, lurching forward and banging on the door. 'I'm here to see Angus.'

The man shrank back, clearly dissatisfied but accepting my response. No further words passed between us as I waited, but his putrid presence still felt oppressive. I prayed Angus would answer. I didn't know whether he was within; he could be on duty for all I knew. After leaving Franny's I had decided against going to the Tolbooth to seek him out. I couldn't bring myself to walk in there, to bear the past and present horrors which echoed within its walls. Besides, even if I had been brave enough, I knew that it wasn't somewhere to be entered willingly by the likes of me. To do so would be to draw unnecessary attention to myself, and Angus. I was certain he wouldn't have thanked me for that.

After what seemed like a painfully long moment, the door swung open, and there stood Angus, bleary-eyed and in a state of considerable undress. I felt my face colour at the sight of his unbuttoned shirt and dishevelled hair.

'Oh,' I exclaimed. 'I am so sorry. I have woken you.'

His tired eyes widened. 'Ailsa? No, no, please don't apologise. I just wasn't expecting you. How did you find me? No, never mind that, please – come in.'

He stepped aside, hurriedly buttoning his shirt. Thank goodness, he'd had the presence of mind to have pulled on his guardsman's red breeches before answering my knock.

'I'm sorry you find me like this,' he continued. 'I was on duty last night. I only returned home at dawn.'

'Oh,' I said again. 'Oh dear. I hadn't even thought about that. Perhaps I should go...'

'No, not at all. Don't go.' He pulled up a wooden chair and invited me to sit. 'I'm glad to see you.'

I sat down, smoothing my dress and taking a moment to glance at my surroundings. His room was a similar size to mine and equally plainly furnished, if indeed furniture could be spied amongst the detritus which decorated it. Clothes, bowls, half-eaten food – I noted it all, along with the stale smell which filled the warm air. I also spotted two beds; one upon which Angus now sat, opposite me, and another across the room, dressed with crumpled and rather filthy-looking blankets.

Angus must have caught me looking. 'I share with one of the other men in the Guard,' he explained. 'A lot of us do – in fact, I'm fortunate that there's just the two of us in here. Sorry - it really isn't a suitable place for a lady.'

I let out a small laugh. 'It could certainly do with a woman's touch.'

He didn't return my smile, and for a moment I feared I'd

offended him.

'Forgive me,' I began. 'I didn't mean...'

'No, it's true,' he said, now looking around himself. 'I live with a pig. His habits are disgusting, he's frequently drunk, and... well, I'd prefer to live alone, but that's not easy on a guardsman's pay.'

'Alone?' I asked. 'Really, I wouldn't recommend it.'

'Well,' he added, looking at me in earnest. 'Of course, I'd prefer the company of a woman. A family, even.'

His directness caught me off guard and I found myself without something to say in response. An awkward silence lingered between us.

'It's good to see you,' he said after a few moments. 'Are you well?'

I nodded. 'Well enough, thank you. I came to apologise for not answering the door to you when you called. I was indisposed.'

'Aye, don't worry. I understand. I'm glad you are better. I presume Franny told you where you could find me?'

'More or less.'

He groaned. 'Well, now you've seen the depths a man such as me must go to, to live in this town.'

Without thinking, I reached over and touched his hand. 'I think we both know that there are worse alternatives. And you forget, I too live modestly. There is not so much of a difference between your home and mine.'

My gesture seemed to surprise him, but he allowed my hand to remain over his. 'Yes, but when I think of the places you must have lived in, in Paris...'

I smiled, withdrawing my hand quite self-consciously from his. 'A different life, Angus. So remote now that it feels as though it was someone else's life that I can recall, and not my own.'

'I know how that feels,' Angus sighed. 'Sometimes I think that Glendrian was just a dream, a place my mind created and now exalts more with every passing year. It's odd - I forget the rain, the cold, the damp stone cottages, the failed harvests, and remember only the smell of the sea, the warmth of the peat fire, the sight of the sunshine rising over the rocky hills. Do you ever find yourself doing that, thinking only of the good parts?'

'I think often about my childhood, which was happy, if a little lonely. Maman's lifestyle was such that I rarely found myself in the company of other children.' I paused, deciding not to mention Pierre again. I still wasn't sure how Angus had taken that particular revelation. 'Nonetheless, I was fortunate. But those last few years before we left cast a long shadow. I'm afraid that it's still the fear I remember most.'

'I don't doubt that you'd never wish to go back there,' he said. 'Whereas my fear is that I'll never see my home or family again.'

'That must be a heavy burden to bear. In that regard, I am fortunate that I'd have nothing to return to in Paris, even if I wished it. What remains of my life is here now, although with Alice's passing it feels somewhat smaller.'

I hadn't meant to start talking about Alice, and the weight of the sympathy in his gaze was almost too much to bear. Ashamed, I brushed away the tears which were gathering in my eyes.

'I'm sorry. I'm sure you could quite do without some mournful woman disturbing your rest today.'

'No, not at all. I'm glad you came.'

He raised his hand towards my cheek then stopped, as though remembering himself. He let it fall, but the ghost of the gesture lingered in the space between us, and I found myself wishing that those fingers had made contact with my flushed skin.

'If you want to talk to me about Alice, about anything, then I am here to listen. We are friends, are we not?'

'Yes,' I replied. 'Of course. I will miss Alice a great deal, even if most of the time she thought I was Joanna and not Ailsa. There was something so endearing about her; I felt this instinct to help her, although in the end my efforts fell far short. I will regret that forever, I think. I will also regret not taking the time to learn more about her, to understand who those people she talked about so often had been to her.'

Angus's face brightened. 'Would you like me to try to find out?

I could ask around, see what I can discover.'

'You wouldn't mind? I shouldn't like you to go to any trouble.'

He smiled. 'It would be my pleasure, Ailsa. I think I told you once before – I like to get to the bottom of things.'

'Thank you, Angus. I would be very grateful. I'm not sure knowing her story will bring me much peace, but I would like to know it, nonetheless.' I rose from my seat. 'And now I shall leave you to get some rest. I have imposed upon you for long enough.'

He followed me to the door. 'You are welcome here any time. If you can stand the state of the place, that is.'

'Thank you for your kindness, Angus.'

I walked out into the dim passage which led back to the stairs. The smell of death still lingered, as did the man. I suppressed a gasp as, once again, he rested that awful, clouded gaze upon me.

'Angus?' I asked. 'What is the name of the other man who lives here?'

'John. Why?'

The man snarled. The bitter fury which flashed across his face was almost too much to bear. Whoever John was, he'd clearly done something to provoke this haunting, but this was hardly the time to warn Angus about it.

'I was just curious,' was all I could manage to say in reply.

I left Angus at his door, looking wearily after me as I headed back down the stairs and out on to the street. The afternoon was bright, and the streets were a hive of activity, encouraged, no doubt, by the warmth of the springtime sun. I lingered in front of Temple's Land, taking a moment to enjoy the air which, although not exactly fresh, was a blessed relief after the stink in the stairwell, and the ripe heat of Angus's room. I pitied him for his circumstances, and for the shame he felt at my knowledge of them. I would never understand why I'd become so exalted in his eyes. Surely, he could see that we lived in the same world.

*But you're not from the same world – you know that. Besides, he cares for you, ma chérie. His pride is all bound up with his passions.*

Passion. There was a notion that never did anyone any good, as my mother knew to her great cost. I pushed all thoughts of passions away as I began to walk, pretending that it was the sun which warmed my face and not the thought of Angus's hand under my own.

'Oi! Watch out!'

The gruff voice and the brittle clack of a cart's wheels startled me. I spun around, ready to dart out of the way, before realising that the warning wasn't directed at me, but at a woman who was walking briskly up the other side of the street. A young woman, finely dressed in white muslin, her cheeks pink, her dark curls bouncing beneath her bonnet as she hurried along. A woman I recognised.

Clara Andrews.

In the midst of everything that had happened over the preceding days, I'd barely spared a thought for Clara Andrews and my strange, unresolved vision about her fate. But now my interest piqued. She appeared to be alone, and flustered, as though she needed to be somewhere. As though she shouldn't be here. What was a young woman of society doing by herself in the West Bow? What business could she possibly have amongst the markets, the caddies and street urchins of the Old Town? It was certainly odd.

I walked on, picking up my pace as I charted the course cleared by the delicate sweep of her dress, reaching the top of the Bow and turning down the Lawnmarket. I'd been going in that direction anyway, I reminded myself. I wasn't really following her. But, if I happened to notice where she was going, that might prove helpful. I might yet come to learn more about this mysterious young woman and her secrets.

# Twelve

Keeping up with Clara proved difficult. She walked fast, maintaining an unfailing pace as she marched down the Lawnmarket, leaving me feeling quickly breathless. As the High Street narrowed through the Luckenbooths, the throng of city-dwellers became so dense that I lost sight of her altogether. I weaved my way through the bodies, trying to pick up her trail again. If she'd gone down one of the wynds, then my cause was likely hopeless. But would a woman such as Clara even consider walking through one of those dark, narrow passages? I thought it unlikely. I searched the crowds as the High Street expanded again, despairing a little as the sea of faces and bodies swam in front of my eyes. It was far too easy to get lost in a crowd; too easy even for a well-dressed woman like Clara Andrews to blend in. I didn't know why, but I suspected that would please her very much.

Finally, after some moments I spied her, quite a distance ahead now, turning the corner towards North Bridge. She must have run to get so far away from me. The idea seemed preposterous; accomplished young ladies of good society didn't go running along the High Street. They didn't run anywhere. They walked, or took a carriage. I recalled Jane's observations about Clara, how she'd noted that she had been behaving strangely. There had to be a reason for her behaviour; there had to be somewhere she was going, and someone she was seeing. I felt sure that wherever or whoever that was, held the key to Clara's fate. I began to run too, then, determined to catch her. Determined to unravel this mystery and to help her, if I could.

By the time I reached North Bridge, I could run no further. I drew to a halt, clutching my sides as I gasped painfully for breath. I was not so young as Clara, nor, it appeared, quite so healthy. I looked around, my heart sinking as I was forced to recall the last time I set foot on this bridge. The memories darted through my mind. Alice, sitting on the wall. Alice, wailing for her lost child. Alice, falling. I shuddered. If it was possible to avoid this place forever more, I believed that I would. But it was the bridge between the towns. I had to confront it. There was no other way.

*Control your grief, Ailsa. You cannot let it overpower you. Remember the lessons you learned when you were grieving for me.*

I remembered. I knew all too well the places that misery could take you. I had walked that dark path, drenched in drink, rambling incoherently to anyone who would listen – alive or dead. I hadn't touched a drop since that time, and in the years hence I'd steadily grown more cautious about who I talked to, from this world and from the next. These days I preferred to talk to my imagination, and to let it answer back.

*You talk to Angus.*

My face grew hot as once again, I recalled our meeting today. I'd touched his hand, and he'd looked squarely at me and as good as told me he wanted a wife. Yes, I talked to him, and he to me. We were mutually bold, but I wasn't sure what good it did us. I wasn't sure that we weren't both in danger of saying too much.

The bridge was busy, a constant stream of people, carts and carriages crossing the chasm between the new and the old parts of the city. My breath had calmed now, and I rushed across, looking for Clara. It quickly became apparent that my search was futile; she'd long since departed from the bridge, and from there, could have gone in any number of directions. Inwardly I cursed; I had let an opportunity to gain some useful information slip through my fingers, and was unlikely to get such a chance again. We lived in different worlds, Clara and I, and rarely did they meet. It would be very difficult to contrive a reason to encounter her again.

I reached the end of the bridge, and found myself standing in front of the Register House, that dome-topped, palatial building which announced my arrival in the place where the monied lived. I allowed myself to gaze at its bright stone splendour, unsure of my next move. Most likely, I would go back to my part of town, but equally, I didn't want to give up hope, just yet.

'Miss Rose?'

The sound of my name being called came from behind me, delivered by the soft but animated tones of a young woman's voice. I spun around to be met by the frenzied footsteps and whispered giggles of Grace Andrews, practically dragging her elder sister towards me. I tempered my smile, conscious that perhaps I looked too happy to see them.

'Oh yes! Miss Rose! It is you!'

Grace gushed out her greeting, her blue eyes bright with delight at having spotted me. Quite what I'd done to earn this woman's unreserved fascination, I'd never understand. Clara looked less thrilled, her pale face managing little more than a tight smile in my direction. I wondered then if she'd noticed me following her, if her swift footsteps across town had been in part an effort to evade me.

I gave a polite nod. 'Miss Grace, Miss Clara. I trust you are well?'

'Quite well, thank you, Miss Rose. Quite well. Indeed, is it not a fine day for a walk around the town? Only, I had just remarked to my sister how very fine a day it is. And warm, too – hotter even than London, I daresay! Truly, I am worn out with it.'

Grace fanned herself, wafting her hand in front of her face to full dramatic effect. Certainly, she did look uncomfortably warm, her cheeks bright pink, a handful of stray blonde curls sticking to her forehead, just below her bonnet. Flustered is how I would describe her. Almost breathless. As though she, too, had been running somewhere. Clara, on the other hand, was a model of composure. She stood taller than her sister, exuding that graceful serenity I'd come to expect from her. Not a part of her white attire was ruffled; there was not so much as a lock of that deep brown hair out of place. Only the dark circles lurking beneath her heavy eyes suggested that anything might be amiss.

'And you, Miss Clara? You are well?'

'Yes, thank you. I am well.' She replied as though speaking to the air, as she would not bring herself to meet my gaze.

'And your mother?'

'Yes, she is also well, thank you.'

'Well, apart from hardly ever leaving that house!' Grace interjected. 'We have barely attended any balls since arriving here, and I have been working so very hard to perfect my steps. Mama says she does not like the society here so much as the society in London, and…'

'Hush,' Clara implored her. 'Miss Rose does not wish to hear of your thirst for country dancing, I'm sure. And Mother has attended the Assembly Rooms with us on many occasions. Your complaints are quite without foundation.'

'Do you like the theatre, Miss Rose?' Grace asked me, apparently unperturbed by her sister's chastising tone. 'We have just walked the vicinity of the Royal in Shakespeare Square, near the bridge. We shall attend our first play there on Thursday evening. It is a romance, and something of a tragedy, too. It would suit your tastes well, I think!'

'I confess, I have so seldom been to the theatre, that I have little experience upon which to base an opinion.'

Clara arched an eyebrow at me, her countenance betraying her surprise. So, I was capable of breaching that chilly exterior and garnering some interest from her; I believed that for a brief moment she even looked me in the eye. I could almost hear her thoughts as she examined the misfit standing before her, no doubt recalling my otherworldly performances in her presence and regarding them as much like the theatre. I supposed she would have a point.

'Really, Miss Rose, you have never been to the theatre?'

I shook my head. 'Not never, no. But I have been only very rarely.'

I gave her a tight smile, not wishing to say any more. It was a pity that of all things, her curiosity had to be piqued over this particular subject. I did not wish to enter into a discussion about why the theatre was not somewhere I had often frequented.

Why I'd been only twice in the past eleven years.

Why both times I'd left before the play had ended, tears running down my face, my head full of Maman.

*The theatre is no place for one such as you, ma chérie.*

Theatres were colourful, bewildering places; those rare spots where the different ranks of a society could gather, sharing an experience alongside one another, even if they did not mingle. Theatres could blur the lines which existed beyond their gilded doors, especially for those who took to the stage. A poor woman with talent and wit could find herself becoming the most celebrated actress in Edinburgh, London, or Paris. She could stand each night on her pedestal, living a multitude of lives as the crowd looked on. One night she might be a witch or a fairy, the next a duchess or a queen. She could capture men's imaginations, even capture their souls, if she was spellbinding enough. And once she had done that, she had triumphed – or so she thought. In fact, it was she who had been caged; dragged from the stage, never to return. Never to take her daughter to see the place which made her, lest she be confronted with difficult truths.

Clara's surprise was justified. Growing up, I think I would have adored the place, with all its embellishments and contradictions. But I, too, was in captivity. I simply didn't realise it at the time.

'Well, I must say, Miss Rose, that it is all the more reason that you must go and see this play!' Grace gushed. 'Mustn't she, Clara? It's called The Spectre in the Woods. They say that there is something very supernatural about it, much like Mrs Radcliffe's novels. Have you read The Mysteries of Udolpho, Miss Rose?'

I shook my head. 'No, I have not.'

'Oh! But you simply must!'

Clara curled her lip at her sister. 'Such wearisome tales – to put the reader through all that terror, only to offer a reasonable explanation at the conclusion. I cannot abide them.'

'Hmm,' I mused, not feeling particularly enthused by the turn our conversation had taken. In my experience, there was little about the dead which could be described as reasonable, let alone be explained.

'Oh! Must you always dampen everything with your gloomy spirits?' Grace asked her sister, waving a dismissive hand at her in a gesture which felt undertaken for my benefit. 'I shall not succumb to her misery, Miss Rose. I shall enjoy this play, and we shall have a merry time. Our mother and father will be there, together, after all! I have high hopes for the evening.'

'Hush,' said Clara, 'Mother would not thank you for discussing such delicate matters in the street.'

'Delicate, indeed! All of town must know about it! Even Miss Rose must know – if she didn't know when she attended upon us to tell our fortunes, she will have asked since and found the answer easily enough. Am I not correct, Miss Rose?'

I smiled, feeling a flush of colour in my cheeks in response to her directness. Grace Andrews might be prone to excitement and self-indulgence, but in some matters at least, she was apparently no fool.

'Nonetheless, I think your high hopes are misplaced,' Clara cautioned. 'It is an evening at the theatre, not a reconciliation.'

'I do hope that you have an enjoyable time,' I interjected. 'Will Mr Turner be joining you?'

A look of irritation flashed across Clara's face, but I couldn't decide whether it was the mention of that name or the impertinence of my question which caused it.

'I do not know,' she replied, her voice ice-cold. 'Mr Turner gives no account of himself to me.'

'Ah! Look, there he is now! And who's that with him, is that Papa?'

Grace peered over my shoulder, staring down Princes Street, wide-eyed with anticipation. I turned around, following her gaze over to two gentlemen who were walking together along that great boulevard, their tall hats bobbing up and down as they made their purposeful march towards us. One was certainly Henry, fair-featured and well-dressed, exuding that serious demeanour I had first encountered in him, rather than the woeful, drunken one I met in the tavern less than a week ago. The other man looked older, towering over Henry from his great height. As he drew closer, I realised that I knew him too. The man I had fallen upon in the street. The man who'd been in the tavern, helping Henry to drown his sorrows in port. The man who'd been so rude, so sneering. That man, apparently, was their father. I must have let out a gasp, for beside me Clara startled.

'It might be best if you leave us now, Miss Rose,' she whispered.

I glanced at her, frowning. Her pale face had gone a deathly white, and I saw that she had clasped her hands together at her waist, her fingers gripping each other for dear life, as though she was engaged in some sort of desperate prayer. I wasn't sure then which of us was more reluctant to meet these two gentlemen in the street.

Grace, of course, was oblivious. 'It is! It is – Papa! This is a jolly surprise.'

The two men reached us, tipping their hats in polite acknowledgement. The older man barely looked at me, but the curl of his lip told me that Henry had noted who I was.

'Papa,' Grace continued, 'may I introduce to you an acquaintance of ours – Miss Ailsa Rose. Miss Rose, this is our father, Mr Charles Andrews.'

'How do you do, Miss Rose?' he asked, setting that steely gaze upon me now as he honoured me with the smallest, sharpest of bows.

I had to force myself not to recoil as he studied me, his keen eye noting every detail from my shabby bonnet, right down to the street muck decorating the bottom of my dress. However, no look of recognition crossed his face. I almost sighed with relief.

'Pleased to make your acquaintance, sir,' I responded with a small curtsey.

He regarded me again, this time with a furrowed brow. 'Your voice – your accent. I recognise it. Have we met before?'

Inwardly I cursed my French lilt for once again betraying me. Beside him Henry gave a restless shuffle; he recalled our encounter in the street, if not the one in the tavern. I could feel my face growing warm, but decided that in the circumstances, it was best to feign ignorance. Something told me that the less this man knew of me, the better.

'I don't believe so, sir.'

'Hmm,' he mused, looking down his nose again, towards my filthy shoes. 'Curious. Pray tell me, Miss Rose, how do you know my daughters?'

'Oh, it really is quite the story,' Grace interjected before I could answer. 'Our maid, Jane…'

'Father won't wish to be troubled with all the details, Grace,' Clara said, her cool tone cutting across the conversation. 'Miss Rose is an acquaintance of our maid, Jane, and has recently been of service to us regarding some household matters. We are, of course, most grateful to her for her assistance.'

Clara gave me a small smile, inclining her head towards me in a carefully performed gesture of appreciation. Her lie was as believable as it was effortless. But then, it was clear that she'd had plenty of opportunity to rehearse such skills recently.

An indignant colour rose in Grace's face and for a moment I feared she might object to her sister's explanation. However, she didn't get the chance. Instead, her father cast the full weight of his disparaging countenance upon me, comfortable now that any insult felt on my part would be without consequence.

'I see,' he said stiffly. 'Alas, Miss Rose, I believe my daughters have humoured you for long enough. They have other matters to attend to, as do I. We bid you good day.'

I watched open-mouthed as he led his daughters away, uttering a few choice words about not associating with servants in the street. Only Clara glanced back, a brief apology flickering across her face before being wiped away by the force of her father's lecture. Insufferable man! Oh, how many people such as Charles Andrews had I encountered in my life, and how many more would I yet have to meet? Those members of so-called polite society who could not muster a kind word for those not so fortunate in birth or circumstances. Those who thought themselves fit to reign over others simply because life had favoured them with the advantages of wealth, land and titles. In Charles Andrews' case, it didn't seem as though he had even achieved the latter. He'd managed to sleep with nobility, but that was as far as he'd got.

*That was as far as I got too, ma chérie!*

'Much good it did you, Maman,' I quipped to myself.

My words bit at me but they were true nonetheless. All those years of dalliances with ducs and comtes and she'd ended up dying on a threadbare sofa, consumed by the twin spectres of poverty and despair. Even the comfort of her only child hadn't been enough for her; she'd preferred death to the loss of those men and the trinkets they'd dangled before her eyes. Well, she was welcome to her eternity with them. She was welcome to share in the death they'd earned for being so utterly abhorrent to the people they'd trampled upon as they'd climbed the ladder of vice and power.

*Arrête, Ailsa! You sound like a sans-culotte.*

I stared after the Andrews' family, watching with disdain until the behatted shape of Charles Andrews disappeared out of sight. Perhaps, if I had stayed in Paris, I would have been a sans-culotte.

*What will you do, then? Will you not help that young woman now?*

I sighed. No, that would not do, as tempting as it might be. Clara was in some sort of danger; my vision had told me that, and everything I'd learned about her since had only given me more reason to believe it. Today she had been at odds with herself; talkative one minute, withdrawn the next. Aloof then agitated, cold then hot by turns. She couldn't stand the mention of her cousin's name, and she paled at the sight of her father and that same cousin approaching. She had shielded me from her father's inquisition for no discernible reason; she owed me no protection, and judging by the cross words she received as a result, her deception did her no good. It occurred to me then that whilst I might still not know the nature of the trouble she faced, Clara Andrews herself just might.

What I did know for certain, however, was where I might see her next. A busy place, where many people might meet, and many conversations might be had. A place where questions could be asked and warnings delivered under the cover of the rowdy, jostling crowd.

I smiled, the seeds of a plan beginning to grow in my mind. Grace was right. That play she mentioned did sound very appealing, after all.

# Thirteen

My first night back in the tavern since Alice's death was strange. Everything felt so disconcerting, so disconnected – as though a week ago I'd walked out of there as one person, and tonight had walked back in as another. I suppose I was altered; I could feel the grief still hanging off my weary limbs and sagging shoulders, and I was painfully aware that my sadness was easily detected by anyone who looked me in the eye. I tried to be cheerful, to allow myself to be buoyed by the jolly atmosphere of my surroundings, but it was hard. It also made little sense: Alice rarely came into the tavern, except to beg or to look for me, on a rare lucid day. There was no lasting association between that old woman and the place where I worked. So why did every drink I poured, every empty smile I gave prompt me to think about her?

Of course, Franny was the first to see that I wasn't quite myself.

'I kent ye'd come back too soon,' she remarked when I dropped a second jug of beer, sending the sweet, sticky liquid splattering all over the floor.

I shook my head, trying not to let her see the tears gathering in my eyes. 'At times like this, it's best to keep busy, is it not?'

'Oh, lass,' Franny sighed. 'I dinnae think there is a best way. There are just ways, an' we manage somehow. If ye need tae go home, just tell me, alright? It'll be nae problem.'

I nodded weakly. I didn't want to go home. What was there for me, other than memories to dwell on, and silence to wallow in? There would be no Alice in the stairwell, no Alice knocking on my door, scavenging for scraps from my paltry table. Home was a reminder of how alone I was, and I didn't want to think about that. I wanted to keep myself occupied, in body and in mind, no matter how clumsy I might be or how miserable I might appear. I might not be good company, but I needed to be among people, even if it was a group of strangers getting merry on a Wednesday evening. Perhaps their merriment would rub off on me. Perhaps, if all else failed, I would join them.

*Ailsa, no. Remember...*

I remembered. But maybe Franny was right; maybe there was no best way forward. Maybe there were only ways, and that was mine.

'Angus said he'd be in tonight,' Franny told me, giving me a pointed look. 'That ought tae put a wee smile on yer face.'

'He's been a good friend to me. You both have.'

'Aye! But I daresay his reasons are different fae mine,' Franny retorted with a chuckle. 'I ken I've said it before, but he's a guid man. And there isnae so many o' them in the world as there should be.'

I nodded. That was certainly true. My encounter with Charles Andrews yesterday had been a testament to that. Such an unpleasant man; so much so, that even his own daughter seemed to visibly shrink at the prospect of his presence. Why was that? And why had she been so frosty when I mentioned her cousin's name? I still didn't know what to think about Henry Turner. He seemed to me to be a typical man of his position; arrogant, self-important, poised to make his way in a world, content in the knowledge that he could bend it entirely to his will. Yet he had argued with Clara, and her manner about him yesterday told me that the rift hadn't healed. He had also, in Charles's words, made a fool of himself. Could the two matters be connected? Was it possible that he was in love with Clara? Had she refused him?

It was possible, of course. But it was Clara's love I had sensed, and hers which had featured so prominently in my vision. She was in love with someone, but nothing about her behaviour suggested to me that it was Henry. Indeed, her behaviour – running about alone in the old parts of the city, using dancing classes as a ruse for her disappearances – suggested it was someone else altogether. Someone she didn't want her family to know about. Someone quite unsuitable.

But who?

And why would that cost Clara her life?

I didn't know, but I felt I knew enough now to tell her I'd foreseen danger, to warn her. I didn't intend to go into the detail of it, but hoped that a few cautionary words would suffice, that she would know how to apply them to her circumstances. I also couldn't see how else to progress. Whatever Clara's secrets were, they were well-hidden, not just from her family, but from me, too. I could only hope that my warning would be enough.

*

Angus came into the tavern much later, not long before last drinks were served and Franny began to close up for the night. He looked exhausted, rubbing his face more than once in an apparent effort to refresh himself. Even in the dim light I could see that he was very pale, and that his usually bright eyes were weighed down by lack of sleep. I must have been wearing my concern on my face, because when he caught me looking, he made a point of giving me a huge grin, as though such a silly expression might be enough to banish tiredness. I found myself laughing in response, and felt my spirits lift a little. Perhaps there was some power in the act of being cheerful. Or perhaps it was Angus's presence which had caused the change in me.

'It is good to see you smile again, Ailsa,' he remarked as he supped his ale.

'Aye, well, she's no' all mended yet,' Franny observed, 'but I daresay ye'll help with that, Angus,' she added, winking at us both.

I rolled my eyes, but Angus only grinned even more. He seemed different tonight; I couldn't quite find the right words to describe it, but there was a boldness, a confidence about him that I hadn't seen before. He'd dropped the deferential 'Miss Rose' when addressing me, of course, but it was more than that. It was the way he smiled, the way he looked at me and didn't avert his gaze when I met his eye. I thought about our meeting yesterday; we'd both been so frank, so familiar with each other. I supposed lines had been crossed. I wasn't sure that I could draw them again. I wasn't sure that I wanted to.

'I'm just glad she's back,' he replied, partly to Franny and partly to me. 'This place hasn't been the same without her.'

Franny laughed, muttering something about how it had only been a week and how foolish young men could be. I was glad when she wandered off to tidy the tables at the other side of the room. I loved her dearly, but her presence sometimes felt suffocating, especially when accompanied by her excruciating remarks. I turned my attention back to Angus, who was once again staring unashamedly in my direction.

'I'm sorry for turning up at your door yesterday,' I began.

He frowned. 'Sorry – why?'

'I woke you, and forgive me for saying but you look like you need all the sleep you can get.'

'Aye,' he said, pressing his fingers to his temples, 'I feel like I'm never away from guard duty, and when I am...'

His words surrendered themselves to a sigh, and he gulped down the last of his beer. I took his mug away, trying to read his expression. He looked weary, yes, but worried too, his brow etched with lines as he ruminated on whatever it was that troubled him. He noticed me looking, but this time he didn't try to mask it with a silly grin.

'What is it?' I prompted him.

He waved a dismissive hand in front of his face. 'It's nothing. I'm not sleeping well, is all. John – the man I share the room with –

he's not an easy person to get along with. I'm tired of his squalor, and his noise.'

'Noise?'

'Aye – when he's sleeping, I don't know what it is, he – he cries out, Ailsa, like he's terrified of something. I've never heard anything like it.'

I thought of the spirit I saw yesterday, standing outside his room, his malevolence poisoning the air. 'Do you know what it is that he fears?'

Angus shook his head. 'John has little to say for himself, most of the time. I know that he was in the war for a time; he was discharged, although I don't know why. I suspect it's that which haunts him. Men see things in war which no man should have to see.'

'And women,' I added quickly. 'We might not sail to other lands to fight, but when a country goes to war with itself, we all see the horror of it – men, women and children, too.'

I shuddered, the spectre of the guillotine casting its shadow over my mind. The tavern had grown empty now; the candles were low, and the hour was late. I began to clean the tables, scrubbing their surfaces hard as though I might manage to erase my memories as well.

'Sorry. Yes, of course, you're right. I can't imagine the things you must have seen in Paris.'

I gave a grim smile. 'We've all had our troubles to bear. I am sorry for John, and for whatever ails him.'

I turned away and continued to clean. I couldn't risk looking Angus in the eye at that moment; I was terrible at deception, and I didn't want him to see that I was withholding something. I couldn't tell him about that spirit; it might be haunting John, but the knowledge of it would surely haunt Angus, too. I couldn't put that on to his already burdened shoulders.

'I've started making some enquiries about Alice, so I will tell you as soon as I discover anything. Don't worry, I haven't forgotten.' He grinned at me, lifting a few stools and placing them upside down on the tables.

'I didn't think for a moment that you would. I'm grateful for anything you manage to find out. And you don't have to do that – you drink here, you don't work here.'

'She's right, Angus,' Franny said, reappearing from the back room and wiping her wet hands down her apron. 'It's lang past closin' time. Why don't ye get yerself home?'

'I thought I might wait for Ailsa,' he replied. 'I thought I could walk with you, if you'd like?'

'But my home is in the opposite direction to yours.'

'That's alright, I don't mind. I feel as though the night air would do me good.'

He looked at me so hopefully that I could hardly refuse him, even if I wanted to. I glanced at Franny whose flushed, round face was beset by the largest grin I'd ever seen. I could see that there wasn't going to be any point in arguing with either of them.

'That's awfy kind of ye, Angus. Isn't it, Ailsa? I've just aboot finished cleaning up back there, so off ye both go and get yourselves home.'

'Alright,' I said to Angus, giving him a small smile. 'If you can wait a moment, I will go and fetch my shawl.'

Franny followed me into the cramped back room, where my shawl lay strewn across an old chair. She was still smiling, and humming a merry little tune to herself. I tucked the ageing woollen cloth around my shoulders and rolled my eyes at her, which caused her to laugh, sending her great jowls dancing in the candlelight.

'Och Ailsa, I'm so happy for ye,' she whispered.

'He's walking with me, Franny, not offering me his hand.'

'No' yet,' she retorted.

'Franny!' I hissed. 'Angus will hear you.'

'Would ye accept him, if he asked ye?'

'I think you've got it all wrong, Franny, but in truth I'd never thought to marry. I'm not sure what I would do if anyone asked me.'

Her smile dissolved quickly into a frown. 'This isnae anyone,

Ailsa, this is Angus. If ye dinnae return his feelings, ye should be honest. He's too guid tae have his heart broken.'

'It's not that,' I sighed, it's just...'

'Just what? Och, dinnae be a fool, Ailsa! Now, go on, dinnae keep Angus waiting.'

I nodded, deciding there was little point in saying anything further. Indeed, I didn't know what I could say. Franny was right; Angus was so good, and so kind, and we had grown closer over these past weeks. But still I hesitated, still I denied to myself that we could have anything more than friendship – why? As I walked out of that little room and towards the tavern door where Angus was waiting, I wondered what was the matter with me. I wondered why, no matter how much I disliked my solitude, I seemed determined to cling to it, nevertheless.

\*

The night outside was pleasant; the air was still, tinged with a chimney smoke scent which served to mask the city's more fetid odours. Above us the sky was black and strewn with the fog of the day's fires, but it was clear enough in parts to see its handfuls of bright little stars. I thought back to that night, mere days ago, when I had named them for those I'd known. I imagined Alice up there now, with her Rab and Joanna, looking down and watching me. I imagined Maman, and Pierre. I wondered what they would all think of my friendship with Angus. I wondered what they would advise me to do.

*You know what I would advise, ma chérie. You shouldn't be alone.*

Of course, she would say that; she could never stand to be alone. She used to tell me that she would wither and die for want of company. For want of men was what she really meant, and I suppose she was right – losing them did kill her, in its way. I thought about the day I found her, stretched out on that sofa, ghost-white, an empty glass stuck in her cold grasp. Perhaps it was then that I decided I would never be so dependent. Perhaps it was then I decided that reliance on others was a weakness.

'There's talk of war again,' Angus said.

We'd been walking in silence since leaving the tavern, subdued by the emptiness of the streets. Occasional noise drifted towards us from the closes as we passed, but on the High Street itself few souls were around, dead or alive. Our presence felt out of place, as though the sound of every step we took and every word we spoke disrupted the rare tranquillity which the heavens had bestowed. The stars twinkled and I breathed in deeply, possessed by a sudden desire to walk to the crags beyond my home, to sit upon them and gaze up at the vastness of it all.

'Some of the men were talking about it in the guardhouse yesterday,' Angus continued, 'saying that the peace won't hold, that Bonaparte is up to his old tricks again. I hope they're wrong.'

'They won't be wrong,' I said quietly. 'Peace never lasts when men only want more and more. More power, more land. It's never enough. And so, there is war.'

'Are you so resigned to it? What if they invade?'

I shrugged. 'I try not to think of it. There is little you or I could do, so it seems to me that there is no point in torturing yourself with possibility.'

He glanced at me, and in the fading lamplight I could just about see his smile. 'Aye - very wise. Come then, let us speak of happier matters. When are you next working at Franny's?'

I laughed. 'You suggest a more pleasant conversation, then ask when might I next be serving you ale!'

'Well – it is the only time I may see you, isn't it? Except for one outing to an exhibition, and when you appeared unexpectedly at my door yesterday. That cheered me for the rest of the day, you know.'

'Oh,' I replied, unsure what else to say. It was fortunate that it was so dark, that he couldn't see me blush.

'Will you not be in the tavern tomorrow night, then?'

'No – not until Friday. Franny doesn't want me there all the time. She thinks I've come back too soon as it is. Tomorrow evening I was actually… actually thinking of going to the theatre.'

'Alone?'

I couldn't see it, but I could detect his frown from his tone.

'Yes – that is, unless you'd like to accompany me? I'm not sure if the play will be to your taste. It's called The Spectre in the Woods.'

'Sounds ominous. I'm surprised that interests you, given your particular gifts.'

I flinched, taken aback by his directness. It was the first time he'd made reference to my abilities since I'd told him of them. Once again, I felt unsure how to answer him, and wished for that earlier easy silence to return.

'I'm on duty early on Friday, but I could manage to see a play before getting a few hours' sleep, I think. It would be my pleasure.'

'Thank you,' I replied. 'I'm obliged to you. It isn't a great deal of fun, going to the theatre alone.'

We reached Anstruther House under the cover of almost complete darkness. No light came from within, and only one or two of the sparse scattering of lamps were still burning their wicks. The moon was absent, and growing cloud must have covered the stars because I could no longer see them. And they, in turn, could no longer see us.

'Goodnight, Angus,' I whispered.

His cool hand reached for mine and raised it briefly to his lips. He leaned towards me; I smelled ale, the tang of it thick on his breath, and felt the brush of his skin against mine as he placed the gentlest kiss upon my flushing cheek. Still he held my hand, and for a short moment I closed my eyes and absorbed it all: fear, courage, warmth.

'Goodnight, Ailsa,' he whispered, and then he walked away.

# Fourteen

The evening sun warmed the dusty square with its orange glow, casting an ethereal light on to the theatre's pale stone walls. Above me William Shakespeare gazed down from his perch, watching the comings and goings of people and carriages as the audience arrived to enjoy tonight's play. Like the rest of this side of the city, the theatre building was a palatial incarnation of fine pillars and large windows, its roof rising to a dramatic point whereupon the statue of the bard sat. Two further statues had been placed at either side of him, although what they were meant to resemble, I could not tell. My mother might have known, but then this was her world, not mine.

More carriages whizzed past, the ceaseless clopping of horses making my heart beat faster. All of the town's most fashionable residents seemed to be out tonight, enjoying the spring air from the comfortable vantage point of their barouches and landaus; tops down, best evening dress on show. Some stopped, and I watched as ladies and gentlemen disembarked, the men self-consciously distinguished in their dandy cravats and dark coats, the women swishing beside them in gowns of muslin and lace. They would occupy the boxes and galleries tonight, looking down on the play as they looked down on the rest of us, watching from the pit. I wondered when the Andrews family would arrive. I had tried to look for Clara, but I had seen nothing of her yet. She hadn't seemed very enthused about this evening when Grace had spoken of it. I hoped she hadn't changed her mind.

'Do you think we should go in yet?' I asked Angus, feeling suddenly unsure of the etiquette.

'The sooner, the better, I'd say. I hear the pit fills up quick, especially if the play is popular.'

'I've no idea if this one will be or not,' I mused.

Angus laughed. 'I've still no idea what attracts you to this particular play,' he remarked, 'but I am happy for that question to remain unanswered. It is simply a nice thing, to spend an evening with you.'

He smiled at me and squeezed my hand, before immediately relinquishing it. During our walk here he had been very courteous and attentive, making me aware of his admiration with small gestures and kind words, but from a polite distance. I still didn't know what to think about it, or how to respond. Perhaps he sensed this; perhaps that was why he seemed so cautious towards me. Certainly, he hadn't made the advances he made last night, when he was emboldened by drink and cloaked by darkness. Nor had he mentioned the kiss, although its ghost remained there, on my cheek, causing me to remember, and to think of what might be.

Thankfully there was no great crowd at the pit door, and we obtained tickets easily enough before moving inside to find ourselves a good seat. I wanted to position us towards the middle, hoping that would be the best vantage point for locating Clara in the areas above. However, the pit was filling up, and the only seats were benches, scattered along the perimeter. Angus looked at me quizzically when I refused a vacant bench in favour of standing more centrally, but a few vague words about a better view of the stage seemed to satisfy him, and he acquiesced.

'You know, this is the first time I've been to the theatre,' he said.

'The first time ever?'

He laughed at my incredulity. 'It's not so surprising. Theatres are found in the towns and cities, and those are in short supply where I come from. And since I came to Edinburgh...I don't know, I suppose I have occupied myself in other ways.'

'I'm not much different,' I replied. 'I've only ever been a handful of times.'

'But your mother was an actress, wasn't she?'

The same surprise rang in his voice as I had detected in Clara's when we'd had this conversation. The reminder prompted me to look around once more, to see if I could find her amongst the growing crowd. Like the pit, the galleries above were filling up, and a myriad of faces gazed down, their laughter and chatter a growing chorus. I sighed. Finding her here seemed almost impossible. Angus seemed to notice that my concentration had wandered from him, and I realised I needed to be more discreet.

'My mother – oh, yes, she was, although I was very young when she left the stage, and we seldom attended a play when I was growing up. I suppose Maman had other interests.'

He raised his eyebrows at that, and I realised there was no need for me to elaborate.

'And you?' he asked. 'What were your interests?'

'Reading, learning, playing cards. Music, although I played the piano very poorly. I led a solitary life, as I think I've said before. Maman was never keen to have me out in society, even once I was of age.'

Around us the crowd packed in ever tighter, and the light began to dim as candles were extinguished in readiness for the play to begin. I took a slow, deep breath, feeling uncomfortable at being surrounded by so many warm, jostling bodies. I looked up, letting my eyes run along the length of the gallery as I searched once more for Clara, or even Grace. Still I couldn't find them. I felt my plan begin to unravel; even if I did locate Clara, how was I meant to convey any message to her, from down here?

'Are you alright, Ailsa?' Angus asked me. 'You seem distracted.'

'Yes, yes – of course. I'm fine,' I assured him, fixing my face with a smile. 'Tell me, what did you like to do when you were a boy?'

He let out a wry chuckle. 'Well, I didn't have my nose buried in books, if that's what you're wondering, although I had some learning, of course. I think my father put me to work on the croft the moment I could walk – at least, that's how it felt. Life was the croft, and the croft was life – we had plenty of mouths to feed. When I got older, any time not spent labouring was spent looking for more work, especially in leaner times. What I liked to do didn't really come into it, if I'm honest.'

'How different our two lives have been,' I pondered.

'Aye,' he agreed, 'and funny how they collided in a High Street tavern. A blessing, indeed,' he added, grinning at me.

I smiled back as the light faded further, darkening the recesses of the theatre and allowing the candelabras above to illuminate the stage. In the pit, the crowd's chatter shrunk to a murmur, although they didn't fall completely silent. Depending upon how they liked the play, they might grow rowdier again yet. In the boxes and galleries polite society sat, suspended above us, their presence more muted as they waited for the spectacle to unfold. Throats were cleared and handkerchiefs were grasped, ready to dab weeping eyes or shield an overwhelmed face from further vexation. Expectations, it seemed to me, were high.

The first scene commenced on the stage, which had been transformed into a woodland. A woman wandered through the trees, a black cape draped over her shoulders, her face stricken with terror as creaks and groans disrupted the quiet. The sharp sounds provoked gasps from the boxes nearest to the stage, and a woman giggled loudly. I looked up, my heart lifting as I realised that I recognised that laugh. And sure enough, there was Grace Andrews, resplendent in a low-cut pale pink gown, her fair curls shaking as she shared a private joke with her father. To her other side sat her mother, who looked sternly at them both, shifting in her seat before returning her attention to the play. Finally, at the end, were Clara and Henry. Clara was prettily dressed in a soft blue, her neckline more modest that her sister's, and her face more serious, too. She appeared unaffected by Grace's high spirits, her slender frame stiff, her lips pressed together, her dark eyes focussed intently upon the stage - perhaps even beyond it, for she looked so deep in thought. Beside her Henry shifted periodically in his seat, glancing to his side to look at his cousin. Once or twice he leaned towards her, whispering a few words. If he desired to garner a response, or to provoke a reaction, then he received neither. Clara merely inclined her head briefly towards him, offering polite acknowledgement but no reciprocation. His efforts weren't even rewarded with a smile. I almost pitied him.

'Do you wish you were up there?' Angus whispered in my ear, and I realised he had been following my gaze.

'Not at all,' I replied. 'I am content exactly where I am.'

Angus reached for my hand. I let him hold it, even found myself leaning a little closer towards him, enjoying his warm proximity as the first scene ended and woods were replaced with the drawing room of a sumptuous manor house. I glanced up once more and realised it was true: in that moment, I wouldn't have traded places with the stony-faced Clara Andrews for all the world.

*

The interval arrived quickly, and I realised I had become quite absorbed in the tale as it unfolded on the stage. It had been a series of spine-chilling scenes in which a woman called Charlotte, played by a very beautiful, petite actress with fiery red hair, was being driven mad by an apparent haunting. After venturing into the woods for a clandestine meeting with her lover, to whom she was secretly betrothed, something had followed Charlotte back out again and had been making its malevolent presence felt ever since. I suspected that all would be reasonably explained in the end, but nonetheless, Charlotte's plight had captivated me, and judging by their relative quiet, the rest of the audience felt the same. I had let my gaze wander a handful of times towards the Andrews' box, amused by Grace's responses as events unfolded; handkerchief clutched against her heaving bosom, her free hand clapped in horror over her mouth. Clara, on the other hand, had remained unmoved throughout, barely raising an eyebrow, never mind emitting a gasp. I couldn't decide whether she was utterly engrossed, or whether her mind wasn't on the play at all.

'I'll get us some drinks,' Angus said, almost the moment the curtain came down to indicate a pause in proceedings. 'What's your preference?'

I made a face. 'Nothing too strong, please.'

Angus laughed, and although probably none the wiser about my choice of drink, left to find us some refreshment. The room around me seemed to heave and strain as hot, sticky bodies jostled about, their gossiping voices growing ever louder as they filled the void left by the play's suspension. I looked up and saw that the Andrews' box had been vacated. They too would have somewhere to go for a drink, somewhere where they might mingle with others in their society. I swallowed hard; it was now or never. Somewhere up there Clara Andrews wandered, waiting for me to find her. I might never get such a good opportunity as this.

Carefully I weaved my way through the crowd and towards the back of the theatre, where I found a staircase leading to the galleries and boxes above. I ascended them with some apprehension, half-expecting to be stopped. I was acceptably attired in one of my better dresses, but I was under no illusion that I could pass for a genteel woman. A few curious eyes were cast over me, no doubt noting the dirt trimming my dusky pink skirt, and the old cream shawl I carried in readiness for the walk home, but no one said a word. Upon reaching the top, I found myself in a long, slim area behind the galleries, awash with people and polite chatter, the air laced with the sweet tang of wine. I walked slowly across the red carpet which cushioned my feet, noting the contrast with the naked floor of the pit. Everything shone, from the glittering chandeliers suspended above, to the bright white silks and satins of ladies' evening gowns as they shimmered around the room. It was like fashionable Paris, only more self-conscious. And more serene.

'Can I help you?'

An older man addressed me in a gruff voice. He was smartly dressed, but something about the roughness of his jaw and the condition of his teeth told me that he didn't belong here either. In his hand he clutched an empty platter, which he tapped on his side, waiting expectantly for my answer.

'I was just looking for something to drink…'

'Drinks for the pit are sold downstairs.'

'I see.'

I walked away, accepting defeat. The play would start again soon, and Angus would be returning with our drinks. I felt the heat of shame rise in my cheeks, felt my breath quicken. What a fool I had been, thinking I could simply wander up here and find Clara among this great swathe of finely dressed bodies, one looking no different from the next and me, standing out against them all! I paused at the top of the staircase, head bowed, clinging to the rail as I tried to compose myself. I couldn't allow Angus to see me like this. I would have his questions to answer, as it was.

'Miss Rose?'

I looked up, and there she was, coming up the stairs towards me. The chill of the evening air outside hung from her, as did the presence of Henry, who hovered closely by her side. He raised an eyebrow when he saw me, but said nothing.

'Miss Andrews, Mr Turner,' I replied with a polite nod.

'My sister's cajoling was successful, then. You decided to see the play,' Clara observed, an amused smile playing at the corners of her mouth. 'I hope you are enjoying it.'

'Very much, thank you.' I glanced at Henry. 'And I hope you, too, are having a nice evening.'

She nodded, then turned towards her cousin. 'Henry – I have a sudden desire for a glass of wine before the interval is over. Would you be so kind?'

A look of reluctance flashed across his face, but of course, he couldn't refuse. He took his leave of us with a small bow. Finally, we were alone.

'Miss Andrews,' I began. 'We don't have much time. I must tell you...'

'Why were you following me through town on Tuesday?' she asked, her question cutting through my words.

I hesitated, taken aback by her directness. 'I wasn't following you.'

'Yes, you were. What do you want, Miss Rose?'

'I want – I want to warn you, Miss Andrews. When I read your leaves, I saw some things – some events in your future. I have tried to make sense of them but truthfully I cannot, so I want to tell you what I saw so that it might help you.'

She frowned. 'What sort of events? Why didn't you tell me what you saw at the time?'

'If you recall I fainted, and when I awoke, I was very confused. I also thought it best to try to understand my vision, but now I find I cannot so I must tell you all I saw. Miss Andrews,' I continued, lowering my voice now, 'I saw that you are in love, I know not with whom, and I saw that this love will lead to your demise.'

'My demise?' she repeated with a gasp. 'You mean my – my death?'

I nodded. 'I believe so. I caution you to be very careful in your dealings, Miss Andrews.'

I'm not sure what sort of response I expected to illicit; indeed, at first, I wasn't sure what sort of response I was receiving. For a few moments Clara simply stood still in front of me, her pale face frozen, her wide eyes staring at me, her lips pressed together. I wasn't sure if I should say more; I wasn't sure what more I could say. Would it help her to know the exact manner of her death? Would such detail help her to avoid it, or would it haunt her?

'I saw you on a staircase, and...'

But Clara just put up her hand, stemming the flow of my words. I saw then that she was shaking, that a handful of tears had begun to fall from her brown eyes.

'Vile creature!' she hissed. 'They asked you to do this, didn't they? Get away from me! Go on – go! Go back to where you belong!'

Alarmed, I took a step back, nearly tumbling down the stairs. I caught myself, grasping the railing and twisting my ankle painfully in an effort to stay on my feet. In the pit the crowd cheered as the stage curtains opened once more, indicating that the interval was over. Behind Clara, the room began to empty as people returned to their seats. But Clara remained, staring down at me. I couldn't look away; it was as though her shock and fury had stunned me, left me stranded like a boat with no tide to free it. Pain shot through my ankle, and I groaned aloud. The stairs were sand, and I was sinking fast.

Then, from behind me, I felt a hand come to rest upon my shoulder. Finally, I forced myself to turn, wincing with discomfort as my gaze came to rest upon Angus. I watched as he looked from me up to Clara and back again, worry and confusion etched upon his flustered face. I wondered then how long he had been looking for me. I wondered what he must have been thinking, what he must have feared.

I wondered, to my great shame, why I hadn't wondered about him before.

'Ailsa,' he said. 'What is going on?'

# Fifteen

I had done my duty, and it felt terrible.

I ran out into the cool Edinburgh night, all thoughts of returning to watch the rest of the play now abandoned. Angus followed closely behind me, saying my name over and over, asking me to stop. I hurried across the square, forcing myself to keep moving despite the searing pain in my ankle, determined to put some distance between myself and that place. Between myself and her. Before I knew it, I was back on the bridge, clutching the low side wall, my breathing ragged and my heart hammering hard inside my chest. The sun had set, and the valley below looked deep and dark. I found myself thinking about Alice, about her descent into that place. I wondered if she was down there now. I wondered if she'd managed to find Joanna.

'Ailsa? Ailsa, what has upset you? Who was that woman?'

I didn't look at him. Couldn't look at him. I tried to walk on, but my ankle finally betrayed me, refusing to take my weight. I slumped to the ground, a deep sob rising from my throat and escaping into the night. I had made an awful mess of everything, and now I couldn't even go home to hide from it all.

In less than a moment, Angus was down at my side. 'You're hurt,' he said, lifting my arm over his shoulder and helping me back on to my good foot.

'I can't…I can't…' was all I could manage to say. Couldn't what, I didn't really know. Couldn't walk. Couldn't help. Couldn't explain.

'You need to sit down properly,' Angus said, helping me over to the wall. 'You need to rest that foot.'

I sat down on the wall, although it was the last place I wanted to be. I thought again of Alice, of how she'd allowed her feet to dangle over it, of how she'd allowed herself to fall. Of all the times I'd seen that thin, smiling man fall as the bridge disappeared beneath his feet. Tonight, the air on the bridge was remarkably still; nevertheless, one unexpected gust was all it would take to send me drifting over. Then I would fall, too. Perhaps that was what the bridge wanted.

*Don't be ridiculous, Ailsa. A bridge cannot want anything from you.*

'Did you know the first bridge they built here collapsed?' I asked Angus, not particularly expecting an answer.

'Aye,' he replied. 'I've heard about that. About thirty or so years ago, I think.'

'I see a man here sometimes. I think he died when it happened. I see the bridge crumble and then he disappears. I've not seen him for a while, though. I don't know why.'

'Perhaps because you've had other matters on your mind.'

Angus wrapped the shawl I'd been carrying around my shoulders, but it didn't prevent me from shivering. He sat down beside me, close enough that I could feel his warmth. I could feel him looking at me, too, and I sensed he was trying to read me, trying to understand what was going on. I avoided his gaze, staring instead at my injured foot and wondering again how on earth I would ever make it home tonight.

'Ailsa, what has happened? Please, tell me. Perhaps I can help.'

'It's too late for that, Angus,' I muttered. 'I've been such a fool. I fear I've done more harm than good.'

'What do you mean?'

*You're going to have to tell him, ma chérie.*

I let out a heavy sigh. 'That woman – her name is Clara

Andrews. A number of weeks ago I did a reading for her family. It's not something I commonly do, but Jane – do you remember Jane from the tavern? She works for them now, and she asked me, so…anyway, that's not important. What is important is that whilst reading Clara's cup I had a vision about her – about her death.'

Finally, I raised my head, daring myself to look at him. The light around us was dim, but in the shadows, I could see his eyes, wide and expectant, taking in all that I was telling him. What he thought of it, I couldn't tell.

'Since the reading, I've been trying to find out more about Clara, to understand what the vision meant. I observed her and her family from afar, I talked to Jane, and I looked for clues. My vision showed me that she is in love, and I thought this might have something to do with her demise. However, no matter which way I turned, I seemed always to find myself at an impasse, and I just couldn't piece her story together. So, tonight, I decided I would tell her what I saw, and that I would warn her to take care. I realised that there was little more I could do. Now it seems that even that action was futile. She told me in no uncertain terms to leave her alone. I doubt she listened to a word I said.'

'She certainly looked very upset. I recognised her, but I can't recall why.'

'The exhibition,' I said quickly. 'She was there when I ran out of that room. That was a coincidence, though – I hadn't known she would be there. She goes to dancing classes upstairs. In my vision, I saw her fall down a staircase which looked exactly like the one in that building. I think that might be where it happens.'

'Did you tell her that?'

I shook my head. 'I didn't get the chance.'

Angus tapped his hand on the wall. 'Clara Andrews,' he mused. 'Andrews. Why do I know that name? Someone was talking to me about an Andrews recently.'

I groaned. 'You read the newspapers, don't you? You read about those criminal conversation trials? Clara's father is Charles Andrews. He was involved in one of those trials recently.'

'Oh, aye, that's him. A financier, really disgraced himself down in London with some aristocrat's wife – cost him more than a few coins, as well. Men like that can't help themselves; I'm sure I read that his wife is a gentleman's daughter from the north of England. You'd have thought he could content himself with as good a match as that! So, the Andrews family is here now, escaping the scandal I expect,' Angus added with a wry chuckle.

'They're here so Mrs Andrews can get a divorce,' I replied, 'or so Jane tells me.'

Next to me, I felt Angus bristle. 'You asked me about that not long ago, in the tavern. Why didn't you tell me all this then? You know I would help you with anything.'

I shrugged. 'I wasn't sure what to do for the best, and besides, we weren't – we weren't so acquainted as we are now.'

'Acquainted,' Angus repeated, shaking his head. 'So, what happened tonight, you saw that she was here and you decided you had to act? Thinking about it, you did keep looking up at those fine people sitting upstairs. I thought you just wanted to be up there, among them. I even asked you, didn't I? You could have told me then that you wanted to speak with her. You could have saved me the horror of coming back with our drinks and finding no trace of you. Do you have any idea what went through my mind? What I imagined might have happened to you?'

'I'm sorry, Angus, I – I wasn't thinking. It was wrong of me, but I was so preoccupied with looking for her, trying to understand how I could make sure that our paths crossed.'

'Looking for her? You mean, you knew she would be here tonight?'

I nodded. 'I met her and her sister, Grace, on Princes Street earlier this week. Grace was very keen to tell me all about the play, about how I should see it. It seemed like the perfect opportunity.'

He got to his feet then, throwing his arms up in the air. 'And what was I in this plan of yours, Ailsa? Your chaperone? Your useful acquaintance?'

I winced at how he spat the words, shrinking back from his

anger. 'No – no, not at all. I had intended to come alone, remember, until you...'

'So, I was an inconvenience? An obstacle to overcome? It gets worse.'

'No, Angus, that's not what I meant. All I meant was that I didn't need a chaperone; I never have, and I wouldn't have dreamt of asking you for that reason. I enjoy your company, but I don't need someone to take care of me. I don't need someone to fret when I leave a room. I've been alone for a long time. I am accustomed to looking after myself.'

'I see. But you enjoy my company,' he repeated.

'Yes, of course I do.'

'But not enough to trust me with information about someone whose life might be in danger. Not enough to let me help you.'

I hesitated. 'Please understand, having abilities like mine means being cautious. I'm not in the habit of asking for help. I'm in the habit of not talking about what I see and hear. They might not burn women like me anymore, but they'd just as soon lock me up for vagrancy or madness. I tend to think handling these matters by myself is for the best.'

'Well, that's where you're wrong, Ailsa,' Angus retorted, 'because from where I'm standing, it looks like you've made a dreadful mess of this.'

\*

The walk back to the Canongate was painful on two accounts. The first was the keen throbbing in my ankle, which persisted despite the long rest on the bridge wall. The second was the silence which hung between Angus and me as I hobbled home, leaning heavily against him. His nature meant he couldn't leave me to fend for myself, and my condition meant that I couldn't insist upon it, but neither of us wanted to be there anymore. Neither of us wanted to speak to each other, to stoke the tension which had already grown between us. The embers of it smouldered as we walked, the quiet enduring between us, punctuated only by our footsteps.

A dreadful mess, that was what he had called it. And he was right; I had achieved nothing tonight. My warning to Clara had been met with resistance and anger, and the clumsiness of my actions had brought cross words and bad feeling into a blossoming friendship. Yes – a mess was the right way to describe it. But still, I hadn't needed Angus to point it out, and as I limped onward, I began to resent the implication which lingered behind his accusation, that his help would have somehow resulted in a different outcome.

*Perhaps it would have. You know what they say, ma chérie – two minds are better than one.*

Perhaps. It hardly mattered now. Clara Andrews had heard my words and rejected them. She didn't want my help. She probably never would.

Anstruther House was a welcome sight, the flicker of candles and rushlights hinting through its many little windows making the old building appear inviting tonight. I longed to be inside, to bury myself beneath my blankets and pray sleep would come. It was not yet so late; there were still waking hours to be had, but I did not want them. I wanted rest. I wanted to leave this day behind. Angus helped me up the stairs, maintaining his silence while I broke mine, littering it with groans of protest at my physical plight. My ankle was still unbearably sore, and my good leg burned with the effort of carrying me alone. Tears began to gather in my eyes; I was tired, uncomfortable and humiliated. I blinked them away, sniffling. If Angus noticed, he said nothing. I glanced at him a couple of times, noting his stealthy avoidance of my gaze, his grim expression, his hardened jaw. The heat of his firm arm around my back as he dutifully helped me home. His anger still burned, yet outwardly he was cold as stone. I'd never seen that in a man before.

*That's because the men you knew in Paris drank their passions.*

I shuddered, thinking then of smashed glasses, of liquor breath. Maybe that was so. Or maybe my behaviour tonight really had proved capable of extinguishing all his warmth. I hadn't known that I could cause such upset. I was guilty of thoughtlessness, of a secretive tendency, but was that really so offensive? It seemed to me that it might be easier to navigate the whims of raging drunks than it was to handle a man who offered chaste kisses under the night sky and who soberly declared he would do anything for you. Perhaps that was why my mother made her life amongst the intoxicated noblesse. Perhaps she learned that there was more to be gained from dazzling simplicity than there was from the nuances of genuine companionship.

*Companionship – is that what you would call it, ma chérie? Is that all you think you might have lost tonight?*

I bit my lip, suppressing the sob which fought hard to flee from deep within my gut. He had left me at my door, and had turned his back immediately, walking back down the stairs without so much as a word to say farewell. I stared after him, helpless. Of course I was at risk of losing more than a – what had I called him? An acquaintance? Someone whose company I enjoyed? Feeble words, but I hadn't had anything else.

'Angus, I...'

I still didn't have anything else. My voice broke and I turned away, unlocking my door and limping inside before I could see if he'd turned back, if he'd acknowledged my words or if he'd just continued walking. I leaned against the door for a moment, listening to Anstruther House straining around me, hearing the scraping of chairs and murmur of voices through its walls and floors. So near, yet so remote, kept separate from me by wood and stone. Out in the stairwell, no one stirred. I sank down to the ground, my legs – and everything else – unable to bear the weight any longer.

Angus had gone. He had gone and I didn't know if he would ever come back.

# Sixteen

I walked gingerly through the kirkyard, lifting my skirt to avoid it meeting with the worst of the mud which squelched beneath my feet. My ankle had now healed, mostly, but was prone to twinges which reminded me to be careful. The past week had brought heavy rain, sending great torrents of water running down the old city's streets, lifting its filth from one place and depositing it further downstream. The streets of the Canongate were blackened with a stinking sludge which, having found itself at the bottom of the hill, now discovered it had nowhere else to go. The clouds still loomed, grey and menacing, and the sun had barely broken through, leaving the spring air feeling uncommonly cold. It was a bad omen, people whispered. Outside the city, crops would fail once more, and the price of grain would rise further. War would come again. Napoleon would come. It seemed that I was the only person who couldn't much care whether the sunshine returned or not. Indeed, the miserable weather suited me just fine, although of course the prospect of widespread hunger did not.

I meandered through the gravestones, all standing to attention like stone soldiers, their greyness dulled further by the poor afternoon light. Normally I avoided these places; they were not somewhere to frequent if you had abilities like mine, unless you wanted to invite conversations with those who might lie restlessly below. Yet today, oddly, this kirkyard was quiet; no more than a handful of souls roamed, and they were little more than shadows, flickering and untethered, and apparently disinterested in getting my attention. Beyond them, to the north, Calton Hill dominated the skyline; lush, green and inviting. I thought for a moment about leaving this place, about walking up the hill instead. About sitting up there and letting it all blow away. But I couldn't – not today. Today I had come to say farewell, to make my peace. I had to do that here, even though I didn't know whether this was the right place. Even though I didn't know whether she was in the kirkyard at all.

I walked on, careful not to tread on the pockets of loose soil and uneven ground which betrayed the presence of a number of recent burials. Apparently, the weather had not prevented the gravediggers from keeping themselves busy. I stared hard at those patches of earth, as though through sheer concentration I might discover who lay beneath. Alice could be buried here, couldn't she? It wasn't beyond the realms of possibility. In Paris, death by one's own hand had seemed alarmingly common, and although condemned, it was said that some would find their way into the sacred ground of the city's graveyards, buried quietly at dawn or late at night. I'd heard my mother and her friends whisper about these matters over games of cards, their tongues loosened by great quantities of claret as they discussed the stories that they'd heard that week. Usually it was such-and-such's maid who'd got with child out of wedlock and thrown herself in the Seine, but sometimes it was someone known to them, rejected by her lover and facing ruin. Women like that didn't drown; they cut their own throats, and they left notes for all of Parisian society to feast upon. Foolish, my mother had once remarked. Foolish to die without ensuring there was any mystery at all. People forget quickly, when everything is explained.

Of course, Maman hadn't left a note, even though by then there had been no one to remember – no one but me. She had no grave, either; at least, none which was known to me. I hadn't seen my mother again after her cold, ashen body was removed from that careworn sofa, and no one had wanted to answer a naïve Frenchwoman's questions. Edinburgh, like Paris, dealt with these matters discreetly.

I leaned against the graveyard wall, carefully unfolding the piece of paper which I had been clutching in my hand. It had been pushed under my door that morning, while I was dressing. No knock accompanied it; no courteous greeting was forthcoming. There was just a rustling sound, followed by the soft tapping of footsteps in retreat. I'd lifted the note slowly, already suspecting who it might be from. The handwriting was unfamiliar, but the contents confirmed my suspicion. My heart had sunk as I'd absorbed those words, and it still ached as I read them again now.

*Alice's husband was a baker called Robert Duff. Some of the older guardsmen remember him. They had only one surviving child, a girl named Joanna. Joanna drowned herself in the Nor Loch over forty years ago. I'm told she would have been no more than twenty years old when she died. Robert seems to have died about fifteen years ago. I hope this is the information you were looking for.*

That was it – an unaddressed, unsigned letter containing the bare bones of Alice's story for me to pick over. A handful of abrupt sentences without polite decoration or commentary, devoid of Angus's own interjections and thoughts. I supposed that I shouldn't be surprised, given how we'd last parted. I hadn't seen him for a week; he'd avoided coming into the tavern, which had not pleased Franny.

'What have ye done tae him, lass?' she'd asked, half teasing and half chastising me about a dozen times.

I'd shrugged off her remarks, feigning ignorance, or suggesting that he was busy with the Guard. Each time she'd narrowed her eyes further, clicking her tongue in irritated disapproval as she bustled off to serve more beer. I knew that she wasn't fooled – how could she be? It was quite clear that he did not wish to see me, and it was clearer still that I didn't know how to change that, such was the extent of the injury I had unthinkingly inflicted upon him. But still, receiving a letter like this hurt more than receiving nothing at all. He had done his duty to me; he had fulfilled a promise he'd made before our friendship had soured. But it was quite clear from the tone that he had detached himself, that he was in possession only of facts now, and that feelings were not involved.

I, on the other hand, felt the contents of this letter like a raw flesh wound. If I'd thought that knowing the facts of Alice's life would soothe my grief or ease my regrets, I had been sadly mistaken. On the contrary, the confirmation of her suffering only made me feel my own shortcomings more keenly. How poor a friend I had been to her; how little comfort I had seen fit to provide. Tears fell from my eyes, smudging the careful loops of Angus's writing. I folded it back up before any further damage could be done. The letter was painful to read, but I would keep it.

'Forgive me, Alice,' I whispered. 'Please forgive me, and rest in peace.'

I moved away from the wall, startling the handful of crows which had been pecking curiously at the ground. The frantic flapping of their wings broke the kirkyard's silence, and I found myself listening for other sounds. A voice. An answer. A sign that Alice had heard me, that she accepted what I had said. But, as ever, when I wanted to hear from the dead, they were decidedly silent.

I walked back through the kirkyard, intent on returning to the living part of the town. I felt as though I'd spent much of these past days trying to make amends, but today was the first time I'd come close to finding some solace in it. Yesterday, I'd had a visit from Jane, and certainly the silence and stillness of the graveyard felt infinitely more comforting than anything she'd had to say to me.

'What were you thinking, seeking out Miss Clara like that?' she'd asked, pacing up and down my room. 'I knew it – I knew you'd seen something at that reading. If only you'd spoken to me first, I could have advised you how to proceed. But it's too late now - you've upset her, and you've left me in a real quandary too. I hardly know what to say to them – I am the reason they ever met you, after all!'

'I'm very sorry,' I'd replied, and kept replying after every cross word she spoke.

'Yes, well, you must stay away from now on. You are not welcome, and in any case, your readings and predictions are not needed, since there is now great happiness all around. Mr and Mrs Andrews have reconciled, and the divorce will not happen now. And Mr Turner and Miss Clara are to wed.'

'Engaged?' I'd repeated. 'Henry and Clara?'

Jane had nodded. 'Yes. It was quite a surprise to us all, as we thought they really rather disliked one another. But it seems he has asked, and she has accepted him.'

Well, his feelings were now clear, at least. I'd been right to wonder if he held some affection for her. Clara's intentions, however, remained a mystery. I'd ruminated on this information, but only briefly, before reminding myself that it was no longer any of my concern.

'If the divorce is no longer proceeding, might the family make plans to return to London?' I'd asked, half-musing and not really expecting a response.

Jane had jolted at that, as though the thought hadn't previously occurred to her. 'Well, if they do then I may go with them. I can only hope that my acquaintance with you hasn't harmed their opinion of me too much.'

I'd nodded at the remark, and apologised again. Jane had left with a final, exasperated sigh, flouncing out of my room and shutting the door hard behind her. Despite my best efforts, peace between us had not been restored. My words to Alice had been met with silence, but my words to Jane had undoubtedly fallen upon deaf ears.

And then there was Angus. What was I going to do about Angus?

I stared at the ground, concentrating on where I was standing as I made my way back to the kirkyard gate. All my efforts to help others had failed, and I'd done far more harm than good. Jane was right; it was best that I keep far away from the Andrews family from now on. I had done all that I could for Clara, and it did seem that her life was now taking a different course from that which I'd seen. Perhaps I had been wrong. Or perhaps my warning had served some of its purpose; perhaps accepting Henry meant that she had changed her fate. I was still certain that Henry was not the object of the love which had dominated my vision. But if she didn't love him, why had she accepted him? I shook my head. It didn't matter. There was nothing more I could do for her now.

I was so deep in thought that I hadn't noticed the young man leaning against one of the taller headstones. In fact, when something finally caught my attention in that direction it was not him at all, but the ghost of a man who darted around in front of him, waving his arms about and remonstrating at the young man for how he had so casually positioned himself over his final resting place. The young man, naturally oblivious, merely grinned at me.

'Madame,' he said, with a polite nod.

The French greeting intrigued me, and I found myself walking towards him.

'It might be best if you stop leaning on that grave like that,' I said to him. 'The dead tend not to like it.'

He gave me a strange look, but nonetheless he did as I suggested and took a step back. The spirit, satisfied that his dignity had been restored, gave me a nod and drifted away.

'Vous êtes française?' he asked me, clearly detecting my accent.

'Yes, I am French,' I responded, acknowledging the fact but speaking rather obstinately in English, although I wasn't sure why.

'It is good to meet someone else from France in this city,' he remarked. 'We are both a long way from home, ne c'est pas?'

I smiled, but said nothing further. I found myself studying him, noting his slender frame and dark features, his unfashionably long hair, his rather shabby-looking cream shirt and brown coat. There was something familiar about him, but I couldn't put my finger upon what it was.

'So, what are two French people doing in a graveyard in Edinburgh?' he asked, returning my smile.

'I was paying my respects to a friend,' I replied, looking back towards the recently disturbed earth and allowing the gesture to imply something I couldn't possibly know. Would never know, I reminded myself.

The young man must have seen the sorrow in my eyes, as his voice immediately softened. 'Oh. Then, I am sorry for your loss.'

'Merci, monsieur,' I replied with a small nod, then began to walk away.

'I'm Antoine,' he called after me. 'Not monsieur – just Antoine.'

I turned around, not wishing to seem rude. 'Miss Ailsa Rose,' I replied.

Antoine took a handful of steps towards me, hanging on to the threads of our conversation. 'It is nice to meet you, Miss Ailsa Rose,' he said, his thin face alight with a large grin. 'So, you are here to talk to the ghosts?'

'Sorry – I don't know what you mean,' I replied with some haste, and rather too defensively. He couldn't have guessed that from my remarks cautioning him against standing on graves, surely.

Antoine let out a nervous laugh. 'Your friend? You said you are paying your respects. My apologies, my comment was in bad taste. But people do that, you know. I see it a lot. People stand and they talk to headstones as though the person laid below might answer back.'

Oh, they can answer back, I thought, but of course I didn't say it.

'You speak as though you come here often,' I observed.

He nodded. 'Perhaps I do. Perhaps it is a habit I have formed during my time here.'

'So, what do you do – sit and watch people?'

He laughed again. 'You make it sound strange, but yes, sometimes I do. Sometimes I draw them. Sometimes I ignore them altogether and write instead. Sometimes I just think. Breathe. Exist.'

'But why?'

'Why not? It is quiet. It is calm. It is so unlike every other corner of this place, isn't it?'

'But it is full of death. We are French. Surely we have had enough of...' I stopped speaking, feeling suddenly foolish.

He shrugged. 'Perhaps. We have had enough of horror, I think. But beauty? No, not nearly enough of that. And there is beauty everywhere, Miss Rose. Even in graveyards. I like to seek it, to draw it and to capture it in here,' he added, tapping the little sketchbook he clutched in his hand.

'So, you are an artist?'

'I hope to be, one day. I assist an artist. I travel with her and her wax model exhibition.'

I looked at him again, and realised then why I'd thought he seemed familiar. The ticket seller with the intense, dark gaze. The one who'd been so quick to resume his sketching that day at the exhibition. Yes, it was him.

'You work for Madame Tussaud?'

'Oui – you have heard about The Grand European Cabinet of Figures, then?'

'I have seen it,' I replied, trying not to shudder.

'And what did you think of it?'

'I think I saw more horror than beauty in it.'

'Yes, Madame evokes horror very well,' he replied, 'which is to be expected, I think, when one gets so close to it. You know that she took those casts herself, of those heads, fresh from the guillotine?' He paused for a moment, and I thought I saw something like disgust flicker across his face. 'And, of course, she almost met that same fate. She seldom speaks of it now, except to say that she is glad to be here, and for the moment, at least, to have left France behind. Did you meet her, during your visit?'

'No. I recall seeing her there, but we did not meet. However, I share her sentiments. I saw little beauty in our country, before I left it.'

He raised his eyebrows at my remark, and I thought for a

moment he might pursue it. Might ask what else I thought, and where my allegiances had lain, if I had any. But he didn't. Instead, he merely made a study of me for a moment, chewing a grubby index finger thoughtfully before smiling at me once more.

'You should visit the exhibition again,' he suggested. 'You might see something different in it the second time. You might even meet Madame, if you are lucky.'

I thought about my first visit, about the things I saw, how they represented everything I'd fled from, and everything which would have come to me if I'd stayed. It wasn't an experience I was keen to repeat. But perhaps that was the point. Perhaps it was time to confront the past; a past I shared with the likes of Antoine and Madame Tussaud, and my own past, the one which no one had survived but me. I looked around me, thinking again of Alice, of how I'd come here so desperate to make amends. I still had other, much older ghosts to lay to rest.

'Thank you. I will do that,' I replied.

I walked away, leaving Antoine to his silence and his sketches. By the time I reached the gate he was drawing again, his gazed fixed on those circling crows.

'See – beautiful!' he called out to me, pointing at them.

The crows squawked their disapproval. I shook my head at him. They looked mean and hungry, not beautiful at all. I took one last look at the things Antoine couldn't see; the white wisps of spirits drifting around their resting places, the flickers of faces peering out of their tombs. I wondered if he'd find beauty in those, too. Wondered if he'd be curious. Wondered if he'd be frightened.

Wondered if, like me, he'd regret that he could see too much.

# Seventeen

Franny gave me a wide berth in the tavern that evening. I knew that was how it was going to be from the moment I walked in and saw how she pursed her lips at me and offered the frostiest greeting she could manage. I'd wondered if someone had been whispering in her ear, if she knew more about what had happened between Angus and me. Wondered, even, if Angus had been in here himself, drowning his sorrows in her strongest brew. Deep down I knew that wasn't his way, but her bad mood fed my fears so thoroughly that my mind kept returning to the notion, replaying it and embellishing it so that I convinced myself, briefly, that she knew everything. Of course, she didn't – if she had, she wouldn't have been able to resist telling me. Her silence, punctuated only by necessary clipped responses, told me that whilst she was cross with me, she was still guessing as to the exact reason why.

I supposed I only had myself to blame. After all, Angus was one of her favourites, and he hadn't shown his face in the tavern for days. And I had been resolutely unwilling to offer her an explanation as to why, when clearly the fault was mine. I might have lost a friend, but so had Franny, in her way. And she'd lost his custom, too.

Fortunately, the tavern was busy, which provided us both with enough distraction to ensure that our paths didn't meaningfully cross. I was content to keep serving the groups of noisy men who crowded around the small tables, answering their need for endless supplies of drink. I had a lot on my mind, and amidst the bustle of the tavern I could allow it to wander a little, safe in the knowledge that I had neither the time nor the space for my thoughts to turn too deep or too dark.

I'd felt better after my visit to the graveyard earlier; I'd felt a sort of peace come over me, as though Alice might have seen and heard me, as though she might have understood. I'd also been cheered by my chance encounter with Antoine. It had been oddly comforting to speak to someone from my country, to someone who knew at least some of the things I knew, who'd seen what I had seen. I'd resolved to return to the exhibition, just as he'd suggested. My first visit had been traumatic, but a second might fare better. I might, as Antoine had said, see something different. I might see my way to finally making my peace with Paris, with the comte, with my mother.

With everything.

I handed out yet more beers, forcing a smile. I had to try. Since that night at the theatre, I'd felt utterly adrift, as though everything which grounded me here had suddenly been swept away. For the second time since coming to Edinburgh, I felt deserted: Alice was dead, Angus was absent from my life, perhaps for good, and Franny and Jane both had their reasons to be cold and distant. I hadn't even the mystery of Clara Andrews to solve any more, to keep my feverish mind occupied. I needed to find my place here again, to move forward. It wasn't like I had any other choice. It wasn't like I could return to Paris.

*But you could, ma chérie. Just think of Madame Tussaud — she is here, and you could be there. There is peace now.*

Yes, there was peace, for however long that may last. But I wasn't sure that Paris was what I wanted, either. I wasn't sure what I wanted anymore, if indeed I'd ever known.

'Ailsa, would ye serve these gentlemen?'

Behind me, Franny's flustered tone disrupted my inner

monologue. I turn around, putting on another smile even though my cheeks were beginning to ache with the effort of it.

'Yes, of course, what can I -'

My smile faded, and my words stopped. There, in front of me, sat Henry Turner and his soon to be father-in-law, Charles Andrews. I felt the blood drain from my face, felt my eyes widen, my mouth become dry.

'- what can I get for you?' I finished my sentence, my words barely a croak. I swallowed hard, uncomfortably, as though the flesh in my throat was now sand.

'Ah yes, Miss Rose, isn't it? We thought we might encounter you in here.' It was Charles who addressed me first, his eyes flicking up and down my beer-stained attire with a look of disdain. 'Isn't it odd how many times our paths have crossed? Yet I never knew who you were. I know now, of course.'

He gave me a menacing smile, his face filled by yellowing teeth, his eyes beset by the wrinkles which gathered around them and briefly betrayed his age. Unlike Henry he had handsome features, but such a capacity for rendering them ugly with his countenance.

'I'm not anyone, sir. Just a woman who serves drink in a tavern. Now, what can I fetch for you?' I repeated my question, hoping in vain that it might afford me my escape.

'I should have you apprehended, you know,' he continued. 'You're a fortune teller. You should be whipped, at the very least.'

I felt the heat rise in my cheeks at his accusations, and grew aware of the curious gazes falling upon me from the surrounding tables as voices muted and ears attuned.

'No, sir, you are mistaken,' I replied. 'I make no living from telling fortunes. I make my living by working here.'

'Then, pray tell me, what were you doing, calling upon my family?' He turned to Henry, who sat beside him, a smirk playing at the corners of his mouth as he watched my humiliation unfold. 'She was at the house, was she not?'

'Yes. It was some weeks ago now, but yes, she was,' Henry replied.

'I do not deny that I was there, sir. I was there at your youngest daughter's invitation. I'm sure you would agree that it would not have been proper to decline such an honour.'

'No, indeed that would not have been proper,' Charles replied. 'And yet, this is how you repay my family's kindness, is it? By filling my eldest daughter's head with your nonsense and your lies? She was extremely vexed after encountering you at the theatre. She didn't leave her room for several days. Whatever you told her affected her gravely.'

Whatever I told her – I lingered for a moment on those last words. Her father didn't know. Henry didn't know. Clara had kept the nature of my warning to herself. I recalled what she'd said that night, how she'd accused me of colluding with others. I'd let the remark slip by me at the time, too stunned by her reaction to really ponder its meaning. But now I wondered who she thought I'd been in league with. Now I wondered just how little she trusted those around her, if she felt unable to tell them about what I'd said.

'I hear all is well now,' I replied. 'Mr Turner, you and Miss Andrews are engaged to be married, are you not?'

At this, Henry looked pleased. 'Yes, that is correct, we are to wed soon.'

I studied him for a moment, wishing I could ask all the questions which were running through my mind. Something about the steely look in his blue eyes told me that he'd pressed his suit hard. I recalled all that Jane had told me about Henry and Clara, about their quarrel, about them seeming not to like one another. I wondered how many times she'd said no before she finally said yes. I wondered, with no small amount of guilt, whether this time he'd caught her in a moment of weakness as she finally left her room, still reeling from what I'd told her.

'I must offer you my congratulations, sir,' I said.

'And I must warn you to stay away from my family, Miss Rose,' Charles interjected. 'If you so much as look at one of my daughters again, I will see to it that you feel the full weight of the law and its consequences. A stay in the Bridewell should suffice to silence that spiteful tongue of yours. Wouldn't you agree, Henry?'

Henry chuckled, shooting me a look of vicious glee. 'Indeed, sir. Indeed, it would.'

Charles rose from his seat. 'Very good. Now come, Henry, we shall find a better establishment in which to toast your impending nuptials.'

Obediently Henry followed, offering the briefest of smug glances over his shoulder as he left the tavern. He looked so pleased with himself, which considering his engagement, he ought to be. But there was more to his manner than that; he had smirked and revelled his way through Charles's admonishment of me, and his eyes had seemed to shine with triumph as the final threat was delivered. It made little sense; why would he consider me to be such an adversary? Why would he and Charles Andrews feel the need to come here and intimidate me so publicly?

I swallowed hard, conscious of all the eyes in the room which still rested upon me, reading my reaction, studying my next move. I busied myself, tidying tables, trying to soothe the sting of that encounter. Once again, I found myself in the dark, grasping for clues. It was hardly surprising; after all, I'd revealed the contents of a vision I barely understood to a young woman I didn't really know. It had been a foolish thing to do, to get so deeply involved, to abandon my usual reserve in order to deliver what had been, at best, a cryptic warning. No wonder she'd hidden herself away; there was little doubt that I'd given her a terrible fright. I took a stack of mugs away, scuttling into the back room before anyone could see the tears gathering in my eyes. A dreadful mess – that was what Angus had called it. I was only just beginning to realise how right he had been.

*

It was closing time before Franny broached the subject of what had happened between those gentlemen and me. I knew she would have seen and heard it all; she'd been running a tavern so many years that she had a special sense for detecting trouble. I'd spent the remainder of the evening bracing myself for an interrogation, knowing that her curiosity would overcome the displeasure she'd shown towards me earlier. I was just grateful she'd decided to wait until everyone else had gone home. The last thing I needed was another audience.

I decided to be truthful; I had been less than forthcoming about the rift between Angus and me, and Franny knew it. I risked damaging our friendship if I tried to be evasive about this, too. Besides, I owed her a reasonable explanation; I worked for her, after all, and the confrontation had taken place in her tavern. I told her the story from start to finish. There was no harm in it, I decided. The matter was over now; Charles Andrews could not have been clearer about that. I told her about Jane's involvement, about how she'd summoned me to do the reading, and about what I'd seen. I told her that I'd tried and failed to understand my vision, and that in the absence of knowledge I'd decided to warn the young woman anyway. I left the specifics out of it; I didn't offer names or details of places, and I didn't tell her about Angus's involvement, or lack of involvement. I didn't tell her that this was why he was upset with me. That felt like a step too far, and if I was honest with myself, I still feared her reaction. I suspected she would regard what I'd done concerning Clara Andrews as foolish, but I knew that she'd view my behaviour towards Angus as unforgiveable.

'I always said that Jane wis trouble,' she said, clicking her tongue in disapproval. 'Now dae ye see why I discouraged ye from telling her yer tales? Got a real fanciful mind, has that lass.'

I felt a frown flicker across my brow. I didn't recall Franny saying anything of the sort; in fact, at the time she'd seemed more concerned that my chatter might corrupt poor young Jane. However, I decided to let it go.

'Yes, well, it's done now,' I assured her. 'I will heed their warning and I will keep away. It shouldn't be difficult – we live on opposing sides of town. I am sorry, though, for the scene they made. I'm still at a loss as to why they felt the need to come all the way here to speak to me like that.'

Franny drew a deep breath. 'Ye said yerself, the lass is now tae wed one o' the men who came here today. Perhaps he thought that ye'd warned her off him.'

I shook my head. 'But that makes no sense. They're engaged now, so even if I had advised her against marrying him, then it would be clear that my warning had not been heeded. Besides, my vision was nothing to do with that man. It seemed to be about her involvement with someone, but I don't think it was him.'

I rubbed my sweating brow with a sudden weariness as I pondered my own reasoning. I had to admit, it was good to say these things aloud. A relief, even.

'But they dinnae ken what ye ken, dae they? Maybe the wummin has been havin' second thoughts. If he's keen to have his bride then he won't want anythin' getting in the way, will he?'

'Yes, perhaps,' I replied. 'I suppose there are a hundred possibilities, aren't there? And I suppose I will never know.'

Franny chuckled. 'I think you're gonnae have to accept that ye've lost this one, lass. An' I think ye should also heed the warning – from the gentlemen, aye, but also from what's happened. Dinnae get involved in things ye dinnae understand.'

I smiled. 'Thank you, Franny.'

She regarded me curiously. 'For what?'

'For listening. I know that you think all my talk about visions and spirits is nonsense.'

'I do. But more importantly I think it could get you intae trouble, and I would hate tae see that, Ailsa.'

I nodded. 'You're right. I will be more careful from now on.'

'Guid. I'd say ye've got enough o' yer own troubles to be solvin', lass.'

'You would?'

She gave me an exasperated look. 'Angus?'

'Oh, yes,' I said, turning away. 'Angus.'

I expected her to pursue the subject further, but she didn't.

Instead, we finished cleaning up the tavern in silence, Franny doubtless pondering the exact nature of my quarrel with Angus, while I wondered, rather helplessly, how I was ever going to fix things between us. In the case of Clara Andrews, I knew now that it was best to let the matter lie. That could never be the solution with Angus. At some point, soon, I was going to have to face him, or risk losing our friendship altogether.

# Eighteen

The first and only time that the comte had laid his hands on me, I'd hit him. Maman had been sleeping in her room, as she sometimes did in the late afternoons. She needed the repose, she'd say to me, if she was to present herself well at their evening engagements and attend parties late into the night. The comte always insisted upon her company, no matter if she was tired or unwell. She was his diamond, he would declare, when he was in one of his more favourable moods. He couldn't be parted from her. I supposed that he liked to get his money's worth.

This particular afternoon had begun like all the others; we dined, and I watched Maman push food around her plate, her only appetite apparently being for the wine with which she refilled her glass three or four times at least. Shortly afterwards she declared her exhaustion and retired, leaving me to pass the time with the comte. I reached for my book and settled upon the sofa, ready to keep myself occupied. The comte mocked my mother's afternoon habits, but more often than not he would find his own liquor-strewn slumber in his favourite chair. I always made sure to be quiet, and to let his age and intoxication work its usual magic against him.

That day, however, it seemed not to have any effect. Perhaps his sobriety was greater than I'd credited him for, or perhaps he was better rested. Whatever the reason, as I perused the pages of my novel, I felt his eyes upon me, bright and keen above his fat cheeks. He was not handsome; even a wig and a touch of rouge on his cheeks could not improve his sweating, grey pallor, his beaked nose or snarl-prone lips. He repulsed me and so, as I often did, I avoided his gaze, concentrating hard on the story before me, even though his attentions had made me forgetful of its content. Next to me a cool waft of air told me Pierre had moved closer. He'd noticed, too.

Eventually, the comte had tired of what he no doubt saw as my coyness. He got to his feet, ripping the book from my hands in one unexpectedly nimble swoop.

'Your mother lets you read too many of these,' he'd said, throwing my book to the ground. 'She should know better. No one likes a bluestocking.'

I hadn't answered him. I knew better than to do that; I'd seen what happened to my mother when she allowed her tongue to become too loose. I just sat, frozen in my seat, waiting for whatever would come next.

'You're sixteen now,' he said. 'Not a girl anymore. I think it's time for you to learn a few lessons from me, ma petite.'

Before I could move, the comte forced his considerable backside on to the sofa and sat close beside me. He leaned over, draping his arm around my shoulder and giving it a rough squeeze. I kept my breathing shallow, trying not to smell the sickliness of the brandy which fermented on his breath. I looked down, my stomach lurching as I noticed the dried dribbles of the game soup we'd eaten, spattered down his breeches. I felt Pierre still hovering at my side, unsure what he could do. He'd always helped me avoid the comte's advances, but this afternoon things had gone too far. There was no avoiding this. The comte pulled himself closer, and I felt his wet lips on my cheek, then on my neck, then…

'No!' I shouted.

I startled him. He retreated, but only for a moment. Then a lazy smile crept on to his lips and he laughed; a menacing, throaty chuckle.

'You see? You learn quickly,' he said.

'No,' I said again, quieter this time but with a vehemence he couldn't ignore.

I got to my feet, pulling myself away from him. I would go to my room, put some distance between us and hope that he abandoned this dreadful notion until my mother woke. But the comte wasn't in a mood to give in so easily. He grabbed hold of my skirt, hauling me back towards him. So, in that moment, I did all that I could do: I hit him once, then again and again, landing blows in the middle of his chest and across his shoulders with all the strength I could muster. At first it amused him, and he laughed more, but quickly his chortles became groans as he realised the need to defend himself.

'Ungrateful wretch!' he yelled, getting to his feet and grabbing hold of my arms. 'Bastard daughter of a whore!'

Somehow, I shook off his grasp and made another bid to reach my room. I expected him to try to follow me, and he did, lurching at me with the sort of indignant fury he usually reserved for Maman. I continued to flee, my mind so panicked that at first, I didn't absorb the sound of a chair scraping along the floor, or believe my ears when I heard an almighty thud. It was only when I reached the doorway and realised that he was no longer in pursuit that I dared to turn around. There, lying on the floor, was the comte, apparently tripped up by a sofa which had flung itself in his path. And there, standing over him, was Pierre, looking mighty pleased with himself.

'Thank you,' I mouthed. Then I ran to my room and kept guard at the door until, a while later, I heard my mother wake.

I revisited this memory a dozen times or more while sitting in the exhibition room on a rainy Friday afternoon, my gaze fixed on the comte's wax head. He'd never touched me again after that day. My mother, apparently having some understanding of what had happened while she slept, increased her efforts to keep us apart, and to ensure that we were not left alone. But it was more than that. The comte knew, as did I, that the sofa had moved into his path. He also knew that I hadn't moved it. Pierre's actions had saved me that day; I also believed that they'd unnerved the comte, that they'd made him more wary of me. It was the first time I'd really appreciated the power I had. It was the first time that I'd truly seen my abilities as a gift.

Not that any of it mattered now, did it? The comte was dead and I was here, looking at his image, watching him suspended in the moment of death for all eternity. I had despised him, but even I wouldn't have wished to see him meet such a dreadful fate. A fate we had left him to. I shuddered, thinking back to our escape, how Maman hid her plans from all who knew us. She must have really hated him, to have left him behind, to have made us little better than destitute in a foreign land.

*You have to let it go, ma chérie. It's been many years. It is time to move on.*

I thought I had, until recently. Until I found myself confronted by it all again.

'I didn't expect to see you again so soon, Miss Rose.'

Antoine wandered in, sitting down beside me. Today his hands were empty; no book, no pencil to occupy them. He folded them together in his lap, as though keeping them still might prove difficult. I found myself staring at his fingers; long, lean digits wrapped in youthful, unblemished skin. I wondered for a moment how old he was. Younger than me, certainly, but it was difficult to guess with any sort of precision.

'A fine row of horrors, are they not?' he said, nodding towards the bodyless mannequins in front of us. 'Of course, you will know most of them, I think. Carrier, Hébert, Robespierre, Marat...'

I nodded, giving him a grim smile. 'Yes, I think everyone must know those names.'

'But those are not the ones you are looking at.'

He gave me an expectant look, as though he knew already what I was going to say. Around us the room had grown empty, the last of the visitors making their way through this room and back outside. Most hadn't lingered here; their gasps of horror and murmurs of distaste had been largely short-lived. Some had made a greater study of me, perhaps curious that someone would choose to sit for so long in this place. A few had looked positively discomfited by it. Two gentlemen, in particular, had stared at me, eyeing my muddied shoes and petticoat, muttering comments – wasn't it such an awful business, but wasn't it to be expected, when the mob took over? One of them had sniffed the air as he passed me, perhaps mistaking the reek of the streets for the stench of revolution. I could only imagine what he would have done if he'd heard me speak.

'Do you not have to sell tickets?'

Antoine laughed. 'No, no more tickets today. We are closing soon.'

'Oh. Do you wish me to leave now?'

'Not yet, not if you aren't ready. Unfortunately, I don't think Madame will be here today; she has other appointments to keep. I'm sorry to disappoint you.'

I smiled. 'You haven't.'

'I didn't think so. I didn't think it was for Madame that you have sat so long in here. So, which one is it?' he asked me, nodding again towards the row of heads.

'The Comte de Rocrois,' I replied.

'Ah! Noblesse. That is…unexpected. You knew him?'

I hesitated, then wondered why. What possible harm could it do, to admit my connection to him now?

'We were acquainted at one time, yes.'

'The Comte de Rocrois. Arrested under the Law of Suspects at the end of ninety-three. Guillotined in early ninety-four.' He smiled sheepishly. 'When you spend all your time with them, you tend to learn their stories, if you didn't already know them.'

I nodded. 'Yes, well, I'd left France by then.'

'Wise. I remember the Terror too well.' He got up, and gestured for me to follow. 'Come – I have something to show you before you go.'

Antoine led me into the exhibition's first room, the one I'd hurried through today, where nobility and royalty still lived. Marie Antoinette caught my eye, and I found myself thinking about my first visit here, about how delighted Angus had seemed when he saw her. About what a happy day it had been, until my vision in the second room had caused it all to unravel. Now, of course, I didn't expect that we'd enjoy such a day together again.

'What do you think of the Sleeping Beauty?' Antoine asked me, bidding me to come closer to the place where she lay.

I gazed at her for a moment, remembering how Angus and I had stood close together, marvelling at her loveliness. I had recognised her name, tried to recall why. Captivating, I think I'd called her, still looking at her face. Angus had studied me for almost as long.

'She's lovely,' I replied. 'Very beautiful.'

'She was created by Madame's mentor, Monsieur Curtius. He left his collection to Madame when he died. She's my favourite of all the models here. I often find myself standing here, just gazing at her. I have drawn her many times. I cannot resist a pretty face,' he added, grinning at me.

I nodded, recalling how I'd wondered at her presence here when I first saw her. It was satisfying to get to the bottom of a mystery, no matter how trivial. The thought reminded me that another mystery about her still remained.

'Do you know who she is?' I asked him. 'In the pamphlet it says only her name. I forget it now.'

'Madame de Sainte-Amaranthe. She was a salonière, perhaps a courtesan also. She was executed in ninety-four, I think. Those who were associated with the old regime paid a heavy price.'

'Hmm.' I thought of my mother, how she feared for us even before Pierre delivered his warning about the danger we faced. How right she had been. How right they'd both been.

'She owned a gambling salon. It was notorious, or so Madame says.'

Somewhere in my mind, a memory flickered to the fore. A memory of him staggering in, his pockets empty, his belly full of drink. Of Maman eyeing him warily, knowing the cards were stacked against her, too. Now I knew where I would have heard the name.

'There should be more models like this,' Antoine continued. 'It is inspired. Beautiful. Interesting. I prefer to look at this than those morbid heads in the other room. Don't you?'

'Yes, I suppose,' I replied, even though I had spent today doing exactly the opposite.

'For now, I learn from Madame. But one day – well, I have dreams, Miss Rose. I have ideas and I wish to create them.'

I smiled at him. 'I look forward to hearing about you, when you achieve fame and fortune.'

He laughed. 'You flatter me, but I hope you are right. I also hope I have given you a nicer image to leave here with. I would hate for you to go home thinking about a guillotined comte, even if you knew him.'

I nodded, looking once more at the sleeping mannequin. I appreciated the gesture, but it would take far more than a beautiful face to make me forget everything that happened in Paris. Nothing in my life so far had succeeded in that.

*

I left the exhibition a little after four, greeted by a mercifully light drizzle and dispersing cloud. It might yet turn into a fine evening, although that didn't much matter to me; I was due in the tavern soon and would work until closing time. My stomach lurched a little as I found myself wondering whether Angus might come in tonight. I knew it was foolish, but I longed to see him sitting in his favourite spot, sipping his beer and watching the other drinkers with his usual hawkish guardsman expression. I longed to talk to him, to say sorry, and for sorry to be enough.

Could it be enough?

Perhaps I could write him a note, to explain myself. Or, perhaps I could ask Franny for advice; after all, she'd lent me a sympathetic ear last night. But telling her about Clara Andrews was one thing; talking about Angus was quite another. I winced, imagining her keen blue eyes widening, her lip curling in dismay as I told her what I'd done. No - I wouldn't ask Franny for advice. I sighed, lamenting the lack of anyone I could turn to.

*That's because you don't trust anyone, Ailsa.*

That wasn't true. I'd started to trust Angus, hadn't I? I'd told him things about me, things that no one else here knew, about my life in Paris, about Pierre, about the comte.

*But you hadn't trusted him enough to tell him about Clara. Do you not think that you deceived him, that night at the theatre? Do you not see how you would have made him feel like a pawn in your game?*

Yes, I did see. I saw clearly now.

I reached the bridge, bracing myself as I walked into its familiar howling wind. In front of me the Old Town beckoned, its stone tenements climbing up the hill and towards a grey-orange sky. It was a sight I'd never tire of. It was home. I'd realised that today, at the exhibition. I'd stared at the comte's face, and this time no vision had arrived. No voices. No screams. Just silence, and memories which felt remote now. Paris was the past. The future, however, was another matter.

'Ailsa?'

Freezing fingers tapped me on the shoulder; I felt their ice seep through my clothes and on to my skin. I spun around, ready to answer, but no one was there. Then I saw him – a dark-haired boy in an old grey shirt, running towards the New Town. He stopped and turned around; he was some distance away, but there was no mistaking his sombre expression, his petted lip. He'd always looked at me like that, right before he told me something that he knew I didn't want to hear.

'Ailsa,' I heard him whisper. 'Ailsa, you must help.'

'Pierre…' I began, but in a moment, he was gone.

I turned away, continuing my walk home as the first heavy droplets began to fall from those charcoal clouds which crowded together now, blotting out the light. The evening would not be fine, after all; I had been wrong about that. I had been wrong, too, to think that I could lay all my ghosts to rest. Some were determined not to be quiet. It seemed that my past wasn't finished with me yet.

# Nineteen

Following his reappearance on the bridge, Pierre began to disrupt my dreams. I knew it was him, rather than my imagination; the images I saw were too orderly and poignant to attribute to mere coincidence. At first, I recalled memories, of precious times Pierre and I were left to find our own amusement. I dreamt of those afternoons when he would march over to the piano, tinkling a tune off-key, and laugh at my efforts to scold him, and of the evenings spent whispering in my room as we listened to Maman and the comte entertaining and made ourselves scarce. After that, my sleeping mind conjured things I couldn't have seen: Pierre, the living child, running around in the large rooms and wide halls of an apartment much like the one I'd lived in. I saw a younger boy chasing him, giggling; a little brother, perhaps. I saw sunny days spent on dusty streets or playing games with other children on the banks of the Seine. Then, tonight, I saw him fall in. Felt the lure of the current and the weight of the water as it drenched his clothes and filled his shoes. Choked with him as the murky river invaded his lungs. Heard his mother's cries. Saw him sink below. Sensed him slip away.

I woke with a start before dawn, cold sweat pouring from me, barely able to breathe. I'd never known how he'd died. Never known anything of his family, of who had loved him, of where he'd lived. He'd been twelve when it happened; that's all he would say. He'd been twelve then, and now he would be twelve forever. He'd steadfastly refused to speak of the details, but for some reason, he'd chosen to show me now.

But why like this? If he had something to say, why could he not just speak to me, like he used to?

I must have fallen back into a deep sleep, because when I woke again morning had broken, its silvery light hinting behind my curtains. Outside I could hear the rain pattering down; it had barely stopped in days, not since Pierre had turned his back on me on the bridge and those black clouds had gathered overhead. My room was cold and damp; I yearned to light a fire but could ill-afford such extravagance. Franny's effort to lighten my tavern duties in the wake of Alice's death had felt like a kindness at the time, but now it left me somewhat short of money. Instead, I huddled down under my blankets, thinking about Pierre, occupied with the same questions which had troubled me in the earlier hours. Why were his appearances so fleeting? Why did he feel so distant? It was never like this in Paris. There he was my constant companion – so vivid, so present that at times I could forget he was dead.

*But you're not in Paris now, are you, Ailsa?*

Yes, perhaps that was it. He had never lived here, never even visited. There was nothing to tether him to the world I inhabited now.

I sighed, turning over. None of that helped me to understand what it was that he wanted to tell me. On the bridge he'd implored me once again to help, just as he'd done when I saw him near the dancing rooms as I searched in vain for Clara. But help with what? The timing of that appearance and his presence in my vision had led me to believe it was something to do with Clara, but that seemed more unlikely than ever now. I'd never understood why Pierre would have cared about the fate of a young woman in Edinburgh and besides, as far as I was concerned, that matter was settled.

*Your visions and dreams have become blurred, ma chérie. The past, the present, the future, all wrapped up together. Keep them separate, or you will drive yourself mad.*

With a shiver, I dragged myself out of bed. It was true: I was driving myself mad. Ever since I'd held Clara's cup, seen her blood run and heard Pierre's cry, I'd allowed the past to intrude, to lead me to make connections which, I now realised, weren't really there. It was folly and it wouldn't end well.

'This has to stop, Pierre,' I whispered as I dressed. 'I am here and you are there. There is nothing I can do for you anymore.'

\*

I stayed in my room for the remainder of the morning, the unfavourable weather and the lack of anything to do confining me within the bounds of the four uneven, careworn walls I called my home. The landlord, or indeed a previous occupant, had some years ago had the walls whitewashed. Over the years the paint had flaked and cracked in places, leaving my décor a patchwork of greying white and exposed plaster. I had meant to repaint it, but a lack of funds and a tendency to feel daunted by the task had prevented me from ever committing to it. Now, as I found my eye continuously caught by the myriad of imperfections, I felt irritated with myself. I used to live in such a large, sumptuous home, each room as bright and immaculate as the next. How could I tolerate this? How could I not find it within myself to improve the condition of a single room?

Of course, that was not the only matter which bothered me. Having finally put Pierre out of my mind, I'd found my thoughts wandering back to Angus. It had been more than a week since I'd seen him, more than a week since he'd come into the tavern and sat down in his favourite spot. Last night I'd stared at that table and wondered if I'd ever gone so long without seeing him. He'd been such a regular fixture of my evenings at work, and I missed him. I missed the way he rubbed his face as he leaned back in his chair, as though he could chase away the ghosts of last night's watch with his hands. I missed how he grinned at me when I brought him his favourite beer. I missed turning around, and no matter how busy the place was, his eyes would always be on me.

'He thinks the world of you,' Franny had once told me.

She was right then, but not anymore. I missed that too, I realised. I hadn't even appreciated it at the time, and now it was gone.

I dwelt on what might have been for a few moments more, before a brisk knock at the door shook me from my thoughts. I frowned at the intrusion into my morning. I wasn't expecting anyone; indeed, I couldn't think who would wish to call upon me right now. Knocks at my door had become painfully infrequent since Alice's passing.

'Who's there?' I called softly, opening the door just enough to peer round. Momentarily I felt my heart fill with hope. Could it be Angus? Had he decided that we should reconcile?

But it wasn't Angus. Instead, the man on the other side of the door sniffed loudly, and I caught sight of greasy grey hair and a muck-stained shirt. My heart sank.

'Dinnae worry, yer rent's no' late.'

I opened the door wider, forcing a smile to greet Jack Burnhouse. I'd always been wary of Jack; he was a short, corpulent man with a reputation for a bad temper, especially towards those who he considered had not been paying their way. He lived in Anstruther House, in a room on the floor below mine, and worked for the building's owner, a wealthy man whose interest in this old house seemed only to extend to income and expenditure. Of the former, there was much, thanks to Jack and his persuasive means of rent collection, but of the latter, there was very little. I'd long since learnt that owners of buildings such as this had little interest in improving conditions for those who had to live within them.

'Good morning, Jack,' I said. 'What can I do for you?'

'There now, that's better – that's how tae greet someone who comes tae yer door. No' yelling at him aboot the roof leaking like the wee wummin up the stairs. Groanin' on aboot aw the water comin' in last night. I told her tae put her stoup under it – save herself a trip tae the wellhead.' He let out a wicked laugh, then stared at me, his grey eyes challenging me to retort.

'Yes, well, I've no complaints,' I replied, even though I had many. Even though I pitied those who lived on the top floor greatly, especially during inclement weather.

'Guid,' he said, narrowing his eyes at me for the briefest moment. 'Now, what wis I…oh aye, the auld wummin who bided across there…'

I swallowed hard. 'Alice?'

'Aye, that's the one. She's deid, aye?'

'Yes,' I confirmed, as flatly as I could manage. 'That's right. Alice did pass away recently.'

'Her room's gettin' cleared oot for the next tenant. Do ye want anythin' from it?'

'Do I want anything?' I repeated, incredulous.

'Well, aye – I ken she wis yer friend. If ye dae, ye'll need tae be quick – it's aw goin' oot today.'

'Going where?' I asked, although I wasn't sure why that was my next question.

Jack shrugged. 'The parish'll decide that. Dae ye want tae tak a look, or no'?'

I hesitated. On the one hand, it felt so wrong to be digging through a dead woman's possessions. Alice had never invited me into her room, and I had never asked to enter. It was fanciful to think she'd want me in there now. On the other hand, seeing her living space could give me some further insight into someone who I'd spent so much time with but knew so little about. That, I had to admit, was tempting, and besides, my presence in that room might lend Jack a few scruples. I'd no doubt that he would pocket anything which caught his eye.

With this justification in mind, I gave him a thin smile. 'Lead the way,' I replied.

Jack harrumphed his way back across the hall, muttering some choice words about old women without family and why these matters were always left to him. I'd no doubt that he did have better things to do; when he wasn't pursuing tenants for their rent, he was more than partial to a drink and a visit to the doxies on the ground floor.

'Ye might want tae fetch oot yer handkerchief,' Jack said as he flung open Alice's door. 'There's an awful stink aboot this place.'

He wasn't wrong. The smell hit me immediately, catching at the back of my throat and causing me to retch. I'd borne a great many odours in my time as a resident of this ripe and grimy city, but the rotten stink in Alice's room was really quite unbearable. I put my hand over my mouth, wishing that I did indeed have a handkerchief to call upon.

'Jack, it smells like something's died in here,' I said through my fingers.

He laughed. 'Well it wisnae Alice. She went ower the brig.'

The casual way he talked about Alice's demise made me wince. He noticed; indeed, he watched my reaction with a cool, studied silence, seeming almost to relish it. I looked around, letting my hand fall from my mouth now but keeping my breathing shallow. Apart from the smell, nothing about Alice's room seemed to be amiss. It wasn't exactly tidy; her little elm table was beset by empty bowls and tin pint pots, and her bed was unmade, strewn with filthy blankets. Her old fireplace sat cold and empty, its poker disregarded on the floor, and I wondered when either had last been used. On the floor I spied crumbs; remnants, perhaps, of the last bit of bread I'd ever given to her. My stomach lurched at the memory, and I pushed it to one side.

'Have you checked the room for anything else?' I asked him. 'An animal, perhaps?'

Jack shook his head. 'No' found anythin' yet, but yer probly right. Who kens what that mad auld wummin got up tae in 'ere?'

I bit my lip, wanting badly to refute his cruel words about Alice, but not quite daring to stand up to him. I'd seen others get on the wrong side of Jack, and they didn't usually keep their rooms here for long afterwards. Anstruther House was hardly a palace, but I also knew that there were far worse places to live.

Jack wandered over to Alice's bed, lifting up the crumpled mess of blankets which hung over its side. He peered briefly underneath, then stood back up, letting out a deep groan.

'Aye, well, that'd mak the place smell,' he remarked.

'What? What is it?'

'Deid cat. Been 'ere a while, I'd say, fae the look o' it.'

I covered my mouth again. 'I did think it might be an animal,' I muttered.

'Was it hers?'

Jack had turned to face me again now, those eyes of his seeming almost black in the gloom of Alice's cold, barren room. I swallowed hard. The man had a knack for inspiring guilt, even where there was none.

I shook my head. 'I don't know. I never saw her with a cat, but then I never entered her room, either.'

'Never? But she was yer friend.'

'Yes – yes, she was. But what does it matter now, whether the cat was hers or not?'

He shrugged. 'It disnae. I just always fancied she was the sort tae keep a cat. She'd naybody else, efter aw, no' efter Rab passed.'

That remark interested me. 'Did you know Alice's husband?' I asked.

Jack nodded. 'Oh, aye. Aye – guid man, wis Rab. Guid tae his missus, an' aw. They were heartbroken when that lassie o' theirs drooned hersel'. She wis their last one – the others had passed when they were bairns. But the lassie, she wis with child, ken? The faither was a sailor, left fae Leith an' ne'er came back. She couldnae bear the shame o' it, folk said. I didnae really ken her, though we'd have been aroond the same age. But Rab – he was guid. His missus wis never quite right efter he was deid. Her mind, it wis troubled, ye ken.'

'Poor Alice,' I replied. 'Since she died, I've been wondering how she managed here for all these years.'

But Jack wasn't listening. He'd bent back down, and was raking through the other items which were stowed away under the bed, pulling them out and away from the cat's decaying corpse. Several tins, much like the one I'd often seen Alice carrying, were unearthed, along with a small mahogany writing-box, decorated with an intricate rose design. The latter item immediately caught my eye; fine furniture like that normally belonged to the genteel, not to a poor widow carving out an existence in a Canongate tenement. I'd had a box like it in Paris; a gift from my mother, and one of the few things I'd regretted leaving behind in our hurry to leave. For a moment I lingered on the memory of it – the musky smell it contained, the swirling design at its edges. I must have traced my finger over its decoration hundreds of times as I sat, staring out of the window, my mind not really on the task of writing.

Clearly, the box had captured Jack's interest, too.

'Well, noo – what's aw this eh, Alice?' he said to himself, chuckling as he regarded it with a greediness in his eyes.

'I'd like to have that, please,' I said, before I could think about what I was doing.

Jack shook his head, still clutching the box. 'Cannae gie ye this, sorry.'

'But you said I could have anything I wanted from this room.'

'I said ye could 'ave a look.'

I sighed. Of course Jack didn't want me to have it, and I doubted it would find its way to 'the parish', either. I didn't know what had come over me, but for some reason I didn't want him to keep that box.

'Alright,' I said. 'Name your price – in coin,' I added, before he got any ideas.

He grinned at me, showing off a set of grey-brown teeth. 'Four shillings.'

I hesitated, reminding myself that I was living with reduced means already. Four shillings was a fortnight's rent, but it was also a fraction of what I suspected the box was worth. It was far too fine an item to leave to the care of Jack Burnhouse. I wondered again how Alice had come to have it in her possession.

'Agreed,' I said in the end.

Jack handed me the box. 'Ye can pay when we've finished 'ere,' he said, with the usual menace which entered his voice whenever the matter of money was addressed.

He bent down again, turning his attention now to examining the handful of small tins Alice had seen fit to store away. All were empty, except two: one contained a lock of dark hair, held together with string, and the other a handful of coins. Jack snatched the money, pocketing it before I could even see its value.

I frowned at him. 'Surely that should go to the parish, too.'

He laughed. 'Auld wummin wis behind with her rent. That'll cover it.'

'How convenient,' I scoffed.

'Ye can have the other one,' he instructed, his quick fingers placing it atop the writing box before I could say anything further.

I looked at it reluctantly, wanting to object. I wasn't inclined towards keeping such personal items, especially with my gifts. The last thing I needed was the nightly appearance of a spirit at the end of my bed, drawn to its earthly remains.

'It was prob'ly fae that lassie o' hers,' Jack remarked, as though that was supposed to make me feel any better about keeping it.

'Hmm,' I mused. I would decide the fate of the hair later.

'I dinnae think there's much else 'ere,' Jack said with a cursory glance. 'That box was a surprise, but the rest is only guid for the poorhouse,' he added, knocking over a stray pint pot to illustrate his point.

'Yes, I suppose it is,' I replied. 'I've often wondered how Alice managed living here. You said she was behind on her rent. Was that a common occurrence?'

Jack laughed. 'Aye, her an' half this buildin'! But she always paid in the end, seemed tae find the money somehow.'

'Do you know how?'

He shrugged. 'No' ma business tae ken that. No' yer business, either.'

'No, you're right, it isn't.'

'Someone took care o' her,' he continued, now pondering the question I'd so impertinently posed. 'Mibbae the parish. Mibbae Rab. Or mibbae she was far better at beggin' than I thought! An' ye took care o' her tae, didn't ye? In yer own way.'

'Yes,' I nodded. 'I suppose I did.'

Jack gave me a brief, strange look; a sort of smile, lost on a crumpled face so accustomed to scowling. Then he continued his work, gathering up Alice's scant possessions, and muttering begrudgingly about his lot. I took my leave of him, but not before I'd allowed myself one more glance around Alice's room, and one more opportunity to say a silent goodbye.

The dark hallway offered little relief from the gloomy dampness of Alice's space, and I found myself hurrying back towards my room, my fingers wrapped tightly around my inherited possessions. I would have to check what coins I had tucked away; no doubt Jack would be standing at my door demanding payment as soon as his work was done. Inwardly I cursed myself; I had little enough to live on at the moment as it was. I could have just let him have the writing-box, but what would have become of it then? No, it was too fine a thing, and besides, it had been Alice's. I would care for it, just as I'd cared for its owner, albeit in my own imperfect way.

'I hope that's acceptable to you, Alice,' I murmured, hastily unlocking my door.

'Ailsa?'

I gasped, thinking for a moment that Alice had replied. Then I realised that it was a man's voice, calling out from behind me. A voice I knew. A voice I had missed hearing this past week.

I spun around. 'Angus?'

From the top step he stared at me, his posture stiff, his face grave.

'I'm sorry to trouble you,' he began, his formality grieving me even as I relished the soft, musical notes of his accent.

'Angus,' I said again. 'What is it? Is something wrong?'

'Aye,' he replied. 'Aye – it is. That young woman you took an interest in – Clara Andrews. She's gone missing.'

# Twenty

'What do you mean, missing?'

I'd beckoned Angus into my room, putting down the writing box before shutting the door behind us to conceal our words from curious ears. I leaned against it, letting the old wood support me as I listened to Angus's explanation. He spoke quickly, pacing back and forth, seldom looking at me. I found myself wishing that he would stop moving, that he would come a little closer, just like he used to. There'd never been so much space between us as this.

'I was on duty last night. We got word from the constables this morning, just as I was getting ready to leave. Apparently when the family rose yesterday morning, they discovered she was gone. We've been told to be on the lookout for her, and to let the captain know if we notice anything amiss. The family are frantic, as you'd expect, and are making their own enquiries. Folk go missing all the time, but not young women like her, not folk from that side of town. How does someone like that just disappear, unnoticed?'

'That depends,' I replied, 'on whether she's chosen to disappear, or whether this is something more sinister.'

Angus stopped pacing and looked at me. Despite the circumstances, I confess I felt my heart skip a beat.

'I must tell you, Ailsa, that they believe the worst. The family, I mean. They are certain this is a kidnapping. Your name – it has been mentioned, on account of your encounter with Miss Andrews at the theatre.'

I drew a deep breath, feeling suddenly weak, and leaned against the door a little harder. I recalled the visit Charles and Henry paid me in the tavern, how Charles warned me to keep away from his daughters. Of course he would see fit to accuse me now.

'Am I – am I suspected?' I asked.

Angus shrugged. 'I don't know. Not yet, I don't think. The constable who spoke to us at the Tolbooth still seemed to think it likely she'd run away; to elope, perhaps, or to avoid a scandal. But the family have given a grave account of you, Ailsa. The constable knew about you coming from France, and about your fortune-telling.'

I sighed. 'I don't tell fortunes; at least, not usually. As you know, I only visited that family out of goodwill to Jane, although I fear that the whole sorry affair has cost me that friendship. And what does it matter that I am French? Is being French now a crime?'

'Oh, come, Ailsa, you must know how people such as yourself are regarded. Just because you fled from trouble in your country does not make you any less suspicious in many people's eyes. And, if war comes again, as many fear it will, then matters will only worsen.'

'Do you think I'm guilty, then?' I asked him, finally stepping away from the door as an indignant heat took possession of me. 'Do you think I deliberately set out to hurt Clara Andrews, to taunt her with a horrid prediction of her death, to kidnap her? Do you think me capable of all that, simply because I am French?'

'No! No, of course not. I hold no such opinions, Ailsa. I do know a little about prejudice too. Your mother tongue isn't English, and neither is mine. Trust me, there are those who would hear Gaelic spoken and react with the same hostility as they would if they heard French.'

'I'm sorry,' I replied. 'I had never appreciated that. Please, forgive my ignorance.'

He smiled, just slightly, but enough to lighten the mood. I realised that in my brief fury I had moved to stand right in front of him, and now I felt suddenly conscious of his warm presence in my gloomy, fireless room.

'You have taken a risk coming here today and warning me,' I continued, my voice much quieter now. 'You would surely be in a great deal of trouble if the constables found out.'

Angus nodded. 'I think I once told you that I'd help you in any way I could.'

He gazed at me for a moment, his lips parted as though he wanted to say something more. Then he cleared his throat and took a step back, and I felt the air between us cool.

'So, what happens now?' I asked him. 'The Town Guard keeps watch and everyone hopes she reappears?'

'For the most part, aye.'

'Is there anything I can do? I'm aware that I've done a great deal of harm in my dealings with Clara Andrews, and that I might be a suspect in her disappearance before the day is over. However, I'd like to help if I can.'

I sat down at my little table, and beckoned Angus to join me. That familiar comfort I felt in his company had returned, and if I was honest with myself, I did not want to let him go just yet. Over the table our eyes met, and I considered his countenance; paler even than usual, with no hint of colour in his cheeks, and with scant humour in his heavy eyes.

'Forgive me,' I said. 'You said you were on duty last night. You must be exhausted.'

'I am,' he replied. 'But I'd like you to tell me about your vision, please. Tell me what you saw concerning Clara Andrews.'

'I told you what I saw, that night on the bridge.'

Angus bristled. 'Yes. Yes, I know you did, but let's talk about it again, shall we? Right now, there's no trace of that young woman, and your vision is the only insight we've got.'

I paused, wondering who the 'we' he spoke of was. Was it the guardsmen, the constables, or did he mean the two of us?

'Ailsa?' he prompted.

'Yes – sorry.'

I drew a deep breath, ordering my thoughts as I recalled that vision to my mind. I had examined it so many times now that I felt weary of it, but I tried hard to focus, to slow its racing images down and to extract every significant detail from it. After all, a young woman's life, or at the very least her reputation, might depend upon it.

'I saw a dark place, like a hallway, dimly lit, although I could see candles flickering. The walls were yellow. I saw two people together, a man and a woman, embracing. Then I saw a staircase, I think it was in the same place as the hallway, although I can't be certain. I saw a woman fall down the stairs, but it was strange – the way she fell, she didn't resist. There was a softness to her movements, as though she was unconscious, or dead. Then I saw Clara's face, running with blood, and that was it – apart from the appearance of my old friend, Pierre.'

'Pierre?' Angus asked. 'What did he have to do with it?'

I shrugged. 'Nothing, as far as I can tell. I've thought and dreamt about him a good deal recently, and I've even thought that I've caught glimpses of him during my waking hours. For a while I thought that he was trying to tell me something, but now I'm not so sure. He keeps asking for my help, but how can I help him now, when I am here? Our life, his life, was in Paris.'

Angus rubbed his chin, his fingers bristling over unshaven skin. 'Do you think his appearances have anything to do with what you saw happen to Clara?'

'At first, I thought so, but I've come to doubt it. For one thing, there's nothing to connect Clara to Pierre, except me and my muddled mind.' I tried to laugh, but it caught harshly in my throat.

'Alright, let's set the matter of Pierre aside then, and concentrate on what you saw concerning Clara. That night we – that night on the bridge, you mentioned that you thought Clara's death, as you saw it, occurs in the place she attends for dancing lessons. Why?'

'The staircase, and the colour of the walls – that vivid yellow.'

'Are you certain?'

I grimaced. 'I can never be certain, but I'm fairly sure.'

'Alright. I suspect it's somewhere that the family will have already checked, but we can add it to the list to visit, and to see what we can discover.'

'When you say 'we', do you mean you and another guardsman, or you and a constable?' I asked.

He gave me a slight smile. 'No, I mean you and me.'

'I see. Are you sure you want me to get quite so involved, Angus, after I…?'

'I don't see who else can help,' he interrupted me, his tone curt.

His abrupt response seemed to surprise him as much as it surprised me, and he looked away for a moment, drumming his fingers awkwardly on the table. If I had been in any doubt as to how he considered me, I could not be mistaken anymore. That night on the bridge still hung over us like the pungent air of the flesh-markets, infesting everything. I was not forgiven, nor would I ever be, and it stung to realise it. But right now, he needed me. Clara needed me. I had to serve my purpose. It was the least I could do.

'What else do you need to know about my vision?' I asked quietly.

He looked at me again then, and I was relieved to see that a softer regard for me had returned to his eyes.

'You said you saw a woman fall down the stairs. Are you sure it was Clara?'

'Yes,' I replied. 'I think it was. Immediately after seeing her fall, I saw her face very clearly, and she was bleeding.'

'Bleeding from where?'

I stared at him. 'Does it matter?'

'Every detail matters, Ailsa. Please, think – where was the blood?'

'It was running from her nose, and there was some on her forehead. And her eyes – they were wide open, and they looked so empty. I felt sure that she was dead.'

'But you can't be certain.'

'No – as I said, I can never be certain. I can only interpret what I see, and sometimes a vision can have many different possible meanings. In this case, though, it seems likely that what I saw was Clara's death. But that doesn't mean to say that she is certain to die in the manner that I saw.'

Angus frowned. 'What do you mean?'

'I mean that I saw a possible fate, one which seemed to be bound to the first image I saw – that of a man and a woman embracing. Before the vision took hold, I had touched Clara's hand briefly, and felt strongly that she was in love. I interpreted both the feeling and the vision to mean that Clara had a secret lover, perhaps someone her family would not approve of. However, I've recently learnt that she is engaged to her cousin, Henry. Now, I don't believe that Henry was the object of her affection that I had sensed, so by accepting him, her fate may have changed altogether.'

'Or it may not,' Angus retorted. 'It seems to me that she's either been taken by someone, or she's run away. In either case, it's possible that the existence of an unsuitable lover is at the root of it. Her life may still be in danger.'

I sighed; it was hard to disagree with him, however much I wanted to believe that my vision might not be relevant anymore.

'I had hoped my warning to her would be enough,' I admitted, 'but it seems putting myself and Clara through all that unpleasantness might have been in vain, after all.'

'What do you think of the cousin, Henry?' Angus asked. 'Might he have something to do with her disappearance?'

'If you're asking whether I've any insight into the man, then regrettably, I do not. He refused to let me read his leaves, which given everything that has happened since, is a great pity. He struck me as rather arrogant, and I hear from Jane that he's very ambitious. I suppose it's clear that he wishes to marry Clara, either for love or advancement. If it's love, I'm not sure the feeling has ever been mutual. In fact, Jane had previously told me of a rift between the pair, so I was very surprised to hear of their engagement. I do wonder whether Clara's father, Charles, has had a hand in matters there. I've encountered him a few times, and suffice to say he is a deeply unpleasant man, and one who I think is accustomed to having his own way.'

'His affair with a high-ranking member of the aristocracy would certainly suggest so,' Angus scoffed. 'And in the aftermath of such a scandal, Clara Andrews' prospects will have reduced considerably. Perhaps the father thinks that a marriage to the cousin is the best outcome for her, given the circumstances.'

'Perhaps Clara doesn't agree,' I added.

'Exactly.'

I grinned. 'You really must stop reading gossip in the newspapers. You're starting to sound like a society commentator, reporting on runaways and elopements.'

'Says the woman who's spent weeks occupied with the notion of a genteel young lady and her clandestine romance,' Angus retorted.

We both laughed, and I confess I felt relieved to experience some easy humour between us, even if only for a moment. I sat back in my chair, allowing myself to enjoy the smile which broke on Angus's weary face, illuminating his green eyes and bringing some colour to his cheeks. He returned my gaze, and I could almost imagine that he was looking at me the way he used to, that he was thinking as well of me as he'd ever done. I could almost forget that I'd hurt him, that he'd been angry with me, and that he'd stayed away from me since that night.

I wished then that I could undo it all. I wished I could go back to the Andrews' house all those weeks ago and chart a different course, one where I didn't persist in acting alone, even when I was floundering. One where I didn't make matters worse. One where I didn't cause pain to someone who I'd come to care so deeply about.

'Ailsa?'

I realised I'd stopped smiling.

'I was just wondering what happens now,' I lied, hurriedly gathering my thoughts.

Angus ran his hands through his dark hair then rubbed his face, stifling a yawn as he tried to revive himself.

'I think we need to speak to the family,' he said. 'From what you've said, they're at the centre of this, one way or another. We need to find out more about the days leading up to Clara's disappearance, and we need you to spend some time in their company again, to see if you can discern anything...untoward.'

'I doubt they'll let me read their leaves again, if that's what you're thinking. Indeed, I think a visit from me would be most unwelcome. The last time I saw Charles Andrews he expressly forbade me from going anywhere near his daughters. I'm not keen to disobey him, Angus. He threatened to have me locked up.'

'Did he?' Angus replied, raising his eyebrows. 'Alright – we will need to tread carefully, make sure we stress that I am a guardsman and that we wish to help find his daughter. Surely he cannot object to that.'

'You haven't met the man,' I said grimly. 'I assure you, he can.'

'Ailsa, please try not to worry.' Angus's voice was firm, but there was kindness in his eyes. 'I will be with you. All will be well.'

I let out a deep breath. 'When do you intend to call upon them?' I looked at him pointedly. 'We cannot go now. It's obvious that you need to sleep first.'

He shook his head. 'I couldn't sleep, even if I wanted to. No, we shall pay our visit now – unless Franny is expecting you?'

'Not until this evening.'

'Good – then, shall we? If we're going to find this young lady, then we haven't a moment to lose.'

I gave him a grim smile and quietly followed him back out of my room. I wanted to help Clara, of course I did – I'd been trying to do just that since the moment I'd had that unfortunate vision. But the thought of encountering Charles Andrews, and indeed the whole family again, vexed me greatly. Angus was right: the information we had, scant and full of supposition though it was, all seemed to lead back to them. Speaking to them was the obvious, and unavoidable, place to start.

Nonetheless, as we descended the staircase of Anstruther House, I couldn't help but wonder just how much the likes of Charles and Henry might know. I recalled that overheard conversation in the tavern, the hint of a pact between the pair. There's nothing that cannot be resolved, Charles had said. What if he'd been talking about Clara? What if she'd refused to comply with their wishes? What if those now insisting on my involvement in her disappearance were merely trying to deflect attention from their own sins?

As we reached the door and walked out into the bustle of the Canongate, I reminded myself that there was another possibility, one which complicated my involvement even further. What if Clara had managed to escape their plans for her?

What if she didn't want to be found?

# Twenty-One

I kept wondering if we were going to talk about that night. Thoughts of it returned to me as we made our way up the High Street, our footsteps fast, our breath labouring in the thick, damp air. Dreich, Franny would call it, and it was; the city smoke joining with the drizzling rain to laden the streets with a grey mist. Many souls breezed by me, the living and the dead so obscured by the fog as to be almost indistinguishable from one another. Not that I was paying any of them a great deal of attention. My mind had become clouded; overwrought with racing thoughts about Clara, it had turned instead to reliving other scenes, other regrets.

As we reached the bridge, I realised that I must have replayed Angus's angry words dozens of times. And yet, still he said nothing about it. Indeed, he said nothing about anything, but simply marched forward, intent upon his mission. I had to admire his resolve, his determination to get to the truth. I had to wonder at his ability to put all other matters from his mind.

Was it really possible that he was walking across this bridge with me, and not thinking about all that happened between us when we were last together in this place?

'Angus?' I called out as he strode ahead.

He stopped and turned around. I caught him up, wanting to say something. Wanting to say so many things. At least here I could see his face, the mist settling in the valley below rather than reaching up to us. I tried to read his expression, but I could not. It pained me then to realise that it contained nothing for me.

'I just wanted you to slow down,' I lied, losing my nerve. 'I fear you are far faster on your feet than I.'

Beyond the bridge the New Town greeted us, its orderly boulevards and fine buildings remaining stoic against the mist which did not seem to trouble this side of town so greatly. Perhaps the inclement weather knew better than to irk the well-to-do set, I thought wryly. If it did, then it was infinitely more sensible than the likes of us.

*

By the time we reached the corner of Hill Street, I was feeling rather weak. I realised that in the midst of the day's events, I had neglected so far to eat anything. I leaned against the side of the first house, catching my breath and willing my sudden dizziness to pass. Angus, who was still walking slightly ahead of me, seemed to sense that I had stopped, and returned to join me.

'Are you alright, Ailsa?' he asked me. 'What is it – not still your ankle, I hope?'

I shook my head, feeling my face colour at his indirect reference to that night. I wanted to talk about it, and I didn't want to talk about it. I didn't know what I wanted anymore.

'No, my ankle is perfectly fine now, thank you. I'm just a little tired is all. It has already been an eventful day.'

'You have grown very pale. Are you sure you can manage this?'

I gave him a grim smile. 'Of course. As you said, time is of the essence.'

Angus offered me his arm, which I took gratefully, and together we walked the final few yards to the Andrews' house. In different circumstances I would have thought more about the gesture, about the feeling of my arm wrapped around his. But as we approached the family's front door, my thoughts were consumed by what, and who, awaited me on the other side. I took a final, deep breath. I had to hope that I could endure this. Preferably without fainting, this time.

'Nice house,' Angus remarked.

'They're all nice houses here,' I replied. 'Actually, I think it would be best if we called at the servants' entrance.' I gave him a meaningful glance. 'The last thing we want to do is cause any offence.'

Angus muttered something about 'these people' and their 'damned etiquette', but with a sigh he acquiesced. We retraced our steps, walking down the lane which allowed access to the houses' rear doors. My heart pounded as I recalled the last time I was here, and the surprise on Jane's face when she saw me. I could only imagine how she was going to react when she encountered me this time.

Thankfully, it was not Jane who answered Angus's firm knock, but the valet, Mr Collinson, who Jane had mocked on my last visit. I hung back a little as Angus carefully explained our reason for calling, and asked with laboured politeness if we could possibly speak with the family.

Mr Collinson looked unconvinced. 'Wait here,' he replied, after a moment's consideration. 'I will see if Mr or Mrs Andrews are at home.'

'Surely he knows if they're at home,' Angus remarked as the valet closed the door upon us once more. 'He works here, doesn't he?'

'Of course he knows,' I replied. 'What he means is he'll check if they will receive us. As you said – it's the damned etiquette,' I added, rolling my eyes.

Angus smiled. 'I didn't think you'd heard that.'

'Well, I did,' I said. 'And for what it's worth, I think you may have a point. It'd save an awful lot of trouble if people would just say what they're really thinking.'

The moment the words slipped out, I regretted them. I bit my lip, feeling the heat creep into my cheeks.

'Angus, I didn't mean…'

'Ailsa, I…'

The door swung open once more, silencing us both. Mr Collinson peered at us with a superior air, as though he was about to make us go through the ritual of begging an audience with his employers all over again.

'Mr and Mrs Andrews will receive you in the parlour,' he announced, raising his eyebrows at his own words.

He beckoned us inside, indicating with a disapproving glance that we should both remove our shoes. Barefoot, we traipsed behind him, eventually following him up the stairs to the same parlour in which I'd read Grace and Clara's leaves just a few short weeks ago. On our way there I hadn't caught sight of Jane. I supposed it was possible that she was out running errands for the family; it was equally possible that she was avoiding me. Either way, I felt some relief at having avoided one unpleasant encounter, at least.

Mr Collinson ushered us into the room, then abruptly closed the door behind him. Clearly, he felt that whatever was about to take place within this room should not be overheard by the servants. Indeed, we had not walked into a relaxed family scene. Mrs Andrews and Grace both sat in front of the fireplace, clutching their sewing, their faces sombre and their eyes swollen. Charles Andrews, meanwhile, was standing, his hands clasped behind his back as though we had just interrupted him pacing up and down the wooden floor. I noted immediately that Henry was not present, and silently I cursed him for evading me once again. After a moment's awkward hesitation, Angus and I both performed the necessary bows and curtseys.

'Miss Rose – you have some nerve; I will give you that. Was I not clear when we last met? Did I not tell you to stay away from my daughters?' Charles stared hard at me, and for a moment I thought I might crumble under the weight of his gaze.

'With respect, sir, one of your daughters is now missing. I – we – have come to offer some assistance in the search for her.'

'Have you indeed? Miss Rose, you must know that you are suspected! I have no doubt that you can assist. I have no doubt that you could produce my daughter this very moment, if you chose!'

'Sir, with the greatest respect, I can tell you that Miss Rose is not suspected,' Angus intervened in a soft, deferential tone I barely recognised.

Charles turned his severe gaze upon him. 'And you are?'

'My name is Angus Campbell, sir. I serve in the Town Guard.'

'If you are in the Guard, you should be out looking for my daughter,' Charles retorted.

'I am not on duty currently, sir, but I assure you that I do wish to help find your daughter. Miss Rose is an acquaintance of mine. We would both like to help.'

'Oh, Charles, do let them assist us,' Mrs Andrews said, dabbing her eyes with her handkerchief. 'Surely it can do no harm. Indeed, the more people out looking for Clara, the better.'

I winced at her feeble pleading, recalling Jane's crowing about their reconciliation. I couldn't fathom what had possessed a woman of such determined character to submit to returning to such a man. I pushed the thought from my mind, reminding myself that this was not the matter at hand.

'Please, Papa. I assure you – Miss Rose is gifted. I know she will be able to find Clara,' Grace added, giving me a watery smile.

'Gifted?' her father scoffed. 'My dear, this woman is a charlatan!'

'I have wept for the loss of my sister all morning,' Grace replied, her voice uneven as her eyes welled up with tears once more. 'I believe Miss Rose may be our only hope of seeing our dear Clara again. She is good and kind, and she will help us – I am sure of it.'

I gave Grace an appreciative nod. Her confidence in me was heart-warming, but it also made me anxious. What if, after all, I could not?

Charles shook his head slightly, but seemed to relent. 'Well, you do not need my permission to conduct your own search,' he said. 'So, I see no need for your continued presence in my home.'

'We will not take up too much of your time, sir,' Angus interjected, 'but to aid our search, it would help greatly if you could give us a little information.'

Charles raised his eyebrows at him. 'Such as?'

'Such as, how was Miss Clara, immediately before her disappearance? Was she in good spirits? Did she seem vexed at all, or express any concerns about anything?'

'She was the same as she ever was,' Mrs Andrews interrupted. 'Reserved, but serene. A real fine young lady. Oh, my poor, poor dear daughter. What has become of her?' She began weeping again, her shoulders heaving as she sobbed quietly into her hands.

'Miss Grace,' I said, turning my attention to the younger sister, 'would you agree that Miss Clara was unchanged?'

Grace hesitated, and I thought I saw her glance warily at her father. 'Yes,' she said in the end. 'Yes – she was just the same as ever.'

'You see? And that is why I am certain that she has been taken, that she must have been lured from her home on some false pretence,' Charles said. 'She had no reason to run away. She was happy, on account of her recent engagement. She had much to look forward to.'

'And nothing is missing from her room,' Mrs Andrews interjected. 'All her clothes and personal effects are accounted for. What young woman would leave her home without so much as a fresh dress and pelisse?'

I looked at Grace again, trying to read her reaction to her parents' assertions. Her face, however, remained frustratingly impassive.

'And this engagement,' Angus said, picking up the thread of Charles' argument, 'is to a Mr Henry Turner, I believe. And where is Mr Turner now?'

Charles bristled. 'He is out searching the town for her, of course, as I will be again, shortly. He is devoted to her. He will not rest until she is returned to us safely – none of us will.'

Angus smiled grimly. 'I see. Are there any particular places that you have searched for her? Any places that she was known to frequent? I believe she was a dedicated student at Bernard's dancing rooms on Thistle Street – have you checked there?'

'Yes, of course we have,' was Charles' impatient answer. 'Mr Bernard informed us that Clara hadn't attended lessons for almost a fortnight.'

'That's a change in her behaviour then, is it not?' I asked. 'To go from being a keen dancer to not dancing at all.'

'She is soon to wed, Miss Rose,' Charles replied. 'Following her engagement, she doubtless felt she had more important matters to consider than learning the latest dances from London.'

'Indeed,' I replied, hoping I didn't sound too unconvinced. Quickly I counted back over the days. A fortnight: it was almost a fortnight since our dreadful confrontation in the theatre. It was almost a fortnight since I'd warned her about what I'd seen.

Beside me Angus shuffled. I sensed his frustration, and shared it. It was clear that we were not getting anywhere, that they were not prepared to talk candidly. I looked once more at Grace, but she steadfastly avoided my gaze. I wondered what she might know. I wondered what she might not be prepared to share with us in front of her parents.

'Well, thank you, Mr Andrews, Mrs Andrews, Miss Andrews,' Angus said, giving them a small bow. 'I don't think we've any other questions, so we will not trouble you further. We will, of course, let you know if our search turns up anything significant.'

'Yes,' Charles replied. 'Please, do. Until then, I remain unconvinced that you do not know more about this than you're admitting, Miss Rose.'

I bit my tongue at the remark, doing my best to ignore how he looked down his nose at me. I was in the business of harbouring suspicions, too, and when it came to Charles Andrews, I still had many.

Mrs Andrews rang the bell and almost instantly Mr Collinson

appeared to escort us from the house. Silently we followed him back down the stairs; he hurried along, apparently keen to be rid of us. I allowed myself to fall behind a little, using my final few moments here to observe my surroundings in the desperate hope of discerning something, anything which might be significant. Alas, I was out of luck there too, confined to examining the hallways as the doors to the family's rooms were all closed. No noise seemed to come from within any of them; apart from the parlour, the house seemed eerily quiet and empty. I wondered again where Jane was, indeed where all the other servants were. It occurred to me then that perhaps they had joined the search for Clara, too.

We departed via the servants' door and made our way back on to Hill Street. The mist on this side of town had grown thicker now, weighing heavily upon us as we meandered along in no particular direction, unsure of our next move. Even in the greyness I could see that Angus looked deflated, his shoulders hunched, his gaze fixed on the ground.

'We will find her,' I tried to assure him, even though I was far from confident myself.

He stopped walking then, and turned to look at me. 'Were you able to discern anything from that?' he asked me.

'What? You mean, other than the fact that they were not being entirely honest with us? I don't think you need to have my gifts to see that.'

'Aye,' he replied with a heavy sigh. 'When you're a guardsman, you get used to people being evasive. They're just not usually so eloquent about it.'

'So, what do we do now?' I asked him.

Angus rubbed his face. He looked so exhausted, and my heart lurched as I remembered that he hadn't yet been to bed after his night duty.

'Oh Angus,' I implored him, 'you really must get some rest. It's afternoon now. When did you last sleep?'

'I'll be fine,' he insisted. 'I think we should go to the dancing rooms, speak to this Mr Bernard and see what he can tell us.

Perhaps he noticed something was amiss. Perhaps he will be more willing to talk.'

'Miss Rose! Mr Campbell!'

We turned around to see Grace Andrews running towards us, her pink day dress swishing against her hurried movements, her shoes tapping softly on the ground. As she drew nearer, I saw that she clutched something in her hand.

'Miss Rose,' she repeated breathlessly as she reached us. 'I cannot stay for long. I told them I was going to fetch my book, and they will soon notice that I am gone. I need to give you something. It might help you to find Clara.'

Without another word Grace placed a piece of paper in my hands. I unfolded it and found myself looking at a sketch, drawn in pencil, of a young woman's face. I studied her features for a moment, observing her dark curled hair and big, dark eyes. It was an outline rather than a finished piece, roughly drawn with soft pencil strokes, but there was no doubt in my mind that the drawing was of Clara.

'Did Miss Clara draw this?' I asked.

Grace shook her head. 'No, I'm certain she did not. Clara was – is – very accomplished, and is quite the artist, but this is not her style. I believe someone else has drawn this and given it to her.'

'Do you know who?'

Grace shook her head again. 'Sorry, I do not. But, Miss Rose, there is more. Turn the paper over.'

I did as Grace instructed. This time I found myself looking at a handful of words, written in a beautiful, delicate script. The drawing might not be Clara's, but I felt certain that the handwriting was.

'Either she must marry a man she does not love or she must be blamed by the world,' I read aloud. 'Either she must sacrifice a portion of her reputation, or the whole of her happiness.' I frowned. 'Are these your sister's words, Miss Andrews?'

'No, although without a doubt it is Clara who has written them. The words are Miss Edgeworth's, from her book, Belinda. It is one of Clara's favourite novels, and one of mine, too. Indeed, it is one of the few books we were ever in agreement upon!' Grace let out a small, sad laugh, then glanced nervously over her shoulder.

'Did Miss Clara give this to you?' I asked her.

'No, I found it – in a drawer, in her room,' Grace replied, looking sheepish. 'I was looking for clues as to why she might have left or where she might have gone.'

'You don't agree with your father, that she has been taken against her will?'

'No, and he cannot believe that either, not really. He must have seen how low-spirited she has been of late. Clara may be reserved, as Mama puts it, but even she cannot disguise utter misery.'

I glanced at Angus. He, like me, was hanging on to these first threads of truth.

'Do you know what has caused your sister such sadness, Miss Andrews?'

'I cannot say for certain, for she has never confided it to me. Papa says that it was you and whatever you said to her at the theatre, but I do not believe that. I believe it is her engagement which troubles her. I believe she is in love, Miss Rose, and not with our cousin.' She glanced over her shoulder again. 'I must tell you quickly, before I am missed, but for some time now Clara and I have had an arrangement. We go into town together, often crossing the bridge into the old parts, but then we go our separate ways for a while. I believe she has been meeting someone. I believe that was the purpose of it, since the arrangement was her suggestion.'

'Did you ever ask her what she was doing?'

Grace shook her head. 'She would not have told me, and besides, I did not wish to tell her how I had spent my time. I do not mind telling you, Miss Rose, as I believe you will understand – I like to promenade in the graveyards. I am quite taken with the notion of writing a novel, just like Mrs Radcliffe. Clara would say that I am ghoulish.'

'Have a care in those places, Miss Andrews,' Angus interjected. 'A young woman such as yourself walking alone in a graveyard invites trouble from all kinds.'

I bit my lip, suppressing a smile as I thought about my own walk through the kirkyard in the Canongate. I wondered if Angus would issue the same warning to me, if I told him of it.

'Can I keep this drawing, Miss Andrews?' I asked her.

'Of course,' she replied, looking once more towards her house. 'Now, I really must go. Mama will know I've been outside. She misses nothing.'

I nodded. 'One more question before you go, Miss Andrews – if your sister is so against marrying Mr Turner, why do you think she agreed to it?'

Grace gave a small shrug. 'What choice did she have, truly? Papa wishes it, and Henry has been besotted with her for years. Even Mama was in agreement, when the advantages of the match were put to her. She esteems Henry very highly indeed.'

'I see. Thank you, Miss Andrews.'

Grace gave me a grim smile. 'You will find my sister, won't you, Miss Rose?'

I winced. The hope in her big blue eyes was almost too much to bear.

'Angus and I will certainly do everything we can,' I assured her.

We watched as she took her leave of us, blonde curls bouncing as she ran back down the street and into her home, no doubt hastily inventing some reason for her absence. While we were talking, that fine drizzling rain had returned, and now I felt uncomfortable; damp, as well as famished, since I still had eaten nothing all day.

'It seems your instincts about a secret lover were correct, after all,' Angus observed.

I nodded. 'Perhaps. What does seem certain is that she doesn't wish to marry Henry. That alone would be a sufficient reason for her to flee, and perhaps to seek sanctuary with whoever drew this,' I added, carefully folding the paper and tucking it into my palm.

'So, what do you think we should do now? Will we pay a visit to the dancing rooms?'

My mind was racing, ruminating on Grace's words, and on Miss Edgeworth's words, written down in Clara's elegant script. On the drawing of her that I now had in my possession, sketched by an unknown hand. I felt sure that the quotation Clara had transcribed was significant; so too was the identity of whoever had captured her likeness with such flair. I stared back at the Andrews' house, trying to grasp the threads of what Grace had told us, to bind it all together. But my mind was as clouded as the street around me, and hunger gnawed at my empty stomach. In this state my thoughts quickly unravelled, threatening only to tie themselves in knots.

'Ailsa? The dancing rooms?'

I shook my head. 'No, not just yet,' I replied. 'First, I think we need to rest, and eat something, and reflect upon all that we've learned. I don't think either of us are much use to anyone just now. I propose that we return to Anstruther House and consider how to proceed.'

I expected Angus to disagree but he didn't. Instead, he gave me a thin smile, nodding briefly, and I suspected that for once he was simply too tired to argue. As we made our way back towards my home, I tried to calm myself, to quell the unease which had settled deep in my gut. Grace had all but begged me to find her sister, but what if I couldn't? Or, perhaps worse still, what if finding Clara meant condemning her to a life and a marriage she simply didn't want?

The mist still clung to us as we reached the Old Town, and I lamented how nothing seemed to be clear. Indeed, the only thing of which I could be certain, was that whatever we did next, we had to tread carefully.

# Twenty-Two

By the time we arrived back at my room it was the middle of the afternoon. The rain had grown heavier as we'd made our way back towards the Canongate, wetting us both so thoroughly that I felt duty-bound to light us a fire. We sat before it, drying ourselves and tucking into some cheese and oatcakes which Angus had bought us from one of the High Street market stalls. Conversation was sparse as we both occupied ourselves with eating, although every so often I noticed Angus glancing at me, with what looked like a smile twitching at the corners of his mouth.

'What?' I asked him in the end.

'Nothing. I was just thinking how much better you look for the benefit of some food and a warm fire.'

'Yes, well, I must confess I had not yet eaten anything today.'

'Aye – I suspected as much. I also suspect that's something you're accustomed to, from the look of you.'

I rolled my eyes. 'You sound like Franny. She insists I'm going to waste away.'

'Franny has a point. I don't mean to be impertinent, it's just, well, I wouldn't wish to see you sicken. I've seen for myself what a lack of food can do, in times of want.' His face darkened for a moment, and he took another mouthful of oatcake.

I nodded. So had I. In France my life had been sheltered, but not so much that I hadn't noticed all the pale, thin urchins sitting barefoot in the city's streets, or their frail mothers, clutching fretful babes to their breasts. Sometimes Maman would observe them too, pointing out their misfortune from the comfort of our carriage as we passed by. She would remind me then that the world was cruel, that we ought to be glad of what we had. That, if it wasn't for the comtes and ducs whose beds she'd successively warmed, those women and children could so easily be us. I was never sure if it was only me that she was trying to convince.

'Yes,' I said after a moment. 'There was always hunger in Paris.'

'There's always hunger everywhere,' he replied. 'Crops fail, prices rise and ordinary folk cannot afford to feed their families.'

'While the wealthy always manage,' I pondered, half to myself. 'Like Clara's family. And like me, when I was in France. My mother and I never experienced hunger until we arrived here, and the money she'd put by for us began to run out. I suppose that's when I got used to it.'

Angus smiled sadly. 'Aye, going without can become a habit. But you must remember to eat, Ailsa.'

'I know,' I replied, trying not to bristle. He was only showing concern, I knew that, but still, I didn't appreciate the reminder that I wasn't particularly good at taking care of myself.

*He's right though, ma chérie. You neglect yourself.*

Like you neglected me, Maman, I thought. When you left.

I brushed off the prickle of resentment and instead returned Angus's smile, before finishing the last morsel of food on my plate. I had to admit, simple fare though it was, it had been delicious. I watched as Angus took his final mouthful, and found myself thinking that perhaps it wasn't just the food I'd savoured, but the company as well.

'Alright,' he said, rubbing his hands together. 'What do we do now?'

I sighed, sitting back in my chair. 'I don't know. Short of joining Henry and Charles to search every part of this city, I don't see how we're going to find her. We don't have a great deal to go on.'

Angus shrugged. 'We don't, although considering what we've learnt from her sister, I think it's very unlikely that we're looking at a kidnapping. My bet is that Clara's run away, probably gone off to elope with this man that Grace thinks she's been meeting. To be honest, I wish her well. Having now met her father, I'll feel no small measure of guilt if we succeed in returning her to him.'

'I agree, but that doesn't mean she is out of harm's way. Indeed, if she does have a lover like my vision suggested, then I fear the rest of my vision may also come to pass.' I picked up the drawing Grace had given me, unfolding it carefully. 'The words Clara wrote on the back of this must have resonated with her. And they must have been connected to the artist. Otherwise, why would she have written them there instead of, say, in a diary?'

Angus nodded. 'Alright. Let's assume that there is a lover, and that they made this sketch of her as a keepsake. A love token. And she wrote that quotation on the back of it because...'

'Because the quotation is about the difficult choice that she knew she must make,' I said with a sigh. 'I think this tells us more about Clara's state of mind, but nothing about the person who drew her.'

'Aye, other than that they capture a good likeness.' Angus took it from my hand, studying it. 'I'm no judge of these matters, but I'd say that whoever they are, they've got some flair for it. Perhaps that's what they do for a living.'

'Hmm,' I mused. 'An artist would certainly be considered an unsuitable match for a well-bred young woman like Clara.'

'Where would she meet someone like that, though? Surely not at those New Town balls.' He made a face, pretending to pull his collar up high as though he was a dandy. 'What about at those dancing classes she was so fond of? Perhaps Mr Bernard is handy with a paintbrush.'

'Now you're just being silly.' I sat bolt upright, a thought suddenly occurring to me. 'She might have met an artist downstairs though, at the waxwork exhibition. Do you remember the young man who greeted us when we visited?'

Angus's eyes widened. 'The ticket seller? Aye – I remember him. He warned me to take care of the delicate lady I had accompanied lest you suffer a fainting fit in front of one of the more gruesome mannequins.'

'How right he was,' I quipped. 'I remember he seemed distracted by the sketch he was working on. I have met him another time since, and he was drawing then, too. His name is Antoine.'

'It's a good theory, Ailsa. Given the proximity of the exhibition to the dancing school, it is reasonable to suppose that they have met.'

'It would also explain why Clara was so keen to attend Mr Bernard's classes,' I added.

'Until she wasn't.'

'Yes – until she wasn't.' I paused, trying to organise my thoughts as they threatened to unravel in front of me. 'Alright. Let's assume for a moment that Antoine is her lover, and that she was using the dancing lessons as a ruse to meet him. Some weeks ago, when I was trying to understand my vision better, I called at the Andrews' house and spoke to Jane. That morning Clara had gone out alone, allegedly for early dancing lessons. However, when I went along to the dancing rooms on Thistle Street, they were all closed up, as was the exhibition. There was just a woman there, cleaning the place. I suppose it's possible Clara and Antoine were inside too, but what if…'

'What if there was somewhere else that they were meeting?' Angus said, his face growing animated at the possibility.

I frowned. 'Yes, and what if that place is somewhere that they might have found refuge now. But where?'

'You said you'd met Antoine another time since we visited the exhibition,' he asked me. 'Where was that?'

'I've met him at the exhibition twice – once with you and another time after that, when I went alone. I've also met him in the Canongate Kirkyard. He was on his own, though. I can't imagine that he met Clara in graveyards. It doesn't seem like something she would agree to.'

'Pity they didn't,' Angus replied, 'then they might have encountered Grace on one of her ghoulish walks and this whole matter would be a lot easier to unravel.' He shook his head. 'So that's Grace, Antoine and now you who like to spend their time in the city's kirkyards. Is it only me who isn't too keen on those places? I dread going in them at night, checking that there aren't any resurrectionists lurking about.'

I shuddered, thinking of my last visit. The rough, loose soil over those new graves was doubtless an open invitation to body snatchers. Whilst I could see and hear the spirits of the dead, witnessing the disturbance of someone's earthly remains was something I didn't wish to experience, either.

'I went to pay my respects to Alice,' I explained. 'I don't know if she's buried there, but even so, I felt it was something I ought to do.'

Angus's expression softened. 'I'm sorry, Ailsa, I meant no offence.'

I gave him a tight smile. 'I know.'

'Did you receive the information I sent to you about Alice?'

I nodded. 'I did. Thank you for taking the time to look into Alice's past for me. I wasn't sure that you would, after…' I stopped, unsure what more to say.

Angus looked up, his green eyes intent upon me. I felt the colour begin to rise in my cheeks as thoughts of that night flooded back. Not now. Not in the middle of our search for Clara. This wasn't the right time. I tried to push the memories of it away, but to no avail.

'I made a promise to you,' he said. 'I always try to keep my promises.'

'Yes,' I replied, rather dumbly. I didn't know what else to say. I moved to sit back down, but Angus caught hold of my hand. I turned my head away from him, not wishing him to see the shame on my face.

'Please understand, Ailsa. I felt slighted, and I was upset with you. Angry, even.'

'You had every right to be angry,' I replied. 'I did you a great disservice. I didn't trust you, and I should have. Please know that I am deeply sorry for the hurt I have caused you.'

He sighed. 'No, don't apologise. I was wrong to have expected you to take me into your confidence, to have thought you were looking at me in the same way I was looking at you. It was a presumption on my part. I can see that now.'

He released my hand, and I sat down once again to face him. A hundred thoughts were whirring around my head; a hundred things I wanted to say, to express. I didn't know where to begin. I had lost something I hadn't even known I'd wanted, and try as I might, I couldn't put that loss into words.

'It's odd, isn't it? We would not have quarrelled if it hadn't been for my vision about Clara Andrews, and we would not even be having this conversation if Clara had not gone missing.'

'What do you mean?'

'I only mean to say, that everything seems to centre upon a young woman who a month ago meant nothing to either of us. And now, you are here because she needs to be found.'

In the grate the fire spat and smouldered as it took its dying breaths. The sight of it fading chilled me, and I rubbed my arms for want of a shawl. I thought about fetching one but I didn't dare move, didn't dare break the spell between us. In front of me Angus narrowed his eyes for a moment, as though thinking hard about what he might say next.

'If you think I am only here because of Clara, you are wrong. I'll admit, her disappearance was the nudge I needed, and yes, I do wish to solve her disappearance. But I've wanted to see you for days, Ailsa. I've thought of little else. I must have replayed our quarrel a thousand times in my head, must have tortured myself with how I spoke to you, how I let my anger and my pride get the better of me. I've been close to coming into the tavern or knocking on your door so many times.'

'I thought about seeing you too,' I said quietly. 'But I wasn't sure how to proceed, or whether I'd make matters worse. After what happened with Clara at the theatre, I confess I'd become wary of my own actions.'

He gave me a tender smile. 'We are quite a pair, aren't we?'

'We are,' I agreed. 'I do trust you, Angus. And I do care. I was bereft when I thought I'd lost you, and our friendship.'

'I know. Our friendship is important to me, too,' he replied, but the warm sincerity of his words didn't quite reach his eyes. Yet again, I sensed I'd said the wrong thing.

I looked once more at the fire, watching as it finally went out. I felt damp again, even though my clothes were almost dry. There was a coldness seeping under my skin which I couldn't seem to be rid of. I leaned forward, hunching over the table, feeling the extraordinary weight of everything.

Angus peered at me. 'Ailsa? Are you unwell?'

'Forgive me, I am quite overcome. It will pass.'

'Is there anything I can do?'

I shook my head. 'No, I will be fine in a moment. Come, let's return to the matter at hand: Clara Andrews and her whereabouts.'

'Aye, alright. So, assuming she is with Antoine, is there anywhere else in this city you think they might be?'

I took a deep breath, trying again to calm my racing thoughts and work methodically through the information we'd gathered. Clara had left her home, presumably during the night or early in the morning, with little more than the clothes she was wearing. We didn't know if she had money with her – it would have been an indelicate question to ask her family, even if I had thought of it at the time, which I hadn't. If she had no means then she would be reliant upon whatever Antoine could provide for her, which I didn't esteem to be much. They might have sought sanctuary in one of the city's inns, but I thought that unlikely, since they would run too much of a risk of being noticed by a nosy innkeeper. No, they had to be somewhere more discreet. And it had to be somewhere in the city; Antoine's position as Madame Tussaud's assistant surely made that a necessity.

I sighed. No matter how hard I tried to look beyond it, all roads led back to that exhibition, and to the dancing rooms upstairs. Everything pivoted on the place where they must have met. The place where I saw her fall.

*But she isn't there now, ma chérie. Her father told you so himself.*

'Why don't we return to Thistle Street and see if we can't ask this Antoine a few questions, if he's there,' Angus suggested, apparently reading my thoughts.

I groaned. 'It's after four now. The exhibition will be closed.'

'Tomorrow, then. When it reopens.'

'Yes,' I agreed, giving him a grim smile. 'Tomorrow. I'm sorry, that is my fault. I should have agreed to go there earlier, when you first suggested speaking to Mr Bernard.'

'No, not at all,' Angus protested. 'If we'd gone marching ahead, you might never have thought about Antoine. You were right to suggest that we come back here first.' He paused, his gaze returning to the drawing once again. 'It's a pity Grace had no idea where her sister went during all those walks, other than that it was somewhere in the old city. An odd thing to do anyway, if you ask me. Folk like them normally avoid coming over here.'

'I did see Clara here, once,' I replied, still piecing my thoughts together. 'It was the day I called upon you. As I was leaving, I saw her walking up the Bow. I followed her. She was alone, and returning to the bridge to meet her sister.'

Angus sighed. 'Up the Bow. She could have been coming from anywhere. Grassmarket, Cowgate, Portsburgh, even. Doesn't really narrow down our search.'

'No, but…'

I shivered, that chilled feeling crawling over me once again. I clasped my hands together, my fingers tingling as briefly, so briefly, I heard a soft whisper in my ear.

'Ailsa, please…'

From somewhere deep in the recesses of my mind, a memory came to the fore. A memory of the day Alice died; a day which had been utterly shrouded in my grief, until now. A wet day on the

Bow. The sharp creak of an iron gate. The feeling of cold fingers taking hold of mine, their gentle pull as they led me down a close. The house I feared, the shadows of two faces appearing at its window.

At the time I'd assumed those faces had not been of this world. But what if I'd been wrong?

'Ailsa, what is it?' Angus asked.

'I can't be certain,' I replied. 'But I think I have an idea about where they might be.'

# Twenty-Three

That evening in the tavern, time passed unbearably slowly. Franny's was busy, as it so often was, but even the rowdy groups of thirsty men vying for my attention did not keep me sufficiently distracted. Normally I enjoyed my work; I spent so much of my time alone that I relished being in the midst of somewhere so full and alive. But not tonight; tonight, I was restless and distracted, desperate for closing time to arrive so that I could get on with the search for Clara. Even if aspects of what that search would entail filled with me a cold dread.

Franny, true to form, noticed the change in my temperament immediately.

'What's botherin' ye?' she asked me in the end. 'Ye dinnae seem yersel' tonight.'

I decided that a sort of honesty was the best way to respond. 'Sorry Franny, I'm just feeling a bit on edge. Angus is coming in tonight, to meet me after work.'

She raised a curious eyebrow, a large grin illuminating her face. 'Is he? I'm glad tae hear that. He's been missed in here. Say nae more, Ailsa. I ken how yer feelin'. Young love, eh? It's no' withoot its troubles.'

I gave her a small smile, not wishing to point out that we were neither particularly young nor in love. I didn't think it wise to elaborate further; Franny had already advised me against being involved in matters I didn't understand. Goodness knows what she would make of my ongoing involvement with the Andrews family. Goodness knows what she would say if she knew that Angus was now involved, too.

Angus was concerned about tonight, I knew that. He'd listened carefully as I'd unravelled my reasoning before him, remonstrating about that unnerving experience I'd had on the Bow, how I'd been led down that close, how I'd seen two faces at the window. Angus had met my tenuous logic with a furrowed brow, which had only deepened as I named the house in which I believed they may be hiding.

'What, Major Weir's old house down Anderson's Close? You can't be serious. And besides, I thought you'd concluded that Pierre had nothing to do with any of this.'

I'd hesitated for a moment. 'I'm still not sure that he does. If I'm honest, I'd not even been convinced that it had been Pierre leading me down the close at all. But just now, I had the oddest feeling; I was cold and wet, just like I'd been on the Bow that day. Then I heard him, it was like he was right beside me...'

Angus had looked about him nervously. 'What – he's here?'

'No, not really. It's hard to explain. It was as though he was trying to make me remember, as though he wanted to guide my thoughts back to that moment. Surely it has to mean something. I don't know, Angus. As I've said before, I can't be certain about any of this. I can only interpret what I see and feel, and see where it leads me.'

Angus had let out a resigned sigh, and I'd feared he didn't really understand. 'Major Weir's house,' he'd repeated. 'No one's lived in there for a hundred years at least, although some have tried. You must know what they say about that place.'

I'd nodded. 'I've heard the stories, yes. I didn't know that was his name, though. Everyone seems to always refer to him as the Wizard.'

'Aye, that was the name he earned for himself, but his real name was Thomas Weir. He was the commander of the Guard, you know, and a deeply religious man.' Angus had shaken his head then. 'It's a strange tale. To go from all that to such depravity.'

'Do you believe the stories,' I'd asked him, 'about the Major and his sister fraternising with the Devil?'

He'd made a face. 'No, not that. But the rest – his intimate relations with his sister, his servants, his step-daughter, even animals? I've been a guardsman long enough in this city to know that's all perfectly believable.'

I'd shuddered. 'I've always avoided that house, struggled to look upon it, even. When I first saw faces at its windows, I took them to be spirits. I thought I was seeing the Wizard and his sister.'

'That's what concerns me,' Angus had admitted. 'Guardsmen talk, as you'd guess. One favoured tale is of the newlyweds who tried to live in that house – long before my time here, twenty years ago or more. They lasted a night, saw some frightful apparitions. It's hearsay, of course, and I've always been cautious about that. Nor am I one to be enthralled by stories of hauntings, of the dead doing atrocious things - I tend to find the living are capable enough of that on their own. But then I met you and got to know about the things you can see. I worry about what might happen to you there, Ailsa.'

'But what if the stories of hauntings and apparitions are nonsense?' I'd argued. 'What if all I've seen of that place so far is its habitation by two young lovers, hiding in the last place anyone would think to look?'

'Aye, but what if you're wrong?' Angus had answered back. 'What if Thomas and Jean Weir are just sitting at that window, waiting for one such as you to arrive? If they could torment an ordinary young couple, I dread to think what they might be able to do to you.'

Thomas and Jean Weir. Their names whirred around my head, over and over again as I served mugs of ale and bottles of port. The Wizard and Grizel – those were the names that Edinburgh folklore had given them. I had to hope that folklore was the extent of it, that this was simply a story bequeathed to us by the past, and nothing more. I couldn't allow myself to truly entertain the notion of anything else; if I did, I'd never find the courage to walk into that old house and find what I was looking for.

Angus arrived in the tavern just before closing time, making time for a mug of his favourite ale and some chatter with Franny, who could barely contain her delight at seeing him. He wasn't on guard duty again until the morning, and while I was at Franny's, he'd gone home to catch up on some sleep. He looked better for some rest; the colour had returned to his cheeks, although his eyes were still heavy. He'd shaved too, I noticed, and had put on a fresh shirt under his usual brown coat. I must have stared for a moment too long, because he caught my eye and grinned.

'Almost finished?' he asked.

Before I could answer, Franny clapped her hands together. 'Och, she's done fae the night, Angus. Ye just go, Ailsa. Go on – I can manage.'

I gave her a quizzical look; last orders had been called, but the tavern hadn't emptied yet, and the cleaning up had barely begun. However, I decided not to protest. There was never any point arguing with Franny; once her mind was made up, she was immovable. Besides, by now our plans for the night were pressing down hard upon my chest, and seeds of doubt were growing in my unsettled belly. The sooner we made our way to the Weirs' house, the sooner we would find Clara, and the sooner this would be over.

I gave Angus a small smile. 'I'll just fetch my shawl,' I said, wishing I could calm my pounding heart, and shake off my unease.

\*

The night outside was calm and still, the town's lamps glowing bright under a moonless sky. Angus offered me his arm, which I accepted, and we walked together for some time in silence. Around us old Edinburgh readied itself for sleep, the flickering of fires and rushlights through windows gradually growing sparser as we made our way up the High Street. By the time we reached the Old Tolbooth, very few souls were abroad, the living and the dead swiftly deserting the streets. The darkness and the quiet weighed heavily upon me, and I was relieved when Angus finally spoke.

'Busy night?' he asked me in a whisper.

'As always,' I replied. 'Did you manage to sleep?'

'Aye, like a log,' he said. 'John's on guard duty until late so I wasn't disturbed for once. He is worse than ever - screams and whimpers in his sleep, barely speaks or eats when he's awake. I don't know what's wrong with him, but it's taking him down a dark path, whatever it is.'

I shuddered, recalling the source of the man's pain. Recalling his venomous words and poisonous stench. 'There's something I should tell you about John.'

'There is?'

'Yes,' I hesitated for a moment, my eye caught by fleeting shadows in the nearby closes. This was hardly the time or the place, but I had alluded to it now. 'When I visited you, I was confronted by a spirit lingering in the hallway near to your door. His name was Tam, and he said he had business with John, said to tell him that he knows what he did. Suffice to say, I don't think his intentions towards John are pleasant at all. That might account for John's behaviour, especially his fitful sleep.'

In the gloom I saw Angus turn to look at me. 'John's being haunted? Well, that would certainly explain a lot. But why didn't you tell me this before?'

I sighed. 'I'm sorry, I know I should have. I agonised over it, in fact. But it's your home – you have to live there. The last thing I wanted was to burden you with that knowledge, to leave you feeling haunted, too. It's not easy to know what to do for the best when you acquire that sort of knowledge. There are many things I'd prefer never to have known.'

Angus brought his hand over to where mine rested in the crook of his elbow, and gave it a gentle squeeze. 'I know. Thank you for telling me now. I'm not sure what I will do with that information, but I've got more chance of being able to help him now that I know the likely cause of his misery.'

'If I can assist in any way, you need only…'

Before I could finish speaking, Angus had pulled me towards him, placing his lips over mine and stemming the flow of my words. His touch was light, as though he was unsure how it would be received, but he let the kiss linger like the still night air around us. I felt an unfamiliar heat rise in my stomach as he cupped my cheek in his hand, and before I knew what I was doing, my hands had found their way on to the coarse fabric which covered his chest. I felt his heart beating fast, in a rhythm with mine, which also thrummed rapidly as he wrapped his arms around my waist and pulled me closer to him. The kiss deepened, and for a moment I was no longer on the High Street but lost at sea, warm waves washing over me, a strong tide sweeping me away. I went along with it, indulging this longing which I hadn't truly understood I'd had.

By the time I felt the earth beneath my feet once more, Angus had released me. The dim lamplight cast shadows across his face, but there was no mistaking his sheepish grin. 'I hope that was alright,' he said, clearing his throat a little. 'I've wanted to do that for the longest time.'

'It was. I mean, it was…'

I hadn't the words. Indeed, what could I say without seeming too bold? Could I stand in the street with this man at this late hour and talk of otherworldly feelings, of magic, even? Surely, he'd heard enough of that from me.

'It was alright. More than alright, I mean.' I settled awkwardly on understatement and smiled at him, hoping he understood.

He nodded, his smile fading into something unreadable, and I sensed then that he'd hoped for something more. Quietly we walked on, finally reaching the point where the High Street met the top of the Bow, its bent shape stretching ethereally into the night. I'd never seen this part of the city at this hour, never descended this ancient thoroughfare where lamplight was sparse and the darkness plumbed such depths that it might lead to Hell itself. I looked up, feeling as though the old buildings were leaning over us, poised to whisper their stories. I wondered for a moment about the sights they'd witnessed over the centuries. An elderly brother and sister perhaps, besieged by age and infirmity, succumbing to madness? Or a wizard and his accomplice, empowered by the Devil, riding across the city in a coach made of fire?

I shuddered, trying to push the tales I'd heard from my mind. They would do me no good now, given what I shortly had to face.

'Are you ready?' Angus asked me, and I realised then that we were facing into the narrow gloom of Anderson's Close.

I took a deep breath and swallowed hard. 'I think so.'

He took hold of my hand. 'Just remember, whatever you see in here, I am with you.'

I nodded, my mouth suddenly too dry to muster a response, and watched as Angus pushed open the iron gate which guarded the entrance to the close. It groaned loudly, and we both startled.

'At least this close is never locked up,' Angus said. I sensed he was trying to keep his tone light, but I saw how he glanced warily over his shoulder. He knew better than most how creeping around after dark would be perceived if we were noticed. 'Come on, let's go.'

I followed him down the passageway, trailing my hands along the cold stone walls to steady myself. The lack of light was disorientating; there were no lamps here, and not even a sliver of rushlight from a nearby window to guide us. In the courtyard we fared little better, and by the time we'd found our way to the Major's door, my eyes were beginning to ache with the strain.

'I've a candle with me,' Angus whispered, seeming to read my thoughts. 'I'll light it once we're inside. That way, if they are here, they will see who it is and know we mean them no harm.'

I hadn't thought of that. 'Perhaps this isn't such a good idea. Look at the place – it's in complete darkness. If they're inside at all, they're probably sleeping. What if we frighten them?'

'Clara will recognise you, surely?'

'Indeed. Although I don't know whether that's a good thing or not.'

Before I could deliberate further, Angus had pushed open the old wooden door which, like the close gate, was not locked. It occurred to me then that he must have wandered down here many times during the course of his patrols, and that he knew this city more intimately than I could ever hope to. We were both emigrés, in our own ways; I'd come from another old city, and he had come from what I imagined to be a sort of wilderness, but we both walked these streets as incomers. Whilst I had kept my world here small, limited to a room in the Canongate and a tavern a stone's throw up the High Street, Angus's work meant that his had grown beyond what I could imagine. He knew every layer of this place; I had only skimmed its surface.

'Down here used to be a store,' he whispered as we slipped through the door, 'but it's been empty for some time.'

He lit his candle as promised, and I caught the stink of the tallow as he moved it around enough to illuminate our surroundings, which sure enough, were little more than rubble and exposed stone walls. I took a shallow breath; the air was thick and musty, heavy with the dust and dampness wrought by years of neglect. There was nothing else here, however; no sign of life, nor death, was present. Relief briefly washed over me; there was no Thomas or Jean Weir down here, lying in wait, nurturing their malevolent intentions. The only thing which had run wild over the centuries was Edinburgh's collective imagination.

'If they're anywhere, they'll be upstairs,' Angus said, still keeping his voice hushed as he waved his candle gently towards a rotting wooden staircase.

I swallowed hard. 'Are you sure that's safe?'

'Only one way to find out.'

Again, Angus charged on, the old stairs creaking with the weight of his determination. I ascended gingerly behind him, my hesitation growing, and not just because I feared the wood might give way beneath my feet. I became aware of the air around me changing, growing colder and more burdensome. It filled my lungs like ice, and with every breath its frozen shards waged their war within my chest. By the time I reached the top I was almost bent double, and it took every fibre of my being to stand up tall and take a look around. I followed the trail blazed by Angus's candle, and my heart sank. Up here, too, was empty.

'Someone was here – until recently, I'd say.'

Angus walked around, scouring the detritus which was scattered on the floor. In one corner of the room several blankets lay in a rough heap, the remnants of a makeshift bed. There was a table, too, turned now on its side and facing towards what remained of a hearth. I moved to stand beside Angus, who was examining its sorry state - crumbling and partially obstructed by its own stones, I doubted that the unfortunate inhabitants of this place could have used it, even if they'd wanted to.

'There's nothing here, is there?' I said, trying not to sound as devastated as I felt. I'd wanted so desperately to find them here; instead, the trail had gone as cold as the air around us. I shuddered, the pain in my chest sharpening again.

Angus shuffled around once more, casting candlelight in every possible direction. I felt the floor crunch underfoot and I realised I'd stood on the hardened remnants of someone's leftover bread. Nearby I heard rodents squeak, no doubt eager to return to their meal. Then something else caught my eye.

'What's that over there?'

Angus shone the candle in the direction I'd pointed, illuminating what appeared to be a handful of papers discarded at one side of the chimney breast. We darted over, examining them greedily. There were about a dozen sheets in total, all bearing variations of the same image: a woman with long, black hair and an intense dark stare, lying naked on an opulent sofa.

'Just like the Sleeping Beauty,' I gasped.

'What?'

'We saw something like this at the exhibition, except that lady was fully clothed. When I visited the exhibition a second time,

Antoine was very keen to show me that particular wax figure. He called her the Sleeping Beauty.'

'So, he's drawn one of Madame Tussaud's figures, but without clothing?'

I narrowed my eyes, sifting once more through the sheets of paper. My movements were slow and painful; the pain in my chest had spread down my limbs, which felt so cold I might have believed I had frostbite. In the end I handed the papers to Angus and clawed at my shawl, pulling it tighter around myself as I desperately sought some warmth.

'Not exactly,' I replied, trying to speak through chattering teeth. 'She's not sleeping, for one thing, and this isn't the same woman. The Sleeping Beauty had fair features, but the lady in these drawings is dark. It's like the sketch Grace gave us. This is Clara. It has to be Clara. They were here, Angus. They were here.'

'I agree, but…Ailsa? Are you alright? You're shaking.'

I looked down, realising then that he was right; every part of me tremored with a growing violence. I could no longer feel anything in my limbs; my legs, my arms, even my fingers were numb. The only thing I could feel, in fact, was the searing pain in my chest. It was as though someone had taken hold of my heart and was squeezing it, suppressing its beat and causing the life which flowed within me to congeal. Weakened and breathless, I fell down, closing my eyes in a stuporous half-slumber.

Then, behind my eyelids, I saw him. I saw his long, black cloak, his crooked walking stick, his pilgrim hat. I saw his smile spread itself indecently across his face. I saw the heat of madness in his eyes. Somewhere within the recesses of my addled mind, I heard him speak my name.

'Ailsa,' he said, taking hold of me with his mottled hands. 'Come with me.'

I'd been so cold, but his touch was like fire, and the smell of brimstone laced his breath.

'Come,' he said again. 'Come.'

After that, there was only darkness, and the sense of falling through never-ending depths.

# Twenty-Four

A shrill cackle rang in my ears, punctuated by the sound of clopping hooves. The ground shook beneath me, and I found myself grasping at it, trying to stop myself from rolling back and forth. I felt the roughness of wood beneath my fingers, but it was hot and pungent, as though it was aflame. My eyes were still closed; I did not dare open them. I did not dare to confront the horrors which I sensed were eagerly awaiting my gaze.

'She's a pretty one,' a woman's voice said.

My skin crawled as someone – the owner of the voice, perhaps – cupped my face in their hands. Their touch was cold and brittle, as though it was not flesh I could feel, but bone. They pinched my cheeks hard, and despite my best efforts, I let out a pained yelp.

'Ah! She still lives,' the woman said, triumphant.

'Of course she lives, sister,' a man's voice replied. 'She tricks us, is all.'

A sharp pain surged through my stomach, and I realised that I had been kicked. I groaned loudly once more.

'Get up!' the man's voice barked. 'Open your eyes and get up!'

Reluctantly I allowed my eyes to flutter open, and immediately wished I hadn't. All around me was fire; I could see its light and feel its heat, but it didn't burn me. Phantom flames licked at my feet and my legs, which were bare. My dress was torn and my shawl and bonnet were gone. I pulled at what remained of my skirts, trying to cover myself, and groped around, finally managing to get myself upright. The ground still moved beneath me, and I realised that I was in some sort of carriage. Through the flames I glimpsed the Old Town's familiar streets, dark and silent, and apparently unperturbed by our fiery spectacle.

'So very pretty,' the woman's voice said from behind me.

I felt her bony hand caress my shoulder, but I didn't dare to turn around to look at her, or him, for I felt sure he was by her side. I kept my gaze fixed in front of me, found myself staring hard at the black outline of the horse which drew us. It was an odd shape, and it took me a few moments to realise that it was only part of a horse, with legs and a torso but no head. I looked down, pulling at my dress again, my legs feeling chilled despite the inferno which surrounded me.

'What have you done to me?' I croaked. 'Where is Angus? Please, take me back to Angus.'

'Is that your lover?' the man asked, amusement dripping like honey from his words.

'A sin! A sin!' the woman screamed. 'So full of sins, so many sins to eat and we shall be forever sated. Oh, brother, the sins!'

'I know who you are,' I said. 'Major Thomas Weir and Jean, his sister – I've heard much about you. But you are long dead. You cannot harm me.' I wrapped my arms around my bare legs, praying that was true.

The Major let out a deep, rumbling laugh. 'Oh, those like you know much, and at the same time, nothing at all. You think you see, but you are only ever peering through your fingers.'

'So very pretty, isn't she, brother?' Jean interjected again. 'Just like the one who lived in our house. We'd not had one like that for years. A ripe peach, indeed. And now we have another!'

'You mean Clara?' I asked. 'What have you done to her?'

Jean giggled, and my blood ran cold. 'I watched her, is all. I watched when she ate, when she slept, when she brushed those long curls of hair. I watched when she gave herself to that skinny

Frenchman. Very disappointing. No meat on those bones. She noticed me, of course. They always do in the end.'

'You showed yourself to her, sister. You could never resist.' The Major's tone was deep and disapproving. 'You chased her away.'

'It is no matter,' Jean bit back. 'We have another now.'

'What do you want from me?' I asked. I could see that we'd left the city now, the fire illuminating the country which sprawled before us, its lengths and possibilities seemingly endless. 'Where are you taking me?'

A pair of hands squeezed my shoulders, hard. His hands. 'Turn around,' he instructed me. 'If you want to see, then turn around.'

I drew a deep breath, sensing I had no choice. I needed to find my way out of here, and back to Edinburgh. Back to Angus. If I was going to manage that, I was going to have to look behind me. I was going to have to confront the evil which held me captive.

'Mother, give me strength,' I whispered.

'Mother?' Jean repeated, her voice mocking. 'Mother! Not the Lord, not the saviour, but Mother?'

I ignored her, listening for a moment; begging, willing Maman to answer me. But of course, there was silence. There was always silence, unless I chose to imagine otherwise, and even I could not conjure her voice right now.

'Look at me,' the Major insisted again. 'If you want the truth, you must look.'

Slowly, carefully, I turned around. The fire seemed to blaze ever harder, and I could feel the intensity of its heat on my face. The carriage jolted, and I felt the horse buck; for a brief moment I anticipated his braying until I remembered that the poor creature had no means to make sound. Hesitantly, I raised my eyes towards the two figures which were now in front of me, and drew a sharp breath as I looked into their dark, hollow eyes. Jean let out a laugh, a manic smile spreading across her ashen, skeletal face as she writhed around in a dress so torn that it barely covered her. She extended a marbled hand, stroking her brother's cheek. He remained serious, like a phantom in his large hat and dark cloak, never taking his eyes from me, as though the intensity of his gaze was sufficient to blacken my soul and drag me straight to Hell.

'Now you shall see,' he said.

From nowhere a pitch blackness came down in front of my eyes, as though he'd cast his cloak over me. The smell of brimstone intruded and I was immediately overcome, gasping and choking as a vision grew in my mind. Images of unspeakable acts came to the fore, and I saw the depths of his violence and depravity towards his sister, his servants, even his animals. Pain pulsed between my temples as the vision ran rampant; I saw his cruelty grow and witnessed his sister's descent into madness, but I saw no magic, no hand of the Devil. No enchanted walking stick; no witchcraft. I saw only human corruption, only earthly evils. In life at least, there had been nothing otherworldly about the Weirs.

The veil lifted, and the Major sat before me once more.

'Are you not horrified?' he asked, giving me a brief, sickening smile. 'Are you not afraid?'

I looked at him again, studying his pinched face, his bulbous nose, his marked flesh which was so discoloured in places as to seem half-eaten by decay. He seemed smaller now, somehow, like a shadow of what was once a man, held together only by gloomy fabric and eternal wrath. I thought about the other men I'd known, other men I'd seen and heard about. The ducs and comtes who'd drink too much wine or lose too much at the card tables and make their wives pay for it. The great nobles of the land who'd beat and bed my mother on a whim. The men who'd make whores of their maids, and make beasts of their whores. The men who'd abandon mistresses with child, leaving them to choose their own end. The men who'd assume that any woman, whether working in a tavern, or a shop, or as a bonnet-maker, was really just selling herself.

'No,' I said in the end. 'I was raised in Paris. I'm the daughter of a courtesan. There is nothing you can do which will shock me.'

The Major stared at me, his lips pursed but no answer forthcoming. He seemed to be getting smaller still, and after a moment I realised that the distance between us was growing. An odd feeling overcame me, as though I was being pulled away by some invisible, powerful force. The surrounding flames began to dampen down and as the air cooled and cleared, I realised I was no longer in the carriage. Wherever I was, it was dark and silent, and I couldn't see the Weirs now - somehow, I had left them. I got to my feet, realising I had been sitting in the same position all the time. I hadn't moved, and yet something or someone had enabled me to escape.

'Maman?' I called. 'Is that you?'

'Ailsa,' a voice replied. 'Ailsa – you must help.'

It wasn't my mother, but it was a voice I knew. Candlelight grew around me, and I saw that I was standing at the bottom of a set of stairs, looking up at a bright yellow wall.

'Pierre?' I shouted his name. 'Pierre, why can I not see you? Why have you brought me here? I need to get back to Angus. He – we can help, but I must return to him first.'

'I know.'

The candles flickered in unison, and there he was, sitting right in front of me, a few steps higher than where I stood. He looked just as I remembered; impish face, large brown eyes, long limbs dressed in a crumpled grey shirt and faded brown breeches. When we first met, we'd been about the same age, and I recalled how he'd seemed to tower awkwardly over me. That hadn't lasted, of course. I'd grown up, whilst he never could. He always said it didn't matter to him, but I knew it did. I could always tell when something bothered him.

Something was troubling him now.

'Pierre...' I began, but words quickly failed me. I had so many things I wanted to say. I wanted to tell him how I'd missed him, how I was sorry I'd had to leave him behind. How I still thought about him, my dear friend, all these years later. All of it competed in my head, but none of it would come to the fore. Instead, I just stood there, dumbstruck, staring at him.

Then, above us, I began to hear voices. Raised voices. Heated words.

Pierre glanced up. 'We don't have much time, Ailsa. They don't have much time. You must help them. Remember the vision. Think about what I showed you.'

'I did, but it makes no sense, Pierre. Clara's family have already checked Bernard's dancing rooms. She wasn't there. She isn't here, either. Why did you lead me here, to this horrible place?'

'She was here, Ailsa. You were just a little too late.'

Pierre stared at me, his dark eyes so sad and heavy that my heart lurched. The image of him began to flicker and fade, and instinctively I reached out, trying futilely to grasp hold of him, to keep him here with me. But I couldn't, I knew that. The distance between us now would always be too great.

'Please, just tell me what I need to do,' I called out to him.

I saw his mouth move to answer me, but the sound which emerged was so muted that I couldn't make out his words. He faded more and more, until eventually all I could see was his outline, still sitting on the stairs but blank now, as though the rest of him was somewhere else. Somewhere far from me. I remembered the day we drove away in our carriage, remembered seeing the bereft expression on his face as he gazed down at us through the window. Now I understood how abandoned he must have felt. A fresh wave of grief hit me, and I felt a solitary tear slip down my cheek.

'Pierre, come back,' I whispered. 'Tell me what I need to do.'

'You need to wake up.' A different voice answered me.

'What?'

I spun around, trying to see where the voice was coming from. At the same time, I felt a strange sensation, as though someone was tapping gently on my cheek. I touched my face, trying to grab hold of the invisible hand.

'Who's there?' I called out. 'Pierre? Is that you?'

The tapping against my skin became more insistent.

'Ailsa, wake up,' the voice said again. 'You need to wake up, Ailsa. Wake up!'

'Pierre?'

'Please, wake up!'

My eyes flew open, and the candles went out. I gasped, and the cold night air shocked my lungs. I felt the dampness of the ground beneath me, and realised I was staring straight up at a starless sky. As my sight adjusted to the darkness, I realised too that there was a face staring down at me; a man's face, his familiar, handsome features possessed by panic.

'Angus?'

'Oh, thank God!' he breathed, his expression softening into relief. 'I thought I'd lost you. I didn't know what to think, I...'

I gasped, the memories of where I'd been and of what I'd witnessed suddenly flooding back. In the gloom I forced myself upright, clawing at my dress, searching for torn fabric and bared flesh. The heat of shame rose in my cheeks as terror gripped me – the sort of terror I hadn't felt since I'd had to fight off the comte's advances, all those years ago.

'Ailsa, what's wrong?'

'My legs,' I babbled. 'I need to check if my legs...'

'You're alright, Ailsa, I promise. When you fainted, I brought you straight out here. Whatever happened in there, whatever you saw, it can't hurt you.'

'No,' I replied, my voice trembling. 'But he let me think that he had.'

Angus didn't question me any further, but instead pulled me towards him, holding me close. I allowed my head to sink into his chest, listening to the sound of his heart beating, absorbing the warm comfort he offered. I felt him push back my bonnet and bend down, kissing me tenderly on the forehead. I turned my face up towards his and our lips met for a second time that night, but with greater urgency now, as though we both wanted the gesture to express something words could not.

'They stayed here, you know,' I breathed, glancing warily towards the house which, once again, had fallen back into darkness. 'Clara and Antoine – they really did stay here. I don't know how they bore it.'

Angus helped me to my feet. 'Did you see them when you fainted? Did you have another vision?' he whispered.

'Not exactly,' I replied, struggling to put into words what I had seen. I was reluctant to relive the horror of it, but I also knew that what I'd learned was important. 'Jean Weir told me. She also said that they've gone now. For good, I think,' I added. I realised my voice was shaking.

'So, you saw Jean Weir – I feared as much.'

'I saw her brother, too. Let's not dwell on that now, though. I also saw someone else again – someone more important. I saw Pierre. He was trying to tell me something about Clara and Antoine, but I couldn't hear him, and then I woke up.'

'Your instinct was correct, then. It was Pierre trying to guide you here.'

I rubbed my face, still feeling drowsy. My temples had begun to throb as the after-effects of my vision began to build in my skull. I willed the growing headache to abate, to allow me some time.

'I think so. I also think he has been trying to send me a message all along. I think they're in danger; Pierre told me that there isn't much time left, and that he wants me to help them. He told me to think about my first vision and what it showed me. When I saw him this time, he was sitting on the stairs of that same building on Thistle Street. I remember seeing the yellow wall, and hearing raised voices above us. I think that's where they might be. It's surely the only place they can be, after being forced to leave here – if not the dancing rooms, then the exhibition rooms, which Antoine will have access to.'

Angus groaned. 'Rather them than me. The thought of having to bed down with a load of wax mannequins makes me shudder.'

I looked over my shoulder at the Weirs' house once more. 'Better than sleeping beside malevolent spirits,' I replied.

'Aye, that's true,' he said, wrapping his arm around my shoulder. He pointed a stray finger up at some of the surrounding tenement windows, which had come to life with dim rushlight and twitching curtains. 'Come on, let's get away from here before someone alerts the Guard. I'm not sure how easily I could explain all of this.'

We slipped back up Anderson's Close and on to the West Bow, and I watched with some relief as Angus pulled the gate shut behind us. I was heartened to see that some of the street's lamps still burned, and sparse though they were, I tried to take some comfort from their glow after spending so long in the darkness. Perhaps sensing my unease, Angus took hold of my hand.

'Do you think we can make it across town to the exhibition without being stopped by the Guard?' I asked him. 'I don't think we can wait until the morning.'

He leaned over to kiss me, his lips meeting mine with determined brevity. 'We have to,' he replied, giving my hand a squeeze. 'Otherwise, we'll be spending the night in the Tolbooth, and I'm certainly not keen on that.'

I sensed that he was trying to make a joke of it, but neither of us managed to muster a laugh. Quietly we walked back on to the High Street, making our way downhill and towards North Bridge with light steps and wary eyes. On both sides of the valley the towns slept, bathed in a growing darkness as one by one, the lamps extinguished. I thought about Clara, imagining her wrapped in Antoine's arms, safe from the Weirs and blissfully unaware that another unknown danger still lay in wait. I couldn't name it, I didn't know its nature, but I had sensed it. I had seen it in Pierre's sorrowful stare. I had seen its consequences in my vision, all those weeks ago. We had to help them. We had to get to them before anyone or anything else could.

'I'm coming, Clara,' I whispered, saying a silent prayer that we would make it to Thistle Street in time, and that neither the living nor the dead would stand in our way.

# Twenty-Five

By the time we arrived on Thistle Street the earlier rainfall had returned, blanketing the night with thick, dark clouds which shed heavy droplets as we took our final, quiet steps towards our destination. My stomach growled noisily; it felt like days since I was sitting in my room with Angus, drying our clothes and eating oatcakes, not mere hours. The anxious rush of getting from the old part of the city to the new undetected had also left me feeling weary, and as we crept to the rear of the building, I found myself clutching the wall, trying to remain steady on my feet.

'Are you alright?' Angus whispered, noticing as I stumbled several times.

'Yes. Yes, of course.'

My assurances sounded hollow even to me; I felt anything but fine. The headache which had been threatening since my vision at the Weirs' house had gathered force, raging through my skull with painful confidence. I needed rest, a meal and a good night's sleep, but there was no time for any of that. I looked up, straining to see any hint of movement through the windows stacked above us, any indication that Clara and Antoine were within, and that we were not too late. But the place was in darkness, and the only sound I could hear was the incessant pattering of rain on the stones beneath our feet. We clung to the building for a moment, seeking any shelter we could find as we caught our breath.

'What now?' I asked, still keeping my voice low.

'It's late,' Angus said. 'If they're inside, they will surely be asleep.' He produced a candle briefly from his coat pocket. 'I still have this. If we can get in, I will light it and we will have a look around.'

'Alright.'

I leaned into the wall once more as Angus went to examine the door which served as the rear entrance. I listened to him fumble and curse under his breath with a thrumming heart and a growing sense of unease. I wasn't sure what I'd expected to find when we arrived – some sort of scene unfolding, perhaps, illuminated by candlelight and the sound of a heated argument. I hadn't foreseen locked doors, complete darkness and silence. I wasn't sure what to make of it. Did that mean we'd arrived too soon, or too late? And if we were too soon, what would we do once we found them? I knew from bitter experience that Clara was hardly inclined to listen to anything I had to say.

*Remember what Pierre told you, ma chérie. To help them, you must remember your vision. Be guided by what you saw. If they are here, then that means they are in danger.*

Indeed, I had seen the danger. I had seen its consequences. What I hadn't seen, and what I didn't know, was its cause. I didn't know what or who was responsible for Clara's demise; if I did, this riddle would be far easier to solve. As Angus tried quietly to break the door's lock, I couldn't help feeling that we were just wandering into yet more darkness, stumbling around and hoping for the best.

'Ah! We're in,' Angus hissed under his breath.

He grabbed my hand and we slipped inside, quietly closing the door to cover our tracks behind us. As promised Angus then lit his candle, briefly surveying the narrow hall we'd entered for signs of life.

'So that's what being a guardsman teaches you, is it?' I remarked quietly, trying to distract myself from my growing nerves. 'How to break into someone's home.'

Angus grinned at me. 'No, in the Guard we just kick doors down, if the need arises.' He gestured towards the staircase which led to the basement. 'Do we check down there first? Or shall we stay above ground?'

'I think we should stay up here. My vision focussed on the staircase. I think they must be somewhere on the upper floors. Perhaps there's more up there than just the dancing rooms,' I mused.

'Only one way to find out. We will need to be careful, though. If they're hiding here, they aren't going to be happy to see us. I imagined they're terrified after their stay at the old Weir house.'

We made our way towards the front of the building, quickly finding ourselves standing in the main hall, the staircase rising at one side of us, and the entrance to the exhibition sitting at the other. In front of me Angus paused for a moment, listening, his candle casting eerie shadows on the walls as he moved it around. I found myself looking at the closed door which led to Madame Tussaud's displays of figures, hoping that we didn't ultimately have to check in there. Angus's earlier remark about sleeping among the mannequins had amused me, but I could also understand his unease. The last thing I wished to see was those wax heads staring at me in the darkness.

Turning away from that door, I crept up the stairs behind Angus, grateful that the solid stone beneath my feet wouldn't give me away too readily. From there we moved along the landing of the first floor, peering into each of the three rooms which greeted us. We found nothing unexpected; the two large, bare rooms were clearly used for Mr Bernard's dancing lessons, while a smaller anteroom seemed to be used as a store. An almost identical composition of rooms greeted us on the second floor, once again clearly in use for dancing. There was no one apart from us in these areas of the building; that was immediately obvious, since there was nowhere for anyone to hide in barren rooms furnished with little more than a piano and a handful of chairs. If they had sought refuge here, they would have had to have gone higher. I paused at the bottom of the next set of stairs, composing myself. It had to be the third floor, or the attic. Those were the only possibilities left.

Angus turned back to look at me. 'Ready?' he mouthed.

I nodded, resisting the urge to draw a deep breath; even that seemed like too much noise to make. I followed the light of Angus's candle up the stairs and on to the landing, my heart pounding so hard that I thought it might leap up into my throat at any moment. The feeling of it reminded me of our escape from France, of how I'd been in the grip of my fears for every long day and night of that journey across land and sea. Of how terrified I'd been of being caught, of being forced to return and of the reckoning which would have surely awaited us. Now here I was, all these years later, stalking around this building at night, looking for a woman who was seeking her own escape, just as my mother and I had done. Pierre was right: I had to help her, but I had to do more than steer her away from the terrible fate I saw befall her. I had to help her to determine her own fate, as well.

We crept along the landing, wincing at every small creak and groan our movements managed to evoke. I wondered for a moment about the wisdom of searching like this, of not simply announcing ourselves. The air up here was warm and stale, laced with that musty scent which settles in any place seldom used. In the dim light I counted the doors – five that I could see, and more rooms meant smaller spaces. If these were used for anything, I doubted that it was for dancing lessons. I paused, watching as Angus reached out, slowly turning the handle on the first door we'd come to. The hinges must have been stiff, as when Angus pushed open the door, it made such a squeal that I startled and gasped with fright.

'Sorry,' I mouthed, cursing myself as I followed Angus inside. After all the things I'd seen in my life, I'd managed to be frightened by a door.

Then, behind me, I felt a rush of movement, followed by the heat of breath, and the coldness of a blade at my throat. Before I could make a sound, a rough hand pressed itself hard over my mouth.

'Put out the candle.'

A familiar French man's voice called out to Angus who, upon turning around and seeing my predicament, immediately did as he was instructed. I watched as the flame died, its grey tendrils of smoke disappearing into the gloom. Unable to speak, I forced myself to keep looking ahead, to breathe steadily, and to remain perfectly still. The sharp metal poised under my chin was sufficient to remind me of the consequences of one careless move.

'What is your business here?' Antoine asked.

'It's Antoine, isn't it? We mean you no harm,' Angus called out.

'I will be the judge of that. Who are you? Who sent you? Was it her father? She does not wish to return to them.'

'No, I can assure you, we are not here in Mr Andrews' service. Antoine, the lady you have hold of is known to you, a French woman who means only to help you and Miss Andrews. My name is Angus Campbell, and I am here with Miss Ailsa Rose.'

'Miss Rose?'

Antoine moved his hand from my mouth, retracting his blade and relinquishing me from his grasp. I moved carefully, turning to face him even though, in this darkness, I knew I could not truly be seen.

'Yes, Antoine, I am here. My friend, Angus, speaks the truth. We are here to help you, if we may.'

I heard Antoine let out a sigh. Relief, exasperation, weariness – I couldn't be sure. I suspected it was all three.

'I am sorry if we woke you,' I added.

'It is no matter. I do not sleep well these days. So, you know Clara also, Miss Rose?'

'We are acquainted, yes. I presume she is here, with you?'

'Oui.' I felt him take a step back on to the landing. 'Follow me. She is in here.'

He led us into a room at the end of the landing, furthest away from the stairs. Without Angus's candlelight I felt disorientated; instinctively I reached for the wall, tracing my fingers along its paintwork as I tried my best to stay grounded. I could sense Angus close behind me; I knew that after the knife incident he would be on his guard. As Antoine opened the door and beckoned us inside, Angus's hand brushed my arm; the gesture was brief, but even through my shawl I felt its warm reassurance. I was stepping into the unknown, and whilst I was acquainted with both Clara and Antoine, it occurred to me now that I didn't really know them at all.

'Clara – some friends to see you.'

Antoine ushered us into the room, closing the door behind us before lighting a single candle which he placed upon a small wooden table. The dim light it offered allowed me to survey the room which they'd made their home. It was small and cluttered; boxes and chests filled the floorspace, along with a number of irregular shapes draped with cloth. At first glance I thought there was no window, then I realised that it had been hidden behind boards. Antoine had been thorough in disguising their presence here. In one corner, on a makeshift bed, sat Clara. She looked much changed; her hair hung loose, wild curls decorating a thick shawl she'd draped over her shoulders, and her expression was dazed, as though we had woken her from sleep. Those dark eyes, however, were unmistakable. They looked at each of us in turn, then settled their disapproving gaze upon me.

'Not friends, Antoine. Certainly not friends. Well, Miss Rose, you have come to return me to my father, no doubt.'

I frowned. 'No, of course not, Miss Andrews. I have come to help you, as has Mr Campbell. He is my friend, and a town guardsman.'

Clara got to her feet, walking over to Antoine and standing by his side. 'Help me?' she repeated. 'Pray tell me, Miss Rose, what is it that I need your help with? More dire warnings, perhaps, so that I might see sense and go home – is that it?'

'No, that is most certainly not the case. What I told you that night was genuine. It was no concoction, no bit of trickery. I saw danger, Miss Andrews, and I saw it in this very place. That is why I am here. I believe you are still in danger.'

Antoine looked at Clara, then at me. 'What danger do you speak of, Miss Rose?'

'She is a fortune teller. She claims to have visions,' Clara interjected before I could answer. 'She accosted me in the theatre, telling me that she knew I was in love and that it would lead to my death. I assumed she was acting on behalf of my family, that perhaps my wretch of a sister had found out about us and had told my father. I thought it was all a ruse to make sure I married Henry.'

'It wasn't,' I said quietly. 'Your sister does have her suspicions, but she has kept them to herself.'

Clara's expression softened. 'Well, that is something, I suppose, but it is of little consequence now. Antoine and I are married. We plan to travel to France, to start our lives together.' She smiled at her husband, placing her hand in his. 'So, you see, all is well. You must understand, Miss Rose, I did not desire the life that was planned for me, trapped in a marriage I did not want. My sister Grace might hanker after a cosseted life of dances and dresses, but it is not for me. I have other interests, other passions. When I met Antoine – yes, I fell in love, but also I began to realise that I could have a different life.'

I smiled briefly, thinking of Grace's clandestine jaunts around Edinburgh's graveyards, and her desire to write terrifying novels. I was not sure that Clara knew her sister as well as she thought.

'I do understand,' I replied. 'My circumstances in life have brought me my independence, by accident rather than design, but I would have it no other way. Please believe me when I say that I would not seek to deprive you of yours.'

Clara nodded, my words seeming to appease her. 'And my family do not know that I am here?'

'No, they do not. They are upset by your disappearance, as you would imagine, and your father is convinced you've been kidnapped. But we have not shared your whereabouts with them, and I have no intention of doing so now.'

'I am sorry to have upset them,' Clara said quietly, lowering her gaze. 'They left me little choice. Henry had been making his intentions towards me clear for some time, which had been difficult enough. When my father returned after reconciling with my mother, the situation became impossible. My father was resolute: I was to marry Henry, he said. He had good prospects; it was a good match. It was as though the two of them had reached an agreement, and I had no say in the matter at all.'

I thought about that night in the tavern, the talk of a stupefied Henry having made a fool of himself, and Charles's suggestion that he would resolve it, if Henry kept his word to him. It seemed likely now that Charles had been talking about Clara. I wondered what Henry's side of that particular bargain had been.

'So, when do you sail for France?' Angus asked them.

'I hope we can leave in a few weeks,' Antoine replied. 'Perhaps once the exhibition here closes and Madame is moving on. I need to discuss with her, but my hope is that we may stay here until then. She rents the rooms on this floor also, so no one should disturb us here. We will have to be discreet, of course, but it will not be for long.'

'I'm not sure it is wise to remain in this place,' I said. 'What I saw in my vision, it took place in this building – I am certain of it. I believe you are in danger whilst you remain here.'

'And of course, the longer you stay in the city, the greater the chance of your family catching up with you, Mrs –' Angus interjected.

'Mrs Desmarais, but Clara will suffice. I am quite finished with the rules of polite society now,' said Clara. 'I'm aware of the risk, but regrettably we have little choice concerning where we stay. The place we stayed in before – we cannot return to it. It is out of the question.' She pulled her shawl tighter around her shoulders, as though suddenly cold.

'It was very frightening for Clara,' Antoine explained. 'She saw terrible things at night, had the most dreadful nightmares. I cannot quite believe I am saying this, but it was as though there was something there, determined to torment us.'

I nodded grimly. 'I know where you were and trust me, I believe every word of what you say.'

Clara let out a heavy sigh. 'I pray that our stay here will be short. I cannot wait to be in Paris. Antoine has told me so much about it, that I am desperate to see it for myself.'

'What will you do in Paris?' I asked.

'We plan to open an exhibition,' Antoine declared, an irrepressible smile spreading across his face. 'Under Madame's tutelage I have learned a great deal, but I have so much of my own that I wish to create. There is enough room on this earth for another wax artist, I believe. Clara will assist me, and she will learn from me, too. She has a good deal of talent, Miss Rose. I can only imagine what an unconstrained Parisian life will do for her artistry.'

'But there is talk of war again,' Angus said. 'How can you be certain that France will be safe for the two of you?'

'There is always war,' Antoine replied, waving a dismissive hand. 'It matters not. In life, we cannot be certain of anything, except that we are here today and gone soon enough. Those preoccupied with war think only of ugliness, whereas I think solely of beauty. Of capturing beauty. Miss Rose, we spoke of these matters when you visited the exhibition, did we not?'

'We did.'

'And I showed you my favourite of all the models on display, the Sleeping Beauty. It was my first great inspiration; the more I have studied it, the more I have drawn it, the more determined I have felt to create my own such wondrous sculptures. And then I met Clara, my second great inspiration.' He spoke fast, almost giddy with enthusiasm as he took Clara by the hand. 'You see how perfect she is, Miss Rose? I sketched her likeness scores of times, but I could not capture her beauty on the page the way I knew I could in wax. And so, I have done it. Would you like to see her?'

'Of course.'

I glanced at Angus, enjoying the bewilderment writ across his face. No doubt I looked the same. The love affair and even the elopement were expected, but a model of Clara – no, I could not have predicted that. I couldn't even begin to imagine what the Andrews family would make of it.

Antoine led us into another room, this one clearly in use as a sort of workshop. There was a table at its centre, bare except for a neat row of brushes and other tools placed next to a small wooden box. Surrounding it in tidy lines at the edges of the room were various odd shapes, some tall, some short, all covered over in white sheets. Antoine walked over to one of these shapes, pulling back the cloth to reveal a table decorated with faces, all staring up at us. I winced at the sight of them, reminded immediately of the gruesome heads I'd been confronted with at the exhibition. I was grateful when Antoine selected just one, taking it out carefully and pulling the cover back over the others.

'Here she is,' he announced, holding up the face with such delicacy that he might as well have been holding a relic.

Even in the dim candlelight it was, quite unmistakeably, Clara's face; he had been right when he'd said that he captured her best in wax. Every feature, every aspect of her beauty had been recorded; slim lips, raised in a half-smile, high cheekbones, and those large, deep brown eyes. He'd left them open, of course; to do otherwise would have been to produce a sort of death mask and this woman's face was nothing of the sort. On the contrary, there was no doubt that this work was full of life, of youth, and of the artist's passion for his subject. Beautiful as it was, I still found the lack of body to accompany it unsettling.

'This is just the beginning, of course,' he explained. 'It is not possible to do more here. But together we have such great plans. You must look at this. I must tell you now, this is not my work. This is Clara's vision of herself.'

In one sweeping movement he'd pulled back another sheet, this time to reveal an easel bearing a painting. It was Clara, again, but this time it was all of her, lying on a sofa, arms draped around her head, wearing nothing more than the blush which hinted in her cheeks. I'd seen an image like this before, lying abandoned in the Weirs' house, but this incarnation of it, with its delicate colours and its detail, was bolder, more complete. More alive. This Clara stared at me, her dark gaze challenging me to stare back. Instead, I found myself looking away.

'Good Lord in Heaven above,' I heard Angus mutter, giving voice to my surprise. Antoine must have heard him too, for he shot him a dark look before tenderly replacing the sheet and covering the painting once more.

'You painted this, Clara?' I asked. 'You painted yourself like this? It is very good but very…daring.'

She nodded. 'I did, and I cannot express how wonderful it was to paint it. Being with Antoine and being able to paint like this is the truest happiness I have ever felt.'

'Our work together will be magnificent,' Antoine interjected. 'You can see the talent she has, Miss Rose. You can see how she captures her own beauty. I cannot wait to take her with me to Paris, to work together and to create her vision in wax. It will be our first great work. I do not believe there will be anything quite so beautiful in all the world.'

'It will be exquisite, I'm sure,' I remarked, 'but are you happy to be seen this way, Clara? Are you happy to be displayed like this somewhere?'

'Of course,' she replied. 'I have never been more certain of anything.'

I regarded her for a moment, meeting her serious, unflinching gaze as it rested on me in the candlelight. She was, without doubt, determined on her course; I could see that. But I could also see the youth in her unlined skin, the girlish naivety in the loose black curls of her hair. I could see how love flushed in her cheeks, how hope and excitement tugged at the corners of her slightly upturned lips. She had been touched by scandal, yes, but nonetheless it was apparent that she knew little about real hardship. She couldn't conceive of how far it was possible to fall, of how deep and dark those depths could be.

'Please, consider,' I urged her. 'I know you say you are finished with society, but it will most certainly be finished with you, if this becomes the talk of the town.'

'I'd listen to Miss Rose, my dear.'

The deep, eloquent voice which intruded caused us all to turn around. I hadn't heard him come in; no one had. He'd seen the candlelight, no doubt, flickering in a window not covered by boards. He'd walked in the door we'd left unlocked for him. He'd climbed several flights of stairs, his footsteps disguised by the sound of our animated voices, which had also acted as his guide. He'd reached the doorway of this room, and now he stared at us, his eyes heavy, his jaw rigid, his fists clenched.

Clara gasped. 'Henry!'

He gave her an icy smile. 'Yes, my darling,' he replied. 'You must have always known that I'd come to take you home.'

# Twenty-Six

'Come, Clara, the hour is late. Your family will be anxious to see you.'

Henry lurched forward, reaching out as though to take possession of her and drag her from this room. Like Clara, he looked much changed since the last time I saw him. Gone was the impeccable dark coat and reserved countenance; in its place I saw only dishevelled hair, a crumpled shirt, and a nasty snarl on those unappealing thick lips. As he pushed past me, I caught his scent; the pungent odour of a man who'd drunk too much and washed too little. If he'd been searching the town as Charles had suggested, then he'd been concentrating too hard upon the taverns.

Clara recoiled, and Antoine moved into his way, placing a warning hand on Henry's chest. 'I think you should leave,' he said gently. 'She does not wish to go with you.'

'This is none of your concern,' Henry spat, smacking Antoine's hand away. 'She is betrothed to me, and she will do as I say. Don't think I don't know who you are! You've been enjoying quite a romance, have you not, Clara? Was it just like those novels you ladies like to enrapture yourselves with? Did you both enjoy making a cuckold of me?'

'Henry, stop-' Clara pleaded.

Henry ignored her, instead taking a step closer to Antoine and staring hard into his face. 'I would demand satisfaction from you for this, except you are no gentleman. If you were going to spoil yourself for me, Clara, you could have at least chosen someone of rank. And someone who wasn't bloody French!'

'Please, Henry, that's enough,' Clara said again. 'We are family, are we not? My mother has been like a mother to you, ever since your mother could not be – God rest her soul. This notion of marrying me is folly. My affection for you is that of a sister towards a brother. I could never love you as a wife should love a husband.'

Henry bristled, stepping back now from Antoine. 'And I could never think of you as my sister. Dear Clara, you know that I adore you. We are a fine match. I might not be an eldest son; I might not have property but I do have prospects. I will provide well for you, and your marriage portion is more than sufficient – your father has assured me of that. I have thought on this a great deal since I discovered this dalliance of yours. Our wedding should proceed as planned.'

Clara's eyes widened. 'How long have you known?' she asked.

'Long enough. I must say, I couldn't believe it was you at first, hand-in-hand with this Frenchman, kissing him goodbye in the doorway downstairs like quite the little adventuress. But then it all made sense: the sudden enthusiasm for dancing, the unexplained outings, your repeated refusal of my affections. Oh, don't worry, I didn't share your filthy little secret with the rest of the family; I kept it to myself, and let the knowledge of it serve me. There will be no scandal; if you come home tonight, it will be as if all of this never happened.'

'What do you mean, you let the knowledge serve you?' I asked. I knew it was indelicate to interrupt but I couldn't help it; after spending weeks considering this puzzle, I was desperate for the pieces to fall into place.

Henry turned to me. 'Ah! Miss Rose, I had quite forgotten you were here. Let us simply say that you are not the only person who appreciates the value of insight. Understanding the root of Clara's objections to me meant that I understood how best to thwart them. After seeing her with this Frenchman, I knew that appeals to her heart were hopeless. I had to start making appeals of a different nature.'

'So, you went to her father,' I said, unravelling it all in my mind. 'And told him what, exactly? That you were desperately in love with her but that, having declared your affections, she'd insisted she wouldn't have you? That you wished for him to intervene?'

Henry laughed. 'Something like that. He was more than happy to assist, of course; he could see the sense in the match, especially now that he has reduced both of his daughters' prospects with his own foolish behaviour.'

'But you agreed to do something for him too, didn't you?' I pressed him. 'What was it?'

'Well, well, Miss Rose, what a lot of knowledge you have, and I didn't even allow you to read my tea leaves,' he scoffed. 'I suppose now that it is all done, I can own my involvement in the recent reconciliation between Mr and Mrs Andrews.'

'You brought Mother and Father back together?' Clara asked. 'I had wondered at her change of heart, given the lengths she'd gone to in bringing us here. Whatever could you have said to bring about such a reversal?'

Henry shrugged. 'As you said, my dear, your mother cares for me like a son. I suppose she listens to me like she would listen to a son, too.' He moved towards her again, pushing Antoine out of the way. 'Now, let us bring this disagreeable matter to a close, and take you home. We can tell your father that you were vexed about the wedding, but that you're reconciled to it now. I'm sure he will agree that a quick marriage would be best, given that you are presently suffering with your nerves.'

Clara moved away from him, pulling herself closer again to Antoine, who was still trying to regain a steady footing after Henry's almighty shove. 'I can't marry you, Henry,' she said. 'I am already married. To Antoine. I am married to Antoine.'

The room fell silent for a moment. The walls seemed to close in around us, and the air grew warm and heavy. Beside me I felt

Angus step forward. He sensed the coming storm, too.

'You cannot be married,' Henry said, shaking his head. 'You have been gone for what, two days? It is not possible.'

'We are in Scotland,' she replied. 'Getting wed is easier here, remember; much like getting divorced.'

'Then a divorce can be arranged,' he spat, his face reddening to the point of grotesque. 'It will be arranged!'

Henry flung himself forward again, and I felt certain that he was going to strike Antoine. I pushed myself into his path, determined to say something, to do something, to calm his growing anger. In truth I was at a loss; I was inexperienced in matters of the heart, and completely naïve when it came to the sorts of passions which were currently running riot in this room. The air smouldered with love and rage. Somehow, I had to dampen it, I had to stop the flames from growing up and consuming us all. I just didn't know how.

*That is not true, ma chérie. You know more than you give yourself credit for.*

Oh, Maman. How I wished you were here to help me now.

'Please, there is no need for raised voices,' I said. 'You will only draw attention to yourselves, and I'm sure no one here wants that – least of all you, Mr Turner, being a gentleman of such good repute.'

'Miss Rose is right,' Angus agreed. 'Believe me, none of you would enjoy a night in the Old Tolbooth.'

Henry stood back, smoothing his hands down his shirt as he looked Angus up and down. 'And who are you?' he asked with no small degree of condescension. 'I don't recall us being introduced.'

'Well, I suppose it was hardly the time for introductions, sir, given the manner in which you presented yourself this evening,' replied Angus, his tone clipped. 'But since you ask, my name is Angus Campbell. I am a friend of Miss Rose, and a town guardsman.'

Henry let out a harsh laugh. 'The Town Guard, indeed? Well then, you will know that the Guard do not patrol the New Town's streets. You have no jurisdiction here; we have our own watchmen, for all the good they serve against the light-fingered ne'er-do-wells from your side of the bridge.'

Angus flinched at Henry's mocking tone. 'I'm aware of my jurisdiction, sir. I am off duty. I come only to assist Miss Rose.'

'I see, and to what end, exactly? What concern is this of yours?' Henry turned his triumphant gaze towards me. 'Did you not heed Mr Andrews' warning to you, Miss Rose?'

Before I could say anything, Clara intervened. 'Miss Rose heard I was missing. She was concerned, and along with her friend she endeavoured to find me, and to assure herself that I am well. She is not yours or Father's to command, Henry, and neither am I. I never was.'

I expected Henry to erupt again at this, but instead he stood, staring, open-mouthed. It took me a moment to realise that he was looking beyond Clara now, that something else had caught his eye.

'What the deuce is that?'

I watched Clara lower her gaze and bite her lip. She didn't turn around, but she knew exactly what he was looking at. We all did. I sensed our eyes move in tandem, coming to rest upon the left side of Clara's self-portrait, her pretty oval face, mesmerising gaze and tumbling dark curls unveiled once more by the slipping of a sheet. No doubt it had been disturbed by the frantic movement in the room. No doubt we were all going to regret that it had.

'It's my painting,' Clara began. 'It's…'

Henry pushed past her, pacing towards it. He pulled the sheet away with the swift flick of his hand, exposing the rest of her. I winced at his sharp intake of breath, and watched for what felt like an eternity as he regarded it, his mouth wide open in disbelief.

'It's you,' he said in the end. 'Good God, Clara, what were you thinking? It's indecent. How could you do this? How could you bring such shame upon yourself?'

'I'm not ashamed,' she replied quietly. 'It is art, and it is the beginning of something wonderful, for Antoine, and for me.'

'It is an outrage,' Henry yelled, striking the painting with the back of his hand and sending it flying from its easel and on to the floor.

'No!' Antoine scurried over, picking it up and clutching it to himself. 'This is Clara's work,' he shouted, his face growing redder. 'How dare you take something which is not yours and treat it like that.'

Henry spun around. 'How dare I?' he asked, staring hard at Antoine. 'You have some nerve, considering what you have taken from me. You shall make a fool of me no more.'

Henry marched forward, grabbing Clara by the arm and dragging her towards the door. She tried to struggle away from him, but he merely tightened his grip. Angus moved to block his path but Henry shoved him out of the way, so hard that Angus fell backwards, crashing into the table and sending paintbrushes flying in all directions. I rushed to Angus's side, helping him back to his feet. He looked at me, stunned. Henry's strength had surprised him.

'Henry, what are you doing? Let go of me,' Clara began, but her protests were soon silenced as he pulled her closer to him, wrapping his arm around her and pressing a firm hand over her mouth. He raised his other arm then, producing a pistol seemingly from nowhere. I gasped as he placed it under her chin.

'I've no desire to use this, my love,' he hissed in her ear. 'Leave quietly with me now and no harm will come to you.'

From behind his hand, I heard Clara whimper, but she protested no more. Henry hauled her out of the room, and they both disappeared into the shadowy gloom of the landing. Angus, Antoine and I all looked at each other, and I wondered if I appeared as strained as they did. Antoine looked utterly wretched, clutching the edge of table, his face ashen, and even Angus had shrunk back in defeat. We couldn't argue with a pistol, we knew that. But we couldn't let them leave, either.

'Think for a moment about what you are doing, Mr Turner,' Angus called. 'You can hardly present Clara to her parents with a pistol pressed to her throat.'

Henry laughed. 'What a pity you've not got your weapon with

you tonight, guardsman,' he yelled back. 'Although I doubt even your axe could stop me from having what is mine.'

We listened as their footsteps grew fainter. They'd have reached the staircase by now, growing further from our reach with every moment that passed.

'We have to do something,' I said.

'He's armed, Ailsa,' Angus replied, 'and he's quite clearly lost his wits.'

'Exactly.' I shuddered, memories of my vision running unabated through my mind. 'We can't just let him leave with her. Who knows what he's capable of?'

'Miss Rose is right,' Antoine said, seeming to come to his senses. He rushed towards the door. 'He can shoot me if he wishes, but I'm not leaving her at his mercy!'

'Antoine, wait...' I began, but he had already dashed out. I could hear the thudding of his feet along the landing; no doubt Henry would hear him too.

Angus and I exchanged glances, and wordlessly he walked over to retrieve the candle which Antoine had discarded near the easel where Clara's precious artwork sat. In the midst of Henry's violent departure, I hadn't notice him replace it. Clara's painted gaze caught hold of me once more, bold and unrelenting in its scrutiny, but this time I didn't look away. An outrage – that's what Henry had called it, but it wasn't. It was quite beautiful, actually, but more than that, it was an expression of her true nature, of the true Clara. That was nothing to be ashamed of.

'Come on,' said Angus grimly. 'We'd better go after them.'

We hurried along the landing and down the first set of stairs, keeping our footsteps brisk but quiet. Below I could hear faint noises, and I strained to identify them, to decipher the creak of a door opening or God forbid, the sharp pop of a pistol going off. Neither were apparent, just the scuffles and thuds of bodies moving around in the darkness, and the creaks and groans of a building acknowledging their presence. I felt reassured that Antoine would still be here, but I wasn't so sure about Henry and Clara. It wasn't beyond the realms of possibility that they'd left here already, that they were halfway back to Hill Street, Henry armed with his pistol and his story of how he'd rescued his fair maiden from her own folly. A small part of me wondered if that was for the best. My vision had shown that the danger to Clara lurked within this building, upon the stairs below us. If she wasn't here, then the fate I foresaw could not befall her, could it?

No, it couldn't - but another, equally dire fate still could. Angus was right; Henry had lost his wits. Letting him leave with Clara wouldn't keep her from danger; it would merely alter its course.

In front of me, Angus stopped. 'Curse it,' he whispered. 'The candle's almost out.'

He turned to show me, and I felt my eyes widen at the sight of its sorry remains, almost completely overrun by melted wax. It hadn't been a tall brown candle like Angus's earlier, fashioned from tallow and sputtering black smoke. It had been a much finer thing than that, the sort of candle which lit genteel homes and exhibits by artists of growing fame. It had been a candle I'd seen before.

It had been the candle from my vision.

Before I could say anything, the candle went out. Then, below us, a pistol fired. I clapped my hand over my mouth to prevent myself from crying aloud.

'Shit,' hissed Angus, discarding the candle. 'Ailsa, please, wait here.'

'No,' I protested. 'You're not going alone. If you must go, then so must I.'

In the gloom I sensed Angus draw a deep breath, poised to argue. 'Ailsa, please…'

'It was my vision that got you involved in this, Angus,' I interrupted. 'I'd never forgive myself if something happened to you because of me.'

Another sigh. 'Alright,' he conceded. 'But stay behind me.'

We moved apace along the landing and towards another set of stairs. The building had fallen back into silence following the gunshot, but not for long. Bathed in darkness and with a growing sense of trepidation my senses sharpened, and once again I began to hear the sound of voices below us. Their tones were deep, sharp and aggressive, and as we drew nearer, I picked out words – few of them bore repeating. It appeared Antoine and Henry had encountered each other once again. I strained to hear more, but I couldn't detect Clara's voice. Perhaps Henry still kept her mouth covered with his hand. Or, perhaps she'd got away from him.

Or, perhaps she had been shot.

By the time we reached the first floor, I could hear every word that they said, every insult they slung at each other. I felt Angus's arm reach out and touch mine, checking I was still behind him. I was both comforted and afraid that he felt the need to act as my shield.

'It's us,' he called out. 'Ailsa and Angus. Please, don't shoot.'

Angus's request was greeted by Henry's laughter. 'I wouldn't waste a bullet on you, guardsman.'

Then, as though emerging from the shadows, there they were, frozen beside each other in the curve of the final staircase, leading to the ground floor. The moon must have risen, and in the silvery darkness I could make out their silhouettes. It was a grim sight to behold. A few steps down stood Henry, clutching Clara in one hand and his pistol in the other, which he pointed at Clara's temple. Slightly above him was Antoine, armed with his knife which he held against Henry's throat. I swallowed hard. This was indeed a deadly impasse.

'We heard a gun fire,' Angus said. 'Has someone been shot?'

'Only the wall,' replied Antoine. 'His aim is poor.'

'Don't tempt me, Frenchman,' Henry retorted through gritted teeth. 'Next time I'll decorate it with your innards.'

From behind Henry's hand, I heard Clara moan – in protest or discomfort, I couldn't tell. She began to move, perhaps losing her footing on the stairs, or perhaps trying to break free. Henry jolted, tightening his grip, and her squirming ceased.

I drew a deep breath and took a step forward, moving myself in front of Angus. He began to murmur an objection and I touched his arm, hoping to reassure him. I had to intervene, to find a way to bring calm into this situation. I had no choice. Everything that had happened over the preceding weeks had led to this point; I understood that now. I knew what Pierre wanted me to do.

'Please, I beg you – both of you. Stop this at once. This cannot end well for either of you. One of you will end up dead, and the other in the Tolbooth on the charge of murder. Is that really what you want? How does that outcome serve either of you?'

'He stole from me,' Henry muttered. 'He took what was mine. He should pay for it.'

'But killing him will not get you what you want. Neither will forcing Clara to divorce Antoine and marry you. Mr Turner, you cannot hope to build a happy union upon such foundations. You must see that.'

In the wan light I saw Henry lower his arm, moving the pistol away from Clara's head. Antoine must have seen this too, because he stepped back, retracting his blade. I allowed myself a brief sigh of relief as I felt the immediate danger pass. But it was only brief. Still shackled in Henry's arms, Clara wriggled again, but this time with greater conviction. From behind his hand, she made an almighty sound; I could only describe it as a growl, such was its deep and feral nature. Henry yelped and staggered backwards, his grip on her loosening. Clara slipped out of his arms and began to run down the stairs.

'Bitch!' Henry yelled.

And then, to my horror, he raised his pistol once more.

'No!' I screamed.

I was hardly aware that I'd flung myself towards him until my hand made contact with the cold metal of the weapon in his hand. I knocked it from his grasp as it fired, its deadly load taking flight in the black night air. I didn't see where it landed; I didn't see anything more of that dark staircase at all. Instead, I could only feel: a searing pain as my head hit the wall, the throbbing of every limb as I tumbled down the stairs, the brittle cold of the stone floor as I reached the bottom. I heard voices crying out my name, I heard my own laboured breath. Both grew distant; I was at sea now, drifting away, the current cradling me, the sun caressing me with its warm glow. I gazed into the light, watching its shape shift until a new image emerged: a boy with dark hair and an old grey shirt, standing on the banks of the Seine.

'Pierre?' I whispered.

He nodded and smiled. The light dimmed, and the cold and the voices intruded once more. Paris faded, along with that boy I once called my closest friend. I knew this would be the last time I saw him.

I knew that, one way or another, this was all over now.

# Twenty-Seven

### Summer 1803

The hot June air was heavy with the earthen scent of the greenmarket as we made our way through the stalls and towards the valley beyond. Around us the voices of traders reached their crescendo, and we offered polite smiles of refusal to those who addressed us as they went about hawking their wares. Underfoot was all dust, wrought by weeks which had brought little rain; I could feel the grit gathering in my shoes, could see it lining the bottom of my dress. In the clear sky the sun bore down, and I was grateful for the shade provided by my bonnet. Grateful too that it was sufficient to cover the patchwork of browns and greys across my forehead. My wounds had almost healed, but the scars would take their time to fade.

'Are you alright?' Angus asked me. It was his favourite question, had been for weeks now.

I nodded, giving him my usual answer as we reached the end of the market and made our way across the uneven grassland which separated the two towns. Behind us the hum of the marketplace faded, superseded now by children's cries and mothers' cautioning as others, like us, enjoyed a walk in the sunshine. Lost souls roamed, just as they always did; I had courteous smiles for them, too. In front of us the great mound of earth loomed, a constant reminder of how this city had changed, how it would continue to change. A loch had become a valley. One town had become two. I stood still for a moment, aware of the baked, dry earth beneath my feet, of the hot wind billowing my skirts, of the stray curl tickling my cheek. Aware of the past, and of the present. For so long I'd avoided coming down here, but where I'd once found distress, I now found comfort. That was something else which had changed.

'Ailsa, you'll tire yourself. Let's sit.'

He wrapped a gentle arm around my waist and brushed a small kiss across the tip of my nose. Two of his favourite gestures, and two of mine, as well. I caught hold of his hand and kept it, even as we seated ourselves in a quiet spot. That hand had been the first thing I'd noticed all those weeks ago when I'd awoken on a bed, in a place I didn't know. That hand and its rough skin, its warmth, its tight grip.

'Are they here?' he asked me.

'Not yet. Soon, I'm sure.'

I traced my thumb across his forefinger, still recollecting. After his hand, I'd become aware of faces gathered at my bedside, white with weariness and terror. Angus, Antoine, Clara, and a woman in her middle years who introduced herself as Marie. I learned that I was in Marie's home, and that I was to stay there until I had recovered. I'd been asleep for more than a day; a physician had attended me and would call again. In the meantime, I had to rest, to avoid agitation. I wasn't to worry about anything, I was told; Marie had taken care of all of it. It was several days before I became lucid enough to realise who Marie was, and several more days before I was able to piece together everything that had happened.

'Is your head alright? Are you in any pain?' Angus asked.

I shook my head softly, offering a reassuring smile. The pains I suffered in my head could be severe. Marie's physician had suggested laudanum; I'd thought immediately of my mother, and declined. Instead, I relied on fresh air, sleep and time. I forced myself to believe that I would heal, that I would be alright in the end. And indeed, as my bruises had faded, so too had my head pains become less frequent. There was hope.

There was always hope.

I'd spent about a fortnight convalescing at Marie's home. Angus had stayed at my bedside, except when he was on duty. Whenever he couldn't be with me, Clara had kept me company. In the aftermath of that night Marie had taken charge of her and Antoine as well, offering them refuge as they took their first tentative steps in married life, although not before chastising them for not coming to her for help sooner. At first weary from her ordeal, as the days marched on, I watched Clara bloom once more as the pieces of her life fell back into place. Henry's long shadow over her began to fade; he had fled the scene after my fall, and hadn't been heard from again. She was reunited with her mother and sister, who reconciled themselves to her marriage, as well as to her impending departure for France. Grace had wept so much that she'd gone through three handkerchiefs, Clara had told me. She also told me that her father had refused to see her. I could well believe it.

I learned other things, however, which took me by far greater surprise.

'Do you mind if I ask, who is Pierre?' Clara had said to me one afternoon. 'After your fall, you kept saying that name – Pierre.'

My eyes had welled up with tears at her question, and I'd had to fight them back as I explained. 'He was my friend, in Paris – a spirit friend, the ghost of a boy who drowned in the Seine. He was the one who sent me the vision about you. He wanted me to help you.'

She'd pressed her lips together at that, her dark eyes narrowing in thought, but she said nothing further. It was only when she returned later, with Antoine, that I discovered the reason for her question.

'When I was a young boy, my mother was a housekeeper for a physician in Paris. We lived with him, in an apartment on Rue Sainte-Claire.'

Rue Sainte-Claire: I'd lived in an apartment there, too. It had felt strange to hear the name again, after so long. 'Go on,' I'd urged him, desperate for the pieces of this puzzle to finally fall into place.

'As well as my mother, I also had an older brother, Pierre,' he'd continued, his expression sombre. 'When I was four, he fell into the river and drowned.'

'How old was he?' I'd barely been able to whisper the question.

'Twelve,' Antoine had replied.

I hadn't been able to hold back my tears that time. Antoine hadn't either.

'You're thinking about it all again, aren't you?' Angus asked me, bringing me back to the present.

'Yes, I'm sorry. I was just thinking about Pierre.'

He squeezed my hand. 'Don't be sorry. I know that you miss him.'

'I suppose that sometimes I feel as though I've lost him all over again.'

'But you were able to help his brother, and his brother's wife. You can take comfort in that, can't you? I know Pierre was always there for you in Paris, but others are here for you now. Franny, me, and even Alice, from where she is now.'

I laughed at that. Something stirred on the breeze, and I wondered if she'd be here soon. With Joanna, of course. She was always with Joanna now.

'There is one thing I'd like to know, though,' Angus said, lifting his hand from mine and wrapping his arm around my shoulder. 'How long exactly did it take you to realise you were staying with Madame Tussaud?'

'You're never going to let me forget that, are you?' I retorted, rolling my eyes. 'Longer than it should have. If nothing else, I should have recognised her from the exhibition.'

He leaned in closer and kissed my cheek. 'I am teasing you,' he said. 'You'd had quite a bang to the head. I'm surprised you knew any of us. You've no idea how relieved I was when I realised that you did.' He kissed me again.

I smiled at his attentions, thinking still about Marie, as she'd insisted on being called. She'd seldom been at home during my stay, understandably preoccupied with the exhibition which, as spring blossomed towards summer, became the talk and the toast of the town. Instead, we'd snatched words here and there; French words about how the weather was improving, how my injuries were healing, how many had visited the rooms on Thistle Street that day. Nothing about how we'd survived, about how Paris haunted us. Those words were left unsaid, spoken only in glances.

'Have you heard news of any of them?' Angus asked me.

I shook my head. Marie had left town at the end of May. I'd heard she was taking her exhibition to Ireland, although no one seemed certain. Clara and Antoine had left earlier in the month, not long after I'd returned home. They'd been London-bound first to settle some affairs, as Clara had delicately put it, before travelling onwards to Paris. I often wondered if they'd made it, and sometimes I hoped they hadn't. The short-lived peace between their two countries had come to an end just days after their departure. Both sought a life without constraint, one filled with art, passion and beauty. I worried they would find nothing so ideal in Paris now.

The warm wind cooled a little, carrying with it a woman's whispered greeting. I smiled. It was always Joanna who spoke first; always her laughter which rang out across the valley, always her favourite questions which filled my mind. How was I feeling now, was I still living alone in my Canongate room, and when were Angus and I going to marry? I always reddened at that, relieved that Angus couldn't hear her. Alice would tell her to let me be, that she was sure all would be well, but that I knew where to come if I needed her. Sometimes she'd remind me that she was sorry, and I would tell her I was sorry too, and then we'd agree that there was no need for any of that. I was just glad to talk to her. I was just glad that I'd had the courage to find her.

'They're here now, then?' Angus asked, observing my grin.

I nodded, breaking into laughter as wisps of them appeared in front of me, swirling around like woman-shaped clouds. Joanna loved to dance, leaping and giggling all around the valley. She didn't stop for a moment; I suspected she didn't dare. She'd chosen to fill her eternity with noise, because the alternative was a void she didn't dare to confront.

'I don't think they'll stay long today,' I remarked. 'Joanna is even more restless than usual.'

I watched as they blew on the breeze, weaving around squealing children and chattering ladies, all entirely oblivious to the ethereal spectacle on display. They reached the edge of the marketplace, and I screwed up my eyes in the sunlight as I watched them disappear beside a gentleman in a smart blue coat, resting lightly on his walking stick. He seemed to jolt slightly left then right, glancing down as though noticing some disturbance around him, then he looked up, straight in my direction. I frowned. He was too far away to see clearly, and yet I could feel the weight of his gaze upon me. I looked away, feeling sure then that he'd seen those spirits, and that somehow, he knew I'd seen them too.

\*

We walked back to Anstruther House as evening drew near, beckoned indoors by the cooling air and our growling stomachs. We had fallen into an easy routine of late, sharing meals together whenever we could, snatching precious moments between his guard duties and my evenings in the tavern. Often, we shared the nights too, and I'd grown so used to his warmth beside me in my small bed that I found the times when he was on night duty lonely. It was odd; I'd spent so long on my own and become so accustomed to it, and yet in a matter of weeks I'd grown to love company, to crave it. As I opened the door to my room, Joanna's words about marriage rang in my ears, and I felt the colour rise in my face once more. I'd once resigned myself to spinsterhood; now I thought about marriage more than I cared to admit.

'There's something here for you,' Angus said, picking up a small envelope which was lying on the floor. 'Looks like it's been pushed under your door.'

I took it from him, checking that it was indeed addressed to me before tearing it open. I took out the letter inside, unfolding it quickly and surveying its contents with haste.

'It's from Grace,' I said, re-reading it more slowly this time. 'She must have had Jane deliver it this afternoon. She writes with news of Clara and Antoine – they are still in London. They haven't been able to secure safe passage back to France so have decided to sail for America. America, indeed! She believes they will sail within the week.'

'That is good news,' Angus said, sitting down at my little table and unwrapping some bread I'd put aside for us earlier. 'They'll be better off there than in France. Can't be safe there right now, not for an Englishwoman anyway.'

'Hmm,' I mused. 'There's more. Grace writes that her father has returned to London. She says her mother and father have separated again, and she believes they will divorce. Grace and her mother will remain here until the matter is settled; once it is, they plan to travel to Mrs Andrews' family estate in Yorkshire, where Mrs Andrews' brother has offered them sanctuary. She says that she hopes her father will return to Edinburgh swiftly so that the matter can be concluded. She also writes that she believes Henry is with her father, although she cannot be certain.'

'That sounds about right,' Angus replied. 'Oh well, both bad pennies have left town. I'd say that's not a bad outcome. Although Henry finding himself locked up in the Tolbooth would have been a better one.'

'She signs off that she hopes I am fully recovered, and conveys her warmest regards to you.' I grinned at him. 'I daresay that Miss Andrews has developed a soft spot for you after news of your off-duty heroics reached her ears.'

He laughed. 'My heroics? I'm not the one who threw herself down the stairs to knock a pistol from a madman's hand.'

I walked over to him, wrapping my arms around his shoulders. 'True, but I don't think Grace would find me half as dashing in a guardsman's uniform.'

He turned his head, his lips brushing my neck. 'Oh, I'm dashing, am I?'

'You know you are, Angus Campbell.'

'Are you going to eat something?'

I stood up straight, examining the letter once more. 'I will, in a moment. I should reply to Grace, thanking her for the news. I want to enquire about Jane, too. I wonder what she will do – she's quite taken with that family, especially Grace. I believe she will want to go with them.'

'You will want to say goodbye, in that case,' Angus observed.

'Mmm,' I replied, still staring at the letter. In truth, Jane maintained a cool distance from me, and I suspected that despite the good outcome, she resented my meddling in her employers' lives. 'I wonder if there's any paper in my writing box.'

I pulled the mahogany box out from under my bed, brushing off the thin layer of dust which had gathered on its surface. I'd barely looked at it since the day I'd taken it from Alice's room. In the wake of Clara's disappearance and everything which came after that, I'd quite forgotten about it until Jack had come looking for his money, not long after I'd returned home. I'd paid him, of course, and apologised for the delay. He'd been gruff as usual, but he'd asked about my health as well, no doubt spotting the colourful mass of wounds still evident across my forehead. I had to admit, I'd been quite taken aback by his concern. I hadn't thought him capable of it.

'That's nice,' Angus said, through a mouthful of food. 'Did you bring that from Paris?'

'No, it was Alice's. I took it from her room when it was being cleared for the next tenant.'

'That belonged to Alice?' His eyes widened with surprise.

I shrugged. 'It would appear so.'

I sat down on the edge of my bed, placing the box at my side before carefully opening it up to view the contents within. To my disappointment there was no paper, only a single well-used quill pen and a small inkwell, which was empty. If I was going to use it, I would have to replenish it myself. I ran my hand around its edges, admiring it again. The rose design which featured so prominently on its exterior was replicated on the inside of the lid. As I studied its intricacies, I noticed a detail which was absent from the external roses. In the middle of each flower were the same letters: G and R. I stared at them for a moment, my mind reeling at the discovery. They were initials. They had to be.

'Well, I think that settles it,' I said aloud.

'What?' Angus asked.

'Look at this.' I got up from the bed and placed the open box in front of Angus on the table. 'There – look at the initials. I don't think this writing box belonged to Alice at all.'

'Aye,' Angus replied. 'She was known to be a bit light-fingered, Ailsa. In all honesty, she probably stole it.'

I bristled, rubbing my arms as I walked towards the window. I knew that what he said was likely to be true, but she had been my friend. She was still my friend. I didn't wish to admit it, not even to myself.

'I wonder who it really belonged to,' I said, staring out at the deepening blue of the sky.

'I'm not sure we'll ever know the answer to that.'

Angus got up, wrapping his arms around me as he joined me at the window. I sensed his eyes fixing upwards, like mine, trying to gaze beyond a skyline strewn with tenement roofs and church steeples. Sunset was still several hours away, and I felt an urge to wander hand in hand up the Salisbury Crags later, to sit together and watch it bestow its pinks and purples over the weary city. I would ask him, and he would say yes. Afterwards I would ask him to stay in my room with me tonight. He would say yes to that, too.

'I could ask Alice about the writing box.'

He drew a deep breath. 'You could, but somehow I doubt she'd tell you.'

I nodded. The living liked to guard their secrets; the same was true of the dead. I looked down, my eyes roaming the street below, picking out people, imagining their stories. A child clutching his mother's hand, looking forward to broses for his supper. A maid rushing back from the market, panicking at the thought of keeping her mistress waiting a moment too long. A young dandy looking forward to a night filled with port and posturing.

An older gentleman with a blue coat and a walking stick. The same man I'd seen just a few short hours ago.

I inhaled sharply as I watched him turn and retrace his steps. I wondered if he'd simply lost his way, or if he'd lost more than that. After a moment he stopped again, removing his tall hat and looking up, scanning the old stones and windows of Anstruther House. I froze, unable to step away, unable to stop myself from staring. In the deepest recesses of my mind a memory stirred, a memory of Paris, of red-brown hair bespeckled with grey and amused hazel eyes mirroring my own. Of hands much larger than mine, lifting me into the air. Of shared laughter echoing down a wood-panelled hallway.

Of a man I'd once known, but had all but forgotten.

I watched as he walked away once more, my gaze fixed on him until his coat was little more than a speck of blue paint, melting into the distance. I wondered what he had been looking for. I wondered if he'd found it.

I knew he'd found it.

Time slid like a rug under my feet, and I felt my past and present collide as my mother's soft whisper echoed in my ear. It was not the voice I'd imagined all these years, but the living sound of her, as though she'd been restored to flesh once more. As though she was by my side. As though she'd never left.

'I knew one day he'd come for you, ma chérie.'

## The End

# AUTHOR'S NOTES

The story and the majority of characters in this novel are fictional, but its context, setting and many of its details are grounded in historical fact. The peace between Britain and France, secured by the Treaty of Amiens in 1802, marked the brief interlude between the French Revolutionary Wars and the Napoleonic Wars. Although the peace was uneasy and lasted just a little over a year, the suspension of hostilities opened up opportunities for travel between the two countries which had not existed for some time.

One notable individual to take advantage of this change in circumstances was the wax sculptor Marie Tussaud, who travelled to London in 1802 to exhibit her work. In 1803 she travelled to Edinburgh; the Edinburgh World Heritage website notes that she set up an exhibition at 28 Thistle Street, an address known as Bernard's Rooms and used for dancing classes. Among her collection of waxworks was The Sleeping Beauty, who was created by Madame Tussaud's mentor Philippe Curtius and inherited by her following his death. Some disagreement about the identity of The Sleeping Beauty persists, with possible candidates including Louis XV's mistress Madame du Barry as well as the salonièrre Madame de Sainte-Amaranthe who I opted for in the novel.

The French Revolution and its bloody aftermath led to a considerable exodus of French citizens, with many crossing the channel and seeking sanctuary in Britain. Although Ailsa Rose is fictional, her story would not have been unfamiliar to the many emigrés who often suffered perilous escapes from their homeland, only to endure poverty and suspicion from both the British authorities and the population at large. In his thesis 'La Généreuse Nation': Britain and French Emigration 1792-1802, Callum Whittaker recounts the difficulties faced by many until the end of anti-emigré legislation in 1802 meant that they were able to return to France.

If the late eighteenth and early nineteenth century world was in a state of flux, nowhere perhaps epitomises this as much as Ailsa Rose's adopted city, Edinburgh. The development of the New

Town, with its orderly grids of streets and elegant neo-classical architecture, would not be completed until the mid-nineteenth century, and was very much still a work-in-progress. Nonetheless, it was sufficiently built to attract the city's wealthier set into its new abodes, leaving the poor to continue to occupy the narrow closes and cramped tenements of the medieval city. Ailsa's home, the Canongate, continued to be a separate burgh until 1856, although the demolition of the Netherbow Port gatehouse and much of the old city walls during the eighteenth century meant that movement between Edinburgh and the Canongate would have been easier than it had been in previous centuries. If you'd like to read more about the transformation of Edinburgh through the centuries, I would recommend *Lost Edinburgh: Edinburgh's Lost Architectural Heritage* by Hamish Coghill.

Throughout the eighteenth century, law and order in Edinburgh was enforced by a system of Constables and a quasi-military Town Guard, with the latter being legally confined to the ancient limits of the city. Increasingly perceived to be ineffective and inadequate, by 1803 the Guard was in its twilight years. In 1805 Edinburgh's first professional police force was established, and by 1817 the Guard was disbanded. Despite its poor reputation, I would like to think that it nonetheless contained diligent individuals like Angus Campbell within its ranks! I am indebted to the excellent work of John McGowan in his book *Policing the Metropolis in Scotland: A History of the Police and Systems of Police in Edinburgh & Edinburghshire, 1770-1833*, in which he explores the complex systems of both law enforcement and justice in operation at the turn of the nineteenth century.

One of the most famous episodes involving the Town Guard was the Porteous Riots of 1736, which are well described by Geoff Holder in his book *Bloody Scottish History: Edinburgh*. His book also contains an interesting chapter on The Wizard of West Bow, a strange story of the supernatural which has passed into Edinburgh folklore. Along with Marie Tussaud, Major Weir and his sister Jean are the only historical figures to feature in this novel.

Finally, law suits and subsequent trials for 'criminal conversation' were a fairly common feature of upper-class life in England during this period, with husbands suing other men for debauching their wives. Divorce in England was difficult and expensive to obtain; it could only be granted by an act of parliament, and only on grounds of adultery. Nor was the law applied equally to both sexes, as a woman could only divorce her husband if his adultery was accompanied by life-threatening cruelty. In Scotland, with its separate legal system, the position was markedly different: divorce was available on equal terms to men and women, on grounds of either adultery or desertion. Scotland's marriage laws were also more relaxed, a fact which famously made the country, and particularly the border village of Gretna Green, an attractive destination for eloping couples. In the same spirit, I enjoyed the idea of a genteel woman making her own dash over the border, but with an opposite purpose – to rid herself of an errant spouse!

If this novel has inspired a more general interest in life during the late Georgian period, I would highly recommend reading *The Time Traveller's Guide to Regency Britain* by Ian Mortimer and *Decency and Disorder: 1789-1837* by Ben Wilson.

# ABOUT THE AUTHOR

Sarah L King lives in West Lothian, Scotland, with her husband and children. Born in Nottingham and raised in Lancashire, her books include the historical fiction novels, *The Gisburn Witch* (2015), *A Woman Named Sellers* (2016) and *The Pendle Witch Girl* (2018), all set during the Lancashire witch trials in the seventeenth century. She is also the author of two contemporary mystery novels, *Ethersay* (2017) and *The House at Kirtlebeck End* (2019). *The Wax Artist* is her sixth novel and the first in the series of Ailsa Rose mysteries set in late Georgian Edinburgh.

When she's not writing Sarah loves long country walks, romantic ruins, Thai food and spending time with her family.

For further information please visit her website & blog at http://www.sarahlking.com/

Lightning Source UK Ltd.
Milton Keynes UK
UKHW011830131121
393907UK00001B/27